THE DOS AND
DONUTS OF LOVE

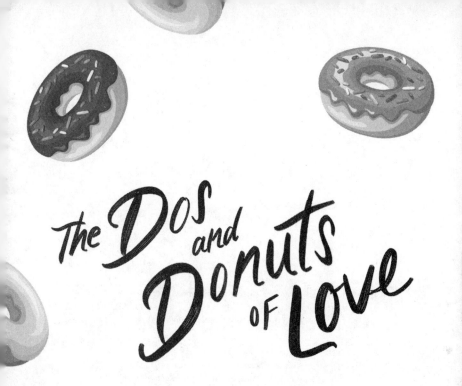

The Dos and Donuts of Love

ADIBA JAIGIRDAR

FEIWEL AND FRIENDS
NEW YORK

A Feiwel and Friends Book
An imprint of Macmillan Publishing Group, LLC
120 Broadway, New York, NY 10271 • fiercereads.com

Text copyright © 2023 by Adiba Jaigirdar.
Donut illustrations © by Naddya/Shutterstock.
Sprinkle illustrations © by Tamara Luiza/Shutterstock.
Whisk illustration © by Anna Beatty/Shutterstock.
All rights reserved.

Our books may be purchased in bulk for promotional, educational, or business use.
Please contact your local bookseller or the Macmillan Corporate and Premium Sales
Department at (800) 221-7945 ext. 5442 or by email at
MacmillanSpecialMarkets@macmillan.com.

Library of Congress Control Number: 2022046370

First edition, 2023
Book design by Maria Williams
Feiwel and Friends logo designed by Filomena Tuosto
Printed in the United States of America

ISBN 978-1-250-84211-4
1 3 5 7 9 10 8 6 4 2

To all the brown kids, queer kids, fat kids,
Muslim kids, anxious kids:

Dream big and don't let anything get in the way of achieving
your dreams.

Not even yourself.

(And to donuts, obviously.)

ONE

This Cookie Won't Crumble

I KNOW THINGS ARE BAD WHEN EVEN DONUTS BETRAY ME. BECAUSE there I am, sitting on my bed, rewatching every episode of *The Great British Bake Off* on Netflix, a box of six donuts from You Drive Me Glazy on my bedside table. Six donuts that I helped Ammu and Abbu create. And the moment I bite into the first, chocolate-hazelnut filling gushes out all over the front of my shirt.

I can only groan and pull myself off the bed where I had finally found a comfortable position. The judges of *GBBO* are on my laptop screen explaining the challenge to the contestants, but I'm a little too busy slipping out of my gross chocolate-stained shirt to pay attention.

My phone buzzes by the box of donuts, and my heart almost leaps out of my chest. Tossing my shirt on the floor, I lunge toward the phone, hoping—

But it's just a text from Fatima.

Fatima: can I call?

I don't reply. Instead, I slip on a new shirt—one without any stains on it—close the lid of my laptop, and hit VIDEO CALL.

Fatima picks up almost immediately. There's a grin on her

1

face but she says, "You look terrible" as a greeting. There's something almost delirious about that being accompanied by Fatima's delighted expression.

I pull a face and tug at the strands of my hair, trying to shift them into something that doesn't make it obvious that I've spent the past few days barely moving from under my duvet cover.

"Thanks, Fatima."

"Sorry." But she doesn't sound particularly sorry as she flicks away a strand of her long, ink-black hair out of her eyes. "Are you still in bed?" There's an accusatory note to her voice, so I try to fill the whole screen with my face so she can't see that not only am I in bed but that my bed is also a mess. Plus, the half a dozen donuts still by my bedside.

"No . . ."

I obviously don't sound very believable because Fatima lets out a frustrated puff of air. "Shireen, I know things haven't been easy but you can't just, you know—" She waves her hands around her like that's supposed to indicate something. But somehow I know exactly what she means.

"Why did you want to call?" I ask, instead of addressing Fatima's pretty valid points.

"Because I read your blog post," Fatima says.

"Oh."

"Yeah." She leans forward so I can almost see up her nostril. Not a pleasant sight by any means, but considering I've known Fatima pretty much since I came out of the womb not an unfamiliar sight either. "First of all, I hope you saved me some cookie dough/brownie ice-cream sandwiches because it's so bloody hot here that just the thought of them made me seriously consider buying a plane ticket and fleeing this country."

"Fati—"

She holds up a finger to silence me. "But second, and most important, you can't tell people in your blog that you're not going to crumble because of your breakup but then spend all of your time in your bed, watching what? Episodes of *The Great British Bake Off*?" She raises an eyebrow, and I'm annoyed that she's guessed exactly how I've spent the past few weeks. Ever since . . .

But that's the last thing I want to think about, even though it's difficult to not think about it. And it's definitely the last thing I want to talk about.

"*The Great British Bake Off* makes me feel better!" I say defensively. In fact, with Fatima gone to Bangladesh for the summer and my ex suddenly out of the picture, it's the only thing that makes me feel better. Well, that and donuts, when they're not leaking out all over my shirt.

"You know what else makes people feel better?" Fatima asks. "Getting out of bed, going outside, taking in the sun, hanging out with real-life people, not people inside your computer screen."

"First of all, you know living in Ireland means taking in the sun is not an option, and second, Nadiya Hussain, the only successful Bangladeshi person in the food industry, is a real-life person, even if she is inside my computer screen, and she's way more inspiring and motivating than any real-life person can be."

"Even me?" Fatima asks, though I know from the almost inhuman screech in her voice that she's not being serious.

I roll my eyes. "Okay, not counting you."

She smiles, though there's still a little bit of worry in her eyes. "You can't spend the whole summer like this, Shireen," she says after a moment. Softer, this time, so I know she's really worried about me. When there's really nothing to worry about. Because I'm okay—or I'm going to be. Like I declared in my blog post—this cookie (and I'm the cookie) won't crumble. Even if it might get a bit disheveled.

"I'm definitely not going to spend the whole summer like this," I say, but Fatima doesn't exactly look reassured. "Tell me about Bangladesh."

Fatima sighs and leans back. "Did I tell you about the heat?"

"I have a thousand texts ever since you got off the plane."

"And the noise. Even at night!"

"Literally a thousand texts since you—"

"And everyone tells me that I speak Bengali with an accent. My cousins literally called me a bideshi. Me, a bideshi!" she says, like the idea of it is preposterous even though Fatima had never even stepped foot inside Bangladesh until a few days ago. It is a little funny that so many of us South Asians call ourselves desi, but the people in our homelands are quick to call us bideshi, just because we don't live in South Asia anymore. Because we have a different kind of culture, a different kind of life.

"You know, even Ammu says she gets called bideshi in Bangladesh," I say, hoping it'll make Fatima feel a little better. "And she was born there, went to school there, spent pretty much her entire life there."

"Until she decided to move to Ireland. And we shouldn't be punished because our parents wanted that life for us!"

I let out a chuckle, but even I know it sounds hollower than usual. Before Fatima can jump in her worry wagon once more, I launch into the only thing (other than *GBBO*) that has been keeping me occupied this summer. "I should be hearing about the *Junior Irish Baking Show* soon."

"Shireen, don't get your hopes up," Fatima says. I know she means well. She doesn't want me to face crushing disappointment. But I know there's no way I'll face crushing disappointment. There's nobody more qualified to be on the show. They *have* to accept me as one of their contestants.

"I know it's your dream to open up your own dessert shop," Fatima keeps going. "And to have your own cookbook and your own baking show, but reality TV is . . . complex." She says it like she knows a lot about reality TV, when Fatima has never even watched a single episode of *GBBO* or *Cake Wars* or *Nailed It!* Not even *Love Island*.

"I'm not getting my hopes up," I say. "My hopes are exactly where they should be."

Fatima sighs like I'm a lost cause and begins to tell me all about her annoying cousins and all of the ways in which she's made to feel like a bideshi in her own family. From not understanding all of the Bengali words that her cousins use to all of their in-jokes and references that she doesn't have a hope of getting. "And Ammu gets annoyed if I'm not always hanging out with them, even though they're horrible to me."

I'm about to point out that having in-jokes and references aren't exactly targeted harassment against Fatima, but then my phone pings loudly. This time, it's not a text. It's an email notification.

"Hello? Shireen?" Fatima asks, a little too close to her camera once more. "You still there? Did the screen freeze?"

"I got an email," I say, my voice barely above a whisper. "I'll call you back, okay?" I can tell Fatima's about to say something else from the way she parts her lips, but I hang up the call before she has the chance. Instead, I stare at the notification bar on my phone. Because it's not just *an* email. It's *the* email.

From the *Junior Irish Baking Show*.

From: Clare Farrin <junioririshbakingshow@ietv.ie>
To: Shireen Malik <shireenbakescakes@gmail.com>

Dear Shireen,

Thank you so much for submitting your audition video and application form to participate in the Junior Irish Baking Show. We loved your audition and would be delighted to offer you a place in the competition.

Though we won't be filming the first segment of the competition until the last week of June, we are inviting all participants to the IETV studio at Donnybrook for a chance to meet the hosts and judges, along with their fellow participants, and for a chance to get to know the format of the show.

As it is the first year the show will be aired, we are very excited to get started.

Please, let us know if you can be in attendance on Thursday, the fifteenth of June at 5:30 p.m. Refreshments and finger food will be served.

Kind regards,
Clare Farrin

TWO

Sweet Dreams

I'M IN.

I'm in!

I'm in!

I don't think I've known true happiness until this exact moment. Until I opened my email and read the words *loved* and *delighted* and *offer*. I do a little happy jig right in my bedroom, and it's all I can do to contain myself for long enough to shoot out a text to Fatima.

I GOT IN!!!!!!!!!!!!!!!!!!!!!!!!!!!!!!!

She texts back with even more exclamation marks: OH MY GOD!!!!!!!!!!!!!!!!!!!!!!!!!!!!!!!!

I put down my phone and fling myself onto my bed, and I'm not even sure why. But as I lay there staring up at my ceiling and smiling so hard that my muscles feel sore, I think it's because there's too much adrenaline pulsing through my body. And lying here makes my heart rate slowly return to normal. I definitely can't tell Ammu and Abbu the news while I'm grinning like a total lunatic. So I try to stop smiling, and as hard as it is I do achieve it!

I can hear the buzz of the TV downstairs as I pull open my

door. Ammu and Abbu are watching a Bollywood movie if the upbeat song is anything to go by. Ammu and Abbu don't have a lot of time to relax. They both give so much to our donut shop in town, You Drive Me Glazy. So, I feel a little bad about the idea of interrupting their only few hours hanging out together, away from donuts and customers and finances. Away from *me*.

But . . .

This is a pretty special occasion, so I don't feel that bad as I skip into the sitting room and flash my parents a bright—but not too bright—smile.

"Guess what?" I ask, waving my arms around as they both try to squint past me at the TV screen I'm blocking.

"Shireen, move!" Ammu says, motioning for me to get out of the way.

"The fighting scene is about to start!" Abbu exclaims, like we don't all know his favorite scenes from Bollywood movies are the romantic ones. He even sheds a few secret tears when he watches them. And when he watches *Kal Ho Naa Ho*, well, his tears are not so secret.

"This is important!" I say. "Pause the movie."

"Ish, Shireen," Ammu groans. Still, she grabs hold of the remote control and presses the PAUSE button.

"Is it an emergency? Are you okay? Are you hurt?" Abbu asks.

"I'm fine, Abbu. I said *important* not *emergency*. I have good news!"

Ammu and Abbu exchange a worried glance between them.

"Okay?" they mumble in unison.

"Can't you guess what it is?" I urge.

"Ish, Shireen, just tell us. We want to go back to the movie," says Ammu, glancing longingly at the TV screen behind me where Katrina Kaif is frozen middance, wearing a sparkly midriff-baring dress.

"I got an email from the *Junior Irish Baking Show*," I say slowly, trying to rile up the anticipation. But my parents just look at me with blank expressions. "I got in! I'm going to be a participant!"

They share another look between them. This one is less confusion and more completely unreadable to me. They've been married for so long that I'm pretty sure they have their own secret language, one that only needs short glances exchanged.

"Congratulations," Ammu says, though it doesn't sound very congratulatory at all.

"We're very proud of you," Abbu says, his voice a little too flat.

"You can do better than that. This is an amazing opportunity and not just for me," I say. "For You Drive Me Glazy too. Imagine!" I throw my hands in front of me, hoping my parents can see the future I'm envisioning for us. "We can put a sign at the front: YOU DRIVE ME GLAZY, WHERE THE WINNER OF THE FIRST-EVER JUNIOR IRISH BAKING SHOW MAKES DONUTS. WHERE SHE LEARNED EVERYTHING SHE KNOWS. And we'll have customers from all over Dublin. No, all over Ireland. No, all over the *world* flocking into the shop, buying up every donut they can just because I—"

"Shireen," Abbu interrupts. "It's an amazing opportunity but are you sure you're ready for this?"

Some of my excitement dissipates. I feel like a balloon that Abbu has just let the air out of with those words.

"Why wouldn't I be ready? If I wasn't ready, I wouldn't have applied. I'm a good baker." I can't have Ammu and Abbu, the two people who have always supported me through everything, not believe in me.

"You've just been so down lately," Ammu adds, like that's an explanation. "You skipped work last week because, you said, 'I can't be around donuts right now.'"

"And when you're not at work, you're up in your room in your bed. Doing nothing," Abbu points out.

"I'm doing something," I say. I can't believe they would suggest rewatching *GBBO* for the millionth time is nothing.

"It's just . . . everything started after you applied to the baking show, and we don't want you to stress yourself out. Being on TV, on a reality show, we know it'll be difficult. Stressful. We don't want you to feel bad about yourself if things don't work out the way you think they will."

"You don't think I'll win?" I ask. Just minutes ago, Fatima was asking me not to get my hopes up about even getting in, and now Ammu and Abbu are doubting my baking abilities. I know they all mean well, but somehow it feels like a personal affront. Like they're telling me I'm not good enough when I know that I am.

"We know you can win," Ammu says. "But it's not just about winning. What was the thing with the donuts?"

I obviously can't tell Ammu why that particular day I had become completely donut averse, so I just shrug my shoulders.

"Shireen, you're perfect the way you are. We don't want you to think you have to be different to be on some TV show. Or that you *have* to be on a TV show or that—"

I groan, realization finally dawning on me. It's funny that Ammu and Abbu can never say the word *fat* or that they talk circles around weight with me. Especially because for the most part, Bangladeshi people love talking about people losing weight or gaining weight. People being too fat or too thin. Sometimes, I'll go to a Bangladeshi dawat, and an aunty that I've spoken to only once before will comment about how pretty I would be if I just lost a few kilos. Like prettiness and weight are all tied up together. In Bangladeshi culture, I guess they are.

But Ammu and Abbu, they've come around to the fact that I'm happy with who I am. I love it, even. Though other people always criticize them for "letting me get fat," they try their best to not let me hear that kind of stuff anymore.

And now, they think I was avoiding donuts because the possibility of going on TV is making me think I need to lose weight. When that's the last thing on my mind.

"I don't want to change or lose weight," I say to my parents now, not sure how to make them believe me when I can't really explain to them why I've spent the past few weeks with an on-again, off-again relationship with donuts and with baking shows and my bed as my only company. "It's just been . . . I've just . . . I miss Fatima." I nod slowly, because that seems kind of believable I think, even though my parents are looking more confused than ever. "If she were here, we would be spending our summer together. We would be going to the park and the movies and doing all kinds of things. So, without her I guess I've just been a little . . . sad."

Ammu and Abbu exchange another glance. If I'm not mistaken, they almost look like they believe me.

"But this show is going to make things better, see?" I say, pasting a grin on my face again. "I'm already feeling better. Excited! Now I have something to do with my summer. Something to look forward to every day."

"And you won't let this stress you out too much?" Ammu asks.

"Psh," I say, waving my hand like I have never been stressed out a day in my life.

"And you'll talk to us if this show isn't what you expected or doesn't go as you hoped or stresses you out?" asks Abbu with a raised eyebrow.

"Obviously!" I exclaim, as if I haven't been hiding a massive secret from them for the past year.

"Good, then congratulations, Shireen. We know you're going to be amazing on the *Junior Irish Baking Show*." And this time, they say it like they really mean it.

THREE
All Zest Up

IN ALL MY EXCITEMENT, I HAD ALMOST FORGOTTEN THAT BEING ON the *Junior Irish Baking Show* poses a pretty huge problem: I have absolutely nothing to wear!

"You have a wardrobe full of clothes!" Fatima cries out through the phone when I tell her about my dilemma.

"But nothing worthy of being on TV, to be viewed nationally."

"Hey, I'm going to be watching from Bangladesh. So, you'll be viewed internationally."

"That makes it so much worse!" I cry, throwing open my wardrobe doors and seeing the chaos inside. Once upon a time, my ex would have reprimanded me for how much of a mess everything here was. Nothing is folded properly, just tossed into different cupboards. Almost everything inside needs an ironing. And it's all so disorganized I can't make out my shirts from my dresses from my trousers. But I know that nothing here is good enough to be nationally—internationally—televised.

"You need to figure out who you want to be on TV and dress accordingly," says Fatima from where I've left my phone on the bed as I rifle through my mountain of clothes.

"What do you mean?" I call back.

"I mean, think about it. Reality TV is not real. There's always that person who's painted as the villain, the one who's talking shit about other people, but they're probably not that judgy in real life. Or at least not any more judgy than anyone else around them. And there's always that one angelic person who you immediately want to root for. But you know that they've talked some shit, that they've manipulated it to make you sympathize with them."

I turn around and make my way back to my bed on my hands and knees, just because I have to see Fatima's expression when I say, "You know a lot about reality TV for someone who doesn't watch reality TV." And I know because it's often been a point of contention for us. When I want to watch reruns of *America's Next Top Model*, Fatima insists that I can absolutely do way better things with my time. When I sit down to watch the newest episode of *Love Island*, she grumbles about how too many people are obsessed with that show.

"I may have watched a few episodes here and there," Fatima mumbles, not looking at me. Which is a really difficult and obvious thing when you're in the middle of a video chat. Plus, with her hijab on, there's no long inky-black hair to distract or hide from her very obvious facial expressions. Like now, when she's obviously trying to appear innocent and not judgmental at all.

"Wow, I can't believe after how much you judge other people for watching reality TV shows—"

"I don't judge."

"—that you've finally succumbed too and didn't even tell me!"

"I kind of watched a bunch of different shows just the last

couple of weeks," Fatima says finally. "Right after you told me about applying to the *Junior Irish Baking Show*. I wanted to make sure you were prepared. I wanted to do something to help, especially because I'm not there." She does look me in the eye now, and from the way her face softens I know she's being sincere. My best friend put aside her hatred of reality TV just for me.

"Thanks, Fatima," I say. "I still don't have anything to wear though."

I turn toward the pile of clothes I've just tossed onto the floor, but nothing jumps out at me. I wish I were the kind of person who could head off for a shopping spree whenever the desire struck. Or on the very rare occasion when I found myself about to appear on reality TV, but realize I don't have a reality TV kind of wardrobe.

There are two issues. One, my parents own a donut shop in town, and they often like to remind me that there are too many donut shops in Dublin. It's difficult to make ours stand out, though I think You Drive Me Glazy does a pretty great job. Still, we're not exactly rolling in riches. My parents came here when they were still young, with only the clothes on their back and bright hope in their eyes. This shop—and me—is what they're staking all their dreams on.

Then, there's the fact that I'm not exactly your average-sized Irish girl. I don't know how many times I've gone shopping, spent hours strolling from shop to shop only to come home empty-handed. Not just because so many shops have nothing in my size but also because so many of the clothes they have for plus-sized people are just not flattering. It's like people make clothing for us that is supposed to cover us up, hide us. I don't want to wear anything that hides me. But cute clothes that complement our bodies are pretty difficult to come by. And most of the time they're expensive.

"You can borrow some of my stuff if you want," Fatima says when I've been sitting in silence staring at my pile of clothes for way too long to be considered normal.

"Because you're going to send them over from Bangladesh?" I ask.

"No, there's still a ton of stuff in my wardrobe. Your ammu and abbu have the key to our house."

"We're not even the same size, Fatima." I sigh, burying my head in my hands. I crawl toward my pile and with closed eyes reach over and grab hold of the first thing I touch. I only open my eyes when I'm holding it up in the light. It's a bright yellow dress with lemons printed across the skirt. Seeing it sends a jolt of pain through me, and I toss it back into the pile almost as soon as I lay eyes on it.

"Maybe I can figure out my dress choices some other day," I say. "I mean, I only have to dress for the meeting at IETV studios, which won't be filmed. I have time."

"Shireen," Fatima says. "That's your favorite dress. You can't just never look at it again because of who—"

"I don't want to talk about it," I cut Fatima off and begin to shove everything back into my wardrobe. I push the doors closed with some effort, though I know I'll regret this tomorrow morning when I have to open it up again and face an avalanche of wrinkled clothes.

"You're going to have to deal with it at some point. She might be at the show."

I know Fatima is right. I know that with my luck she'll definitely be at the show. But there are going to be tons of contestants, and I know I can avoid her. I think I can avoid her. I want to avoid her.

"Look, even if she's on the show, it doesn't matter," I say, though the way my stomach has dropped tells me that it matters to me a lot. But I can't say that to Fatima. I've spent way too long feeling sad about a girl who didn't even care about me enough to help me realize my dreams. A girl who wants to sabotage my dreams. I'm not going to let her take away the little spark of happiness I have this summer.

"Shireen . . ." I can tell Fatima wants to talk about it. Like, really talk about it, because we haven't since everything happened. Since I began my new life of *GBBO*, my bed, and the occasional box of donuts.

"I can deal with her. If I have to," I say. "Don't you have faith in me?"

Fatima sighs, like she doesn't want to be having this conversation any more than I do. "Yes, I have faith in you. I know that no matter what, you're going to do amazing in this."

"Good. Because I'm not letting her ruin this."

FOUR

Meet and Treat

I COUNT DOWN THE DAYS TO THE FIFTEENTH OF JUNE RELIGIOUSLY. Every day that I wake up and it's not the fifteenth of June, my day is a little worse. But I know I have work to do. Just because I'm a contestant on the show doesn't mean things are going to be easy going forward.

I manage to get hold of all of Ammu's recipe books. Some of them are even in Bangla, and I get her to translate as much of it as she can for me. She gives up after the third recipe, but I can't really blame her, considering she never follows recipes anyway. Her instructions to me have always been "andaj moto deo," which basically translates to "follow your instincts." It doesn't really work when you want to try new recipes because things can go very wrong, very fast.

And I'm not looking to trend on Irish Twitter for the wrong reasons.

One morning I wake up, roll to my side to check my phone, and . . . it's June 15. It's the day. But I don't fill up with hope and excitement and the overwhelming sense of joy that I expect to feel. Instead, something presses into my chest. Like a rock or something. And the breath has been sucked out of me. I'm just lying on my bed with my phone faceup beside me, and it's June 15, and I'm supposed to go to the IETV studios because today is the day, but I can't breathe!

I know what I'm supposed to do when I feel anxious like this. I close my eyes and count my breaths. Slowly breathing in and breathing out. Usually, that works. But because it's today, it's like the world has it out for me. No, more like my own mind has it out for me. Because there are a million thoughts buzzing around my head, but I can't pick out a single one, and my chest is so constricted I am pretty sure I'm dying.

That is, until my eyes land on the half a donut necklace peeking out from the mess that is my desk. I can barely make it out from all the way over here, but it evens my breathing somehow. It makes today feel more . . . surmountable. I give it a few more minutes, to make sure I'm not actually dying before I scramble out of bed and head to my desk.

I'd thrown this necklace here a few weeks ago, right after our breakup. I thought back then I never wanted to see it again. Never wanted anything to do with something that was so connected to her and us and our relationship. But now I pick it up from under all the books and Post-it notes and pens and papers and slide it carefully into one of the drawers. Tucked away for a time when I'm ready, maybe? Or maybe for a time when I'm ready to really be rid of it. I'm not sure. I just know that it gives me the courage I need today. Because I'm not going to let my anxiety keep me from my dreams. I'm not going to let anything keep me from them.

Ammu seems almost as nervous as I am when I hop down the

stairs and into the kitchen with a grin, trying to pretend that I wasn't having an anxiety attack just a few minutes ago.

"That's what you're going to wear?" She frowns, looking me up and down disapprovingly.

"What's wrong with this?" I ask, glancing down at my red-and-white polka dot midi dress. It's not exactly reality TV show quality, but I think it's cute. Fatima had agreed.

"You have nicer clothes than that, Shireen," Ammu says.

"First impressions are important," adds Abbu, putting down his phone to consider me with a serious expression. I can't remember the last time my parents thought about what clothes I wore. Other than Ammu trying to buy me new Bangladeshi clothes at every opportunity, my wardrobe is not exactly something they get involved in.

"Shouldn't you both be at You Drive Me Glazy?" I ask instead.

"Raju is watching the shop today, so we can take you to the IETV studio," Abbu says. I think about this for a long moment. On the one hand, Ammu and Abbu taking me to the IETV studios means not having to wait for an unreliable bus and possibly being late. On the other hand, it means having my very loving but slightly overbearing parents by my side. There's also the fact that if my ex is there, they're going to ask questions that I don't want to answer. Like: *Shireen, why is seeing the Huangs' daughter making you have an emotional reaction?* Or: *Shireen, why is the Huangs' daughter glaring at you like you're her sworn enemy?* Or: *Shireen, I didn't know that you and the Huangs' daughter even knew each other?*

And it'll be even worse if Mr. and Mrs. Huang are there because who knows how my parents will react to seeing them.

So, I sit down at the table across from Abbu and perpendicular to Ammu and smile like the most perfect daughter in the world. To Ammu and Abbu, I always have to be that because I am their only daughter, and they have told everyone who will listen to them that I was their miracle baby.

"Abbu, Ammu," I say. "I think if the studio wanted parents to be there, they would have mentioned bringing you with me. It might be awkward if you show up. They might not have space for you."

"But you're our daughter," Abbu says, like he can't comprehend the words coming out of my mouth right now.

"Yes, but—"

"And this is a reality TV show. You can't go on it without our permission."

"Yes, Abbu, but—"

"Because you're only seventeen years old, Shireen."

"I know how old I am Abbu, but—"

"I think Shireen can go on her own." Ammu interrupts this time. Even Abbu seems confused by this, if I were to judge by the speed with which he turns to look at her. I'm surprised he doesn't have whiplash.

"We decided we would go with her and make sure everything was okay," Abbu says.

"We already researched everything, and we looked through the contracts, and we agreed we would give her permission to go. We don't have to go. Shireen can handle it on her own." She sounds so confident that I almost forget about my anxiety attack when I realized it was the fifteenth.

"But make sure you get there early, and you call us if you need us," Abbu says. I know it's his way of saying that he thinks I can do this on my own too.

"Thanks, Abbu."

I'VE NEVER BEEN TO the IETV studios before. Once I get past the car parks and all the different buildings to the room that's been designated to the *Junior Irish Baking Show* contestants, I'm twenty minutes late. Considering Irish people's knack for tardiness, I'm hoping it won't be an issue.

But by the time I register, put on my name tag, and step inside, the place is already filled with people. It's a room that's barely bigger than our donut shop, and there's a little mic placed at the front. Chairs and tables are laid out every which way.

The sight of most of the tables filled makes my heart pick up. There are at least two dozen people here. For some reason, I hadn't really spent much time thinking about the fact that there would be so many other contestants. People who are as good—if not better—at baking than I am. People who are my competition.

I do a sweep for my ex—not that I'll sit with her or even give her more than a quick glance—but she's nowhere to be seen. Relief floods me. Maybe she didn't get in.

With that out of the way, I'm stuck with the predicament of what exactly I'm supposed to do. I can't just join a random table, injecting myself in the middle of people's conversations. For a moment, I just stand there at the back of the room, trying to make eye contact with someone—anyone—in the hopes that they'll take pity on me and invite me to sit with them. It's pretty pathetic, but it's all I've got.

"Hey." A voice interrupts my ridiculous eye-contact plan. I look around quickly and notice a girl with wispy red hair smiling directly at me. She has a pale face full of freckles and a sharp nose. She looks a little like a bird.

"Hi." I approach her hesitantly. Unlike most of the other tables, this one has only this girl at it. It's slightly less intimidating.

"Did you get here late as well?" Her accent has a Northern twang that I can't quite place.

I nod. "What gave me away?"

"The look of someone who has no idea what's going on?" She chuckles. "Do you want to sit with me?"

Relief washes over me, and the smile on my face is almost automatic. "Yeah, sure." I try not to sound too eager, but it doesn't quite work, because when I try to rush to slip onto the seat next to her, I half topple over in all my excitement. I'm pretty sure this is it. Abbu had said first impressions were important and my first impression in this competition is going to be as the girl who can't even sit. But the girl with the red hair grabs hold of my chair at the last minute, until I'm settled all the way into my seat. I can feel my face heat up with embarrassment. Thankfully, I'm dark enough that not even a hint of a blush shows on my face. Bangladeshi aunties may despair that my dark skin will never get me a husband (if only they knew I wasn't looking for one), but this is the number one benefit.

Still, the girl shoots me a grin like I didn't just almost fall flat on my face right in front of her. "My name is Niamh."

"I'm Shireen," I say as confidently as anyone can after that majorly embarrassing almost incident.

"That's a pretty name," she says, her bright blue eyes watching me a little too closely. My cheeks somehow heat up even more.

"Um, thanks. Are you from the North?"

"Belfast, yeah." She nods. "You?"

"I'm from Dublin," I say. "So, you've come all the way here from Belfast? Did the show put you up?"

Niamh chuckles again. She has a nice laugh. "Please, as if they would. I'm staying with my aunt. It's not a big deal anyway, because I was going to come up next year for university, though I'll be staying in residences. But coming up now and getting a feel for things, it's good."

"Which university? Culinary school?" I ask the question a little too eagerly. I've always wanted to skip university altogether to attend culinary school. It's another dream of mine, though I still have to get Ammu and Abbu on board.

Niamh grins but shakes her head. "My ma and da wouldn't let me do that. I promised them coming to this"—she spreads her arms out—"means that afterward I'm going to study hard at university. My top choice is UCD Business to study accounting, but I guess we'll see. There are lot of people here from all across Ireland though."

My stomach drops. All across Ireland. I hadn't even thought about that. "You've already talked to them?" I ask Niamh instead.

"Some. We've got to scope out the competition, don't we?" She has this twinkle in her eye as she says it, and I remember again that this is a competition. Niamh seems nice and, well, cute. But she's probably just trying to figure out how much competition I am to her in this thing. We're all in this to win.

"Is that why you asked me to sit with you?"

Niamh's smile widens. "Not exactly." But she doesn't get a chance to elaborate because the next moment the noise of mic static fills the room.

"Testing, one, two, three."

I turn to the front of the room, where a woman with honey-blond hair and bright red lipstick stands with the mic in her hand. She grins down at us, and her outfit—a navy blazer and blue skirt—makes her look a little too much like a flight attendant. But maybe this is what reality TV show fashion is all about. "Welcome, everyone, to the first-ever *Junior Irish Baking Show*. My name is Kathleen Keogh and I'm so excited to have you all here today. There are so many bright young bakers in our midst. We're thrilled to get started with the competition." As she speaks, Kathleen weaves her way around the room. The click of her high heels sounds too loud against the otherwise deafening silence. She has our rapt attention.

"Now, you're all here today to get the chance to meet me, the show's host." At this, she pauses and glances around. I wonder for a moment if we're supposed to applaud, but since nobody else does, I don't either. Kathleen doesn't seem too disappointed, though, because she continues as if there were no awkward pause. "And you're also here to meet each other, your fellow competitors. Right now, there are twenty-six of you, but there will only be one winner at the end."

My breath hitches in my throat at her words. There are twenty-five people that I have to beat if I want to win this competition. Twenty-five people who are probably just as good at baking as me. I've told everyone that I was guaranteed to get in, guaranteed to win, in an attempt to convince them that I was doing okay—great, even. That this was my great destiny—the path to achieving my dream of opening my own bakery. But now for the first time I'm thinking about the fact that I have competition—and from how serious everyone else in this room looks, everyone here is in it to win it. Just like me.

"Most important"—Kathleen's voice breaks through my anxious thoughts—"we're here today to pair you up for the first round of the competition."

Pair us up? Across the room, the contestants exchange confused glances. Even Niamh looks over at me with a question on her face.

Kathleen plows on like she hasn't noticed our reactions. She takes out a sheaf of envelopes and waves them around for a moment. "In these envelopes you will find the filming schedule and all the rules of this competition. The first episode is going to be filmed on the twenty-ninth, and you will need to work well with your partner in order to win. Every baker needs to know how to work well with others. There is no *i* in baking." Kathleen stops and takes us all in for a moment, and I wonder if she is taking this time to rethink the fact that there actually is an *i* in baking. But instead, she just flashes us another smile and says, "Any questions?"

I glance around the room full of my fellow participants, who seem just as awestruck as I am. I have a million questions, of course, but they're swimming around in my head all jumbled together. I'm not sure I'd make any sense if I actually tried to ask any of them.

Kathleen claps her hands together and says, "Great! So the pairings are at random, and I have a list here. Make sure you use this time to get to know your partner and figure out your first steps in this competition." And before we can say anything more, she begins to prattle off a list of names.

Niamh leans close to my ear and whispers, "This feels like being in school." And it does feel like that. Like in first year when you don't know anybody and the teachers try to pair you up all the time in a weird attempt to help you make friends. It always fails.

I try to ignore the rush of anxiety worming its way through me while listening out for my own name.

"David O'Clery and Ruby Ryan." I watch as a lanky boy with curly brown hair and a girl with bright blond locks and a face full of freckles exchange a grin on the other end of the room. I wonder if they already knew each other before the show or if they've just met and struck up a friendship.

"Niamh Lynch and . . . Séan Brennan." My heart sinks at Séan's name. Niamh shoots me a deflated smile, like she had hoped we would get paired up together too.

"And . . . hm, not sure how to say this name." Kathleen frowns at the list of names. "Sha . . . ron. May-leak?" I wince. Both at the completely butchered pronunciation of my name and the fact that Kathleen did not even try at all. "And Christina Who-aang."

Even though Kathleen completely screwed up the name, my stomach sinks for a different reason.

They paired me up with my ex.

FIVE

We Were Mint to Be

FROM THE FRONT OF THE ROOM, A FAMILIAR FACE MEETS MY EYE. The first thing I notice is just how much she's changed. Her long black hair has been chopped short. Instead of falling all the way to her waist, her hair barely comes to her shoulder now.

It's only been a few weeks since we broke up, and it seems she's already altered her entire look. That thought makes a hole open up in my stomach.

I wonder what else she has changed about herself. I can't make out her expression at all. Once upon a time, I could read Chris like an open book. She glances away quickly, like she can't bear to keep looking at me. I try not to think about it too much as I glance back at Kathleen, who is still smiling down at us.

"Enjoy the food and drink. Prepare for the first episode with your partner, and I will see all of you on the first day of filming." Kathleen gives a perfectly manicured wave of her hand before she click-clacks out of the room and disappears from sight.

For a few minutes, nobody moves. Then, slowly but surely, the contestants begin to drift around the room, looking for their partners and grabbing envelopes. Niamh, though, stays seated right beside me.

"That was a bit anticlimactic, wasn't it?" she asks.

"I guess. I think once we start filming it'll be a bit more excit-ing." I obviously don't tell her that I've been paired up with my ex-girlfriend and the fact that this is making my palms sweaty and my heart beat a little too fast.

"Too bad we weren't paired up," Niamh says. She's completely oblivious to my low-key anxiety attack. I don't know if that's a good thing or a bad thing. "But I guess what were the chances of that, right?"

"One in twenty-five?" I ask.

Niamh grins, but I can't muster up a smile because from the corner of my eye I can see Chris making her way over to us.

Niamh must see my face fall because she glances behind us—then back at me. "You know her?"

"Yeah." I leave it at that. I definitely don't want to hash out my entire history with Chris to someone I just met.

I don't know what Niamh deduces from my singular yeah, but she doesn't ask any more questions. She just leans back a bit, so when Chris finally makes her way toward our table a moment later, there's space for her.

"Hey," Chris says. She gives us both a smile that seems a bit pained. Very *not* Chris.

"Hi," I say, looking at Niamh, then the table, then at the rest of the room. I'm not sure if I can look at Chris—like properly look at Chris—when she's here, right in front of me.

"Hello." Niamh—at least—sounds normal. She even shoots Chris a pleasant smile. "I'm Niamh."

"I'm Chris," says Chris, before clearing her throat and glanc-ing at me. "Shireen, should we?" She motions toward one of the empty tables. I notice that she already has two envelopes in her hands.

The last thing I want to do is be alone with her, but I guess fate has pushed us together, and there's nothing I can really do. In my head, I'm just asking, *Why, fate?* over and over again. But out loud I say, "Sure, yeah."

"Wait!" Niamh exclaims, stopping us in our tracks. She reaches into her pockets and pulls out her phone. "Give me your phone number, Shireen. Maybe we can hang out sometime?"

I glance at Chris subtly, and she looks blank. Like she doesn't care that some other girl has just asked me for my phone number.

"Sure, that would be . . . good. That'd be nice!" I say, typing my number into her phone. Then, too soon, Chris and I are walking away, leaving Niamh behind to meet up with her partner. The walk to the nearest empty table takes only a few seconds. But it's the longest few seconds of my entire life. The silence between us is palpable, and somehow Chris and I manage to keep an entire person's distance between us.

When we finally sit down, we have no choice but to actually look at each other. And I hate that my stomach flips. I'm not sure if it's anxiety or nervousness or familiar feelings rising to the surface again. I hope it's not that last one.

"Looks like you already made a good friend," Chris says, her expression still blank. She slides one of the envelopes toward me while I take her in for a moment.

"Yeah, maybe I did," I say, before glancing down and slitting my envelope open. I start to sift through the contents inside.

There's a schedule for production and another schedule for the show's airtimes. And finally, a single sheet of paper detailing our challenge for the first episode.

"Make something with chocolate," Chris says. When I glance up, she's staring at the same sheet of paper as I am. She looks up at me with a confused expression. "I thought this was supposed to be hard."

"Well, you're one of the participants, so clearly not." I regret the words almost as soon as they leave my lips. I sound so cruel, but I can't take them back now.

Chris looks at me with a smile, though there's no humor in it. "So, this is how it's going to be?"

"I . . . don't know what you're talking about." I glance back at my piece of paper. Reading and rereading the words, even though nothing actually registers in my head. Because I'm a little too aware of the fact that Chris is staring right at me.

"Is there a problem?" I snap after a moment because Chris is still staring at me.

"I don't have one," she says. "Do you have one?"

"You know what, I'm going to ask if we can switch partners." I stand up, and my chair scrapes loudly against the concrete floor. "Maybe I can partner with Niamh and you—" I don't get a chance to even leave my chair—or finish my sentence—because next thing I know Chris's hands are clamped around my wrist. Her grip is tight—almost rough. Still, her familiar touch makes a lump form in my throat. It makes my heart flutter.

I fucking hate this.

I pull away, trying to ignore the weird things my body is doing, and settle her with a glare. "What. The. Hell?"

"We're not splitting up, Shireen. They wouldn't let us anyway."

"Don't touch me," I say. The words are supposed to come out angry and strong, but they come out soft and weak. Like I'm making a plea not giving a command.

Chris's face softens. It's the first time that her guard seems to have come down. She takes a step back. "I'm sorry. Just . . . I know we broke up but I thought . . . I mean, we don't have to be . . . it doesn't have to be like this."

"What did you expect?" I ask, trying to change the hammering of my heart into the anger I should be feeling for Chris. After all, if she had her way, I wouldn't even be here.

"You broke up with *me*, Shireen. You don't get to be angry at me." She actually looks confused at my anger. Like I broke up with her out of the blue for no good reason. Like she didn't betray me or try to stomp all over my dreams.

"Right, because our breakup was so amicable," I say.

Chris runs a hand through her hair and takes another step back. It wouldn't matter how close or far she was—the distance between us is palpable. I don't know how we were together one whole year. Now, it's like we can't even understand each other.

"You know, neither of us is going to make it through this if we don't work together, right?" she says, staring right at me with her warm brown eyes.

I know that she's right. We've been paired up for this first round of the competition, and neither of us can go forward if we don't find a way to work together. But I can't just sit across the table from her, pretending that everything's okay. No matter how many times I tried to convince Fatima that I was fine, I'm not really fine.

"Why did you cut your hair?" I ask, instead of replying to her question.

Chris scrunches her eyebrows together, as if she hadn't expected me to ask this. "I felt like a change, I guess?" She shrugs like it's not a big deal. But it feels like a big deal.

"Because of our breakup?" I ask. Chris's expression shifts back to the void it's been every time I've glanced at her today. I know that neither of us wants to talk about our breakup, that we shouldn't be talking about anything except the first challenge, but I have to understand why Chris is suddenly so . . . different. So unlike the girl that I was with for the past year.

"Why would it be because of our breakup?" Chris asks.

"So, you ended a one-year relationship and then cut off all your hair and the two things aren't related?"

Chris crosses her arms over her chest. "I didn't end a one-year relationship. That was you."

"You didn't answer my question."

She takes a deep breath and looks to the other side of the room. Out of the corner of my eye, I can see Niamh and her partner in an animated conversation. Niamh looks like she's having about as good a time as I am.

"I have wanted my hair short for a long while, but you didn't

35

want me to cut it. So, now that we're broken up, I thought, *Yeah, it would be a good time to make the change*." Chris turns back to me. "So, I guess, in some ways, yeah, it was because of our breakup."

"I never said I didn't want you to cut your hair," I say. And I didn't. She asked me for my opinion on whether she should cut it short or keep it as it was. I just gave it to her.

"You said you thought it looks better long. I wanted you to like my hair," Chris says.

"And I told you that you would look perfect no matter what you did to your hair," I say. And I was right—because even with her hair just above her shoulders, Chris looks . . . well . . . "I was wrong," I tell Chris, glancing down instead of looking at her. "It doesn't suit you."

Chris chuckles, but she doesn't sound amused. "You're really something, Shireen."

"Isn't that why we were together?" I ask, looking up. Chris's face darkens.

"I think we can do this over text. I think that will be best." She doesn't wait for me to reply. Instead, she turns away and hurries toward the door. A few of the other contestants watch her curiously as she passes before their eyes shift over to me at a table all by myself.

My cheeks warm at the attention. I can't believe she just up and left like that. But I also can't believe that I said all of those things to her. But she deserves them . . . doesn't she? Chris doesn't feel like the person I dated—the girl that I was pretty sure I was in love with for the best part of a year. This Chris, the one with the blank expression and short hair feels like someone I don't seem to know at all.

I wait for five minutes before I gather my things and hurry out the door too. All the while, I wonder how getting a chance at my dream suddenly turned so bittersweet.

SIX

Friend, Foe, or Something S'more?

AMMU AND ABBU HAVE A BAJILLION QUESTIONS FOR ME AS SOON AS I get home, but I'm in such a bad mood that I don't want to answer them. I want to go up to my bedroom, get into my PJs, and start watching reruns of *GBBO* once more. But I remember this morning: Ammu said she trusted me to do this. And she and Abbu put a lot of faith in me, letting me go to this competition.

So I put on a bright smile and tell them all about Kathleen Keogh and the first round of the competition.

"And who's your partner?" Ammu asks. "It's a good idea to make friends, you know." Obviously, what I told her about how I was sad because Fatima was gone to Bangladesh really stayed with her.

"Well, she's—"

"No," Abbu interrupts, shaking his head vehemently. "This is a competition, Shireen. You're not there to make friends."

"Just because it's a competition doesn't mean she can't make any friends," Ammu says, sending a small glare in Abbu's direction.

"Shireen wants to win this, don't you?" Abbu turns to me with a smile.

"I do, and—"

"So, in these reality TV shows, you have to watch out for your competition!"

"Can I go to my room?" I rush to interject with my question before Abbu and Ammu can get deeper into their ridiculous argument. I'm pretty sure neither of them have watched enough reality TV shows to be doling out advice like they're experts. Thankfully, they look at me with twin expressions of sympathy and shoo me up to my bedroom.

I call Fatima as soon as my door clicks shut behind me. She's the only person I can really talk to about Chris, and I need to talk about her. And about everything that happened today. I need her to help me figure out a game plan about how to work with Chris.

But Fatima doesn't pick up the phone. It rings and rings and rings. I check the time. It's way past midnight in Bangladesh now. I hate time differences. And I hate that Fatima isn't here right now. So, I collapse onto my bed instead, letting out a groan that doesn't even cover half of my frustration—not even a quarter or an eighth. Because not only did Chris make it into the competition but she also had to be my partner? What kind of justice is that?

That familiar lump rises in my throat again, and this time I'm about to let the tears out. I'm alone in my room. And my ex-girlfriend sucks. And my best friend is thousands of miles away. Why shouldn't I curl up in bed and cry my heart out?

But then my phone pings with a new text, and I swallow back my tears. When I look at the screen, it's not a message from Fatima.

Hey! It's Niamh, from the Junior Irish Baking Show? You left in a rush, just wanted to make sure you were okay?

My stomach flips, but Niamh is probably just being nice because she doesn't know anyone in Dublin. I pick up my phone, but before I can type out a reply another message from Niamh comes in.

Sorry, I probably sound like such a weirdo! Just seemed like you and your partner weren't getting on, and my partner is kind of a dickhead so . . .

I hold back a smile and send out a quick reply.

Me: Hey, I'm . . . okay. Yeah, my partner and I aren't really working great together.

It's definitely an oversimplification, but I can't really explain what things are like with Chris over text. I can barely even explain it in person. It hurts a little too much to even think about.

Niamh: Want to meet up tomorrow and talk shit about our partners?

I can't help the grin on my face. I'm not sure if I'm ready to talk shit about Chris, my ex-girlfriend, yet. But maybe it wouldn't hurt to talk shit about Chris, my unfortunate baking partner.

Me: There's nothing I would like more.

I SPOT NIAMH IN the corner almost as soon as I enter Rise and Grind Café the next morning. She's sitting on a love seat all by herself, cradling a mug in her hands and staring off into the distance. But as I approach, her head snaps up and her face breaks into a smile.

"Hey," I say, and slide onto the love seat next to her. It feels a little strange being here with her when I barely even know her.

"Hi. Aren't you going to get some coffee?" She nods toward the till just beside the front door. There's a short queue of people already lined up.

"No, I don't drink coffee." I wait for Niamh to get judgmental, as people sometimes do. But she just asks, "Tea?"

I hesitate before answering, because admitting that you don't drink tea to an Irish person is basically as bad as admitting to a crime. "No caffeine. My girlfriend says—" I stop myself. Because of course, she isn't my girlfriend anymore, and it still feels strange to realize that. "I mean. My ex-girlfriend used to say . . ." I recover, trying to brush it off instead of thinking about how referring to Chris as my girlfriend when we broke up weeks ago probably means things I don't want it to mean. ". . . that I'm hyper enough without any caffeine, so I really don't need it. And my best friend says I probably have enough sugar in my diet to make up for the lack of caffeine."

Niamh smiles, which is a good start. "I like that everybody has theories about why you don't drink caffeine. But just so you know, I've heard they have really good hot chocolate here. And amazing baked goods. Though, I'm sure they don't compare to what you can do."

I hold back a smile. "I mean, we're both contestants on the show, so . . ."

"We are," Niamh says, leaning back in her seat. "And you know, it's nice to be around people who, like, get it."

"Get it?"

"You know, like, the whole baking thing."

"What? Your friends back home don't like getting free baked goods whenever the whim takes you?" I don't think I've had anyone get weird about my baking obsession. Friendship with me means free baked goods for the rest of their lives—not to mention all the delicious donuts from You Drive Me Glazy. I'm not sure how long Fatima would put up with me if all the complaining and annoying her with all my problems didn't also come with the best chocolate chip cookies to ever exist (her words, not mine).

"Sure, they like *that*, but me talking about it? Not really. I told them about coming on this show and they were excited about me being on TV or whatever, I guess. But, like, they don't really get it. Why it's so important to me and what I really want to do with it all," Niamh says.

"Start your own bakery?" I ask.

Niamh shoots me a grin. "How did you know?" Except, of course, I imagine all of us in the *Junior Irish Baking Show* have this exact same dream. It's not easy to break into the food industry, but with the money and semifame from winning the competition, it can definitely be a lot easier.

I want to ask Niamh why—if her dream is the same as mine—she's going to university to study accounting. If she really wants it, shouldn't her parents support her? But I don't think we know each other well enough to have that conversation yet. So I change the subject to the real reason we're here anyway. "So, your partner . . ."

"Séan." Niamh lets out a groan.

I giggle. "That bad?"

"He's just a bit . . . much," Niamh says. "I think he's one of those guys who's got a bit of a big head or whatever. He already knew exactly what he wanted to make, and he seems convinced that once we get past the first episode, he's absolutely going to win this thing." She rolls her eyes. "I imagine he's the best baker at the tiny home ec class in his all-boys school in Louth or whatever, but he doesn't seem to have realized that he's in a competition with people who can actually tell apart a whisk from a sifter."

"So, not a favorite to win?" I grin.

Niamh shakes her head, like she's already done with him. "I'm ready for the first challenge if only because I need be rid of this bastard. Other than his mansplaining and condescension, he's also tried to flirt with me. Like anyone could be into a prick like him."

I've definitely met enough guys like that in my life to know exactly how frustrating it must be to have him as a partner. Though it's not like being partnered with Chris is a walk in the park.

"But at least he had ideas about the first challenge, right? What exactly did you guys settle on making?"

Niamh shifts in her chair, glancing away from me. "Well, we juggled some ideas and, well, you know."

I don't know—obviously. But I can tell Niamh really doesn't want to tell me. For the first time since we met, it feels like we're competitors. And when the first challenge takes place, Niamh and Séan doing well might mean that Chris and I don't.

The silence between us seems to stretch out for hours, but finally Niamh clears her throat and meets my eyes with a small smile.

"What about your partner?" she asks. "You two seemed to already know each other?"

"Yeah . . ." I'm not really sure how to explain the whole thing with Chris. Not sure I really want to either. "My parents and her parents are, well, competitors, I guess."

That piques her interest so much she leans forward in her seat. "Really? And now you're competitors?"

"Well. My parents own this donut shop called You Drive Me Glazy—"

"Fantastic name."

"Thank you, I came up with it. I am a master of puns."

That gets a chuckle out of Niamh.

"Well, the thing is You Drive Me Glazy is across the street from this other shop. The Baker's Dozen. And, well, it's run by Chris's parents, the Huangs. So, my parents and the Huangs have hated each other for a long time."

"And you and Chris . . ." Niamh looks at me like I'm supposed

44

to finish her sentence for her. For some reason, that makes my heart beat faster.

"What?"

Niamh holds my gaze for a moment too long before shaking her head. "Nothing, never mind. I guess it hasn't been easy working with her."

"Working with her has not been working at all," I say. "We got into a fight and she stormed out. We've figured out nothing, and . . . I don't know how we're going to work together."

"Hey, if Séan and I could figure it out, you and Chris can put your differences aside too," Niamh says. I know she means to be encouraging, but her words send anxiety gnawing through me. Has everybody already decided what they're making for the challenge? I can almost see the twenty-four other people—twenty-four people who are my competitors—spending all their time preparing for the challenge. Coming up with the most creative and original recipes. And practicing. If Chris and I can't even sit together for a few minutes to have a conversation, how are we going to actually work together to make something in the kitchen?

"Hey." Niamh's voice interrupts my thoughts. When I look up, she's sitting a little closer. Her eyes are kind, her expression soft. It's like she can read my mind. It fills me with a sense of comfort I haven't felt since—Chris. But I definitely can't get caught up in this—not with Niamh and not now.

"Thank you." I come to a hasty stand. "It's getting late. I should probably go. Thank you for . . . this." Even though I haven't really figured out what this is yet. I had thought we were just meeting to talk shit about Chris and Séan, but I suspect it was something else to begin with.

"No problem." Niamh smiles. "I'll see you later?"

I smile back, trying to ignore the butterflies in my stomach. "Definitely."

SEVEN

Pudding Up with Exes

I HAVE FIVE MISSED CALLS FROM FATIMA AND A BAJILLION TEXTS asking me for updates about the show. I wait until I'm home to call her, and she picks up after just one ring.

"Where have you been?" she asks, exactly like Ammu does if I'm ever home later than I said I'd be.

"I was, you know, working," I say. I'm not sure why I lie. Maybe because I know Fatima would tell me maybe it's not such a good idea to hang out in a kind-of-sort-of date with someone who is supposed to be my competitor. Especially not when everything with Chris is so fresh. But I don't want to deal with Fatima's logic, and I don't want to hear her lectures. Especially when I'm pretty sure Niamh and I are friends only.

So, instead, I tell Fatima all about Chris and our argument at the IETV studios. She listens with rapt attention, even though I can hear people in the background speaking Bangla, along with the clink of cutlery and laughter. There's probably some kind of a dawat going on in Fatima's house, and she's spending her time listening to me complain about my problems. That's the kind of best friend she is.

After I finish my story, Fatima scrunches up her eyebrow

like she's in serious thought. Then, she says, "Chris was out of line—"

"Right? Like, how could she—"

"But"—Fatima raises a finger to interrupt me—"I think you were kind of out of line too."

I scoff. "How was I out of line?"

"You were kind of mean. Well, really mean," Fatima says. "You said her hair was ugly."

"I said that her short hair didn't suit her, not that it was ugly."

"I don't see the difference," Fatima says. "The point is, you shouldn't have said anything about her hair at all. You should have talked about baking and that's it."

"Easier said than done," I mumble under my breath, but obviously Fatima hears me because my phone is right in front of me.

"Look, I told you it was going to be hard," she says.

"I can't believe you're I-told-you-so-ing me!"

"I'm sorry!" Fatima says, but she doesn't sound sorry at all. "But you have to put your differences aside and figure out how to work with her. I think you should apologize to her."

"I should apologize?" My voice rises higher than I want it to, but I just can't believe that Fatima is taking Chris's side over mine. I know that they were kind-of-sort-of friends when we were dating. But it was just because we were dating. I've known Fatima my whole life. Fatima has barely known Chris for a year, and half that time was just hearing about Chris from me.

"Okay, you need to stop freaking out." Fatima lowers her voice, stealing a glance around her as if to check if someone is listening. "Look, I need to go because we're having a thing here, and Ammu will notice if I'm missing for too long and try to come find me. But I'm just saying if you want to win this thing, you need to figure out how to work with Chris. And being angry all the time isn't going to help you do it. Whatever happened between you two . . . happened. And it sucks. And she was mean yesterday, but so were you. You apologize to her, get through the first round of the competition. Then you can go back to calling her hair ugly all you want."

"But—"

Fatima raises a finger again to interrupt me. "I know it's not ideal, Shireen, but it's what Allah's given you to work with, hasn't he?"

I want to argue and tell Fatima that there's no way in a million years I'm going to apologize to Chris. But . . . somewhere in the back of my mind there's a voice telling me that she is right.

"Okay, now I really have to go," Fatima says, glancing back once more. "Food is served, and I'm not letting my cousins get all the good stuff before me. I'll talk to you later, okay?"

"Sure, yeah." The screen goes blank before I can even say goodbye. I wish for a moment that Fatima were here instead of in Bangladesh. She complains about the heat and the noise, but I know that she's having fun. She's got her cousins, her family. Without her here, I feel like I've got no one.

Instead of dwelling on that, I go to my messages and click on Chris's name. It's been weeks since we last texted each other. I'm not sure how exactly to figure this thing out, but Fatima is right. I have to find a way to work with her. Or else neither of us has any shot in this competition.

Me: can we meet up and discuss the show?

Chris's answer comes almost immediately.

Chris: working 'til late today, but I can meet you tomorrow.
Usual place?

I chew on my lip for a moment. Our usual place was by the gazebo at Stephen's Green Park. But I can't stomach going back there with Chris.

Me: Let's go to a café . . . Kilkenny?

Chris replies with a thumbs-up emoji, and I feel a weight on my chest at the thought of seeing her again. This time, all on our own.

I ARRIVE AT KILKENNY earlier than we had planned to meet. I buy myself the largest piece of coffee cake they have to offer and their most massive mug of hot chocolate and try to ignore the ball of anxiety growing inside me with each passing minute. I choose a seat in a corner overlooking the window. Specifically so I can spend my time peering outside to check for Chris.

When I finally glimpse her my heart nearly leaps out of my chest. Two minutes later, she's climbing up the stairs, and somehow she spots me in my little corner almost immediately.

She approaches the table a little too slowly, like she doesn't really want to be here. I guess she's still angry at me. Which is fine because I'm still angry at her.

"Hey," Chris says, not really looking at me. She takes off her hoodie and drapes it over the chair. Then, she frowns at the cake and hot chocolate in front of me. Usually, when the two of us went to a café together, we would pick one cake and split it between us. Chris said it was because if I had my way, I would try to have a taste of every cake there, and she had to pull me back from my "natural instincts." I wonder if she's thinking about that now.

"Hi . . . do you want to sit?" I ask when she's hovered by the table for way too long.

"Umm . . ." Chris chews on her lips for a moment, like she's really thinking of taking off after she came all the way here. But then she finally pulls out the chair and perches on the edge. It's almost like she's expecting she'll have to leave at a moment's notice.

"So." I pull out my recipe book from my handbag and lay it out in the middle of the table. Chris blinks at it, like she wasn't expecting to see this now. "I've been tabbing a few of the recipes we could maybe make for the first episode. We have to decide I guess. Do we want something that's just full-on chocolate? Subtly chocolatey? Something in the middle? There are a lot of options and—"

"You want to talk about chocolate?" Chris interrupts.

I glance up to find her staring at me. I had hoped that we could go straight into this without talking about what happened at the IETV studios . . . but maybe not.

"I want to talk about the challenge," I say. "So we can get through this."

"This, meaning the first round where we have to work together?" she asks.

"Obviously," I say. For a moment, Chris holds my gaze, like she's expecting something else—something more—from me. But then she heaves a sigh and looks away.

"Fine. Let's talk about chocolate." Her voice is somber, and nobody's voice should be somber when talking about chocolate. But there's also this hint of finality to it. Almost like dejection. Like maybe she had expected something different from our meeting today. Something more than chocolate.

I push my recipe book farther toward her, avoiding her gaze—though I don't have to try too hard. "These are just some of my ideas. If you have any other ideas—"

"Just tell me your top three ideas," Chris interrupts. "I don't have the time to go through your entire recipe book."

"You don't have to go through all of it," I say, pointing at the tabs. "Just the chocolate recipes."

"There are like a million tabs in this thing," Chris says, running her fingers along the side of my notebook. "I know you have ideas, Shireen. Can you just tell me what they are, and then we can get this over with?"

I lean back in my chair and fold my arms over my chest. I don't know why she's being so difficult.

"Fine," I say. "My top three ideas. We could go with something really classic, like a really nice chocolate cake. I have a recipe for a chocolate truffle cake that is, well, divine."

Chris's eyebrow quirks at my description but she doesn't say anything, so I continue.

"Or we could go with something that is more technically difficult, like a chocolate soufflé for example. Though obviously we both need to be skilled bakers for that to work."

Chris lets out what sounds like a low growl, but she still doesn't make any comments. She's definitely glaring at me now though.

"Or, you know. We could play to our strengths and make something that nobody else in that kitchen will make. Something uniquely Bangladeshi or . . . Taiwanese."

"I'm still not very good at making Taiwanese desserts," Chris says. "And I don't think, out of all the Bangladeshi desserts that you've made me try over the years, a single one of them contained any kind of chocolate."

"Okay, so, no to the last one and no to the soufflé. Which leave us with chocolate cake," I say. Which is great because I can make the best chocolate cake ever.

But Chris frowns at me, like she's not happy with the decision at all. "Why do you immediately assume it's a no to the soufflé? I can make a soufflé."

"You can make a soufflé with a time limit while cameras are on us and probably in a very busy kitchen?" I ask.

"Yes. If you can do it, I can do it," Chris says. Like the two of us are somehow on the same level. I want to say as much to Chris, but Fatima's voice in my head pulls me back. We're supposed to try and work together and being snarky to each other is definitely not going to help either of us win this competition.

"Fine. So you want to make a soufflé?" I ask.

"No," Chris says, leaning back and crossing her arms over her chest. "Because a soufflé is way too easy to mess up. Do you not remember all those episodes of *MasterChef* where the soufflé goes flat?"

"But it doesn't always affect the outcome. As long as the taste is there—"

"But they lose points for presentation I bet. The judges always look very disappointed and serious."

I chuckle. "When do the judges on *MasterChef* not look serious? I don't think I've ever even seen Joe smile."

Chris lets out a chuckle at that too. For a moment, it almost feels like we're back to how we used to be. Watching too many reality TV shows about food and complaining. Eating cake. Splitting donuts. Bringing each other bubble tea in the summertime.

Falling in love.

But obviously, that time doesn't exist anymore.

I clear my throat and drag the recipe book back toward me. "So, chocolate cake?"

"Yeah, chocolate cake," Chris says, her voice somber again.

"Great!" I jam the recipe book back into my handbag and stand up. "I guess I'll see you for the first day of filming."

"Wait," Chris says before I can move past her. "Should we wear matching colors or something?"

"Seriously?" I ask. Because Chris is not the type of person who proposes wearing matching colors.

"I know you're into that kind of thing," she says. "Remember the matching donut necklaces?"

I don't just remember. I tucked it out of sight in my bedroom. The thought of it creates an ache in my heart, but I try to push past it.

"You were the person who made them for us."

"But it was your idea," she says. "I just thought maybe you would . . . Don't worry, it was a ridiculous question."

"I'm going to wear pink," I say, even though I haven't picked out what I'm going to wear yet. But pink is a color that suits Chris astonishingly well. She should definitely wear it more often.

She glances up at me one more time, and there's a question on her face. I'm not really sure what it is, and I'm not sure if I have the answer.

So I look away and say, "See you later," before slipping past her, knowing all too well that the next time we see each other will be the first round of the competition. And I have no idea what's in store for us.

EIGHT

Blood, Sweet, and Tears

EVER SINCE MY BREAKUP WITH CHRIS, I'VE BEEN GOING INTO WORK at You Drive Me Glazy like a thief in the night, breaking into the shop that my parents own. Well, I'm not going as far as crawling through windows or anything. But I did make a copy of Ammu's keys, which open the back door of the shop, so I can sneak in through the deserted alleyway in the back. Just on the off chance that strolling in through the front means seeing Chris through the window at her parents' donut shop and going through a roller-coaster ride of emotions.

But now that I'm seeing Chris for the show, I figure it's probably time to stop doing that. So I stroll through the front door, bathing in the bright glow of the pink neon donut in the *o* of You Drive Me Glazy.

The shop is small, but it always feels a little like coming home. In a way even home doesn't. It's the sharp smell of freshly fried dough, the sweet scents of glaze and fillings, the sound of my Ammu and Abbu arguing somewhere in the background, the clinking of pots and pans, the whirring of a machine. It all feels familiar and warm, even on the coldest winter day.

"Hi!" I say to Raju, the only worker in the shop that Ammu and Abbu have actually hired.

"Not coming in through the back anymore?" Raju asks, ducking out from behind the counter and taking off the apron that's his uniform. It has our shop's logo embroidered on it: a cute pink half-eaten donut and the words *You Drive Me Glazy* in cursive handwriting right beside that.

"I decided I needed a change!" I say. Raju doesn't look convinced, though I'm pretty sure he also doesn't know the real reason I've been avoiding coming in through the front door.

"It would be good if needing a change meant coming to work on time," Raju says.

"I'm only five minutes late," I say, checking the time on my phone. That's better than I usually am.

Raju just gives me a disgruntled look, grabs his massive finance textbook, which could probably be used as a murder weapon, and slips outside.

"You know I'm not going to be able to work at the shop as much once the show starts," I tell Abbu when I spot him coming in from the kitchen. "You should ask Raju if he has any classmates who want a job during the summer."

"We can't afford to hire another person," he says. "Your ammu and I will figure it out."

I feel a pang of worry as I look at the empty shop in front of me. Summer is supposed to be our busiest time of year. We usually get so many tourists coming in, and people are enticed by our bright sign and funny donut names. But this year, our customers have dwindled more and more. We went from a shop full of customers at the start of the year to almost none. With so many donut shops in Dublin now, it's difficult for ours to stand out.

It's not the biggest shop in the world anyway. Renting space in town is expensive. I step past the counter to the cluster of tables in the corner, brushing donut crumbs off the tabletops and tossing half-used coffee cups into the bin. Before turning back, I stop to stare at the wall full of Post-it notes: my idea! The Post-its are full of drawings, names, inspirational quotes— anything and everything from the customers who have visited us since we opened up. Ammu and Abbu begrudgingly let me set the Post-it wall up, though when they saw how popular it was, they couldn't stop singing my praises. But now there's nothing new since the last time I was here, like even our Post-it wall has lost its charm.

I make my way to the other side of the shop with our counter of donut displays. From behind the counter I pull out our chalkboard and set it up at the front of the display case. We always have our donut of the month written on the chalkboard, but I'm the one in charge of coming up with the punniest names ever for them and putting them on the chalkboard at the start of the month. This month, the chalkboard reads ORANGEALINA JOLIE, for the new orange-flavored donut that's part of our summer lineup. For good measure, I pick up a piece of chalk and draw an orange slice beside the name, before dusting the white powder off my hands.

"Are you sure you can handle the shop without me?" I ask. Less because I think I'm the most important thing about this place and more because I know that me not being here as much means Ammu and Abbu will be working even more than usual. And they already work themselves to the bone.

"If you can handle the baking show without us," Abbu says with a smile, and I roll my eyes. But I have to smile too. He's right. If I can go on national TV to try and win the *Junior Irish Baking Show*, then I'm sure my parents can hold down the fort without me.

I have to remind myself that this is also the reason I'm doing the show. Free advertising for You Drive Me Glazy means no more empty shopfront with no customers.

Just as I put on my apron and my customer-is-always-right smile, I hear the *whoosh* of the door opening. A tanned and beautiful couple stroll in through the door. The woman has freckles dotted along her nose, and the man has a stoic expression on his face. They're definitely not Irish. Nobody gets this tanned in the Irish sun.

"Hello," the man says. His English is tinged with an accent that I can't quite place.

"Hi!" I greet him cheerfully. "What can I get you?"

"Where is . . . the . . . museum?" the man asks, his eyebrows furrowed like he's really concentrating on picking and choosing his words.

My stomach sinks. Not customers then.

"Um, which museum?" I ask, trying not to sound too dejected, though it's hard.

The couple exchange a glance.

"National?" the man asks, putting the emphasis on the wrong syllable.

"There are a few of those," I say. "Archaeological? Natural? History?"

"History!" the woman says with an enthusiastic nod.

"It's not close to here," I say. "You'll have to get the Luas toward Tallaght and get off at the stop that says MUSEUM."

The couple nod with serious expressions, and the woman notes something down on her phone.

"Thank you!" they say before strolling out into the rare Irish sunshine.

I try not to groan in frustration. They're the first people other than my family or Raju I've seen in the shop, and they weren't even customers.

"Abbu," I say. "Should we do a new summer initiative to get more customers? Like donuts and ice cream!" I can already see it. A scoop of ice cream with a warm donut. Who doesn't love that? And nothing says summer like ice cream.

"Ice-cream machines are expensive, Abbu," Abbu says, using what I call him as an endearing term toward me. It's something Bengalis do that non-Bengalis probably have no hope of ever understanding. It can be confusing I guess, but I've grown up being called Abbu and Ammu by my parents instead of *honey* or *dear*. It always makes me feel warm and fuzzy with love when my parents call me either.

"But think of how many customers it'll bring in over the summer!" I say. "It'll basically pay for itself!"

But Abbu shakes his head, a strange kind of dejection in his face that I've never quite seen before. When he sees me looking, though, he seems to perk up. He puts away the phone he was scrolling through and says, "With you on the *Junior Irish Baking Show*, we won't need an ice-cream machine."

"That's true," I say, though I'm not sure if my being a contestant on the show is as good as an ice-cream machine.

I glance at the empty shop once more. At the bright colorful walls, the corner of Post-it notes, the case full of donuts. I hope the show does change something.

NINE

Baking New Ground

I WAKE UP TO THE SOUND OF MY PHONE RINGING INCESSANTLY ON the twenty-ninth. I groan and grab at it on the bedside table, and nearly send it crashing to the floor, just catching it at the last moment. *That* wakes me up more than the sound of my familiar ringtone. Fatima's name flashes on the screen. Stifling a yawn, I hit the ANSWER button.

"Today is the day!" Fatima exclaims as soon as the call connects. She sounds ecstatic. Probably because she's not the one going on TV and pairing up with her ex. "Are you excited? Nervous? Excited and nervous? Are you—"

"Fatima," I say, rubbing my eyes. Sleep is still weighing on them and on my body, though there's that current of anxiety running through me that kept me up for half the night. To put it mildly, I feel like shit.

"You're going to be amazing!" Fatima's voice is a little too loud.

"Mm. I hope," I say, sliding out of my video call screen to look at my messages. Niamh has sent me about a dozen texts, excited about the show today. A smile tugs at me when I see her name. For the past couple of days, we've been texting almost nonstop, and even though Niamh has asked to meet up more than once, I've kept my distance. But I still haven't told Fatima about her.

"You know, I would have thought you would be bouncing off the walls this morning." Fatima's voice sobers a little. "I mean, you've always said this is your dream."

I sigh, going back to the call screen so I see the way Fatima is examining me a little too closely. I know that I have bedhead and my eyes are probably rimmed red from sleeping restlessly— or not much at all—for the last couple of nights. I'll need lots and lots of makeup before I leave for IETV.

"Not all of it," I say. "You know that."

"Well . . . the good news is I've figured out how to watch it when the first episode airs. I can get the IETV player, so I'll be cheering you on from Bangladesh. I'll probably get all my cousins to watch too. They've heard a lot about you."

"Yeah?"

Fatima smiles. "They're all ready to line up and buy your desserts. Trust me, Shireen, if you open a dessert shop here in Dhaka, you'll have business like no other."

I have to smile too. Of course a dessert shop in Dhaka is something I absolutely wouldn't do. I haven't been to Dhaka in so many years. The only relatives we have left there are second and third cousins, because all of our apon cousins are in the UK or the United States. Plus, I could never deal with all the traffic and heat in Dhaka. Not to mention that Bengali people always prefer Bengali desserts to everything else. And even though I'm learning how to make more Bengali desserts, there's no way I can compete with the likes of Bonoful and Premium.

There's also the whole thing about me being queer, which is not exactly accepted in wider Bangladeshi society. Even though Ammu and Abbu accept that part of me—well, all parts of me—it's not something we share with the rest of the Bangladeshi community.

"Maybe one day I can make some for them," I say.

"After you win this competition, you might be too busy." Fatima grins.

Fatima's confidence in my abilities does make me feel a little better, but I can't help the anxiety still pulsing through me as I get dressed.

I've opted to wear something that's not as bright and flashy as most of my wardrobe, since too many of those clothes hold memories of Chris. But I suggested the color pink and it was difficult to find something muted pink in my wardrobe. Still, I manage to find a blush pink dress with lace sleeves. I'm not sure if it's exactly reality-show ready . . . but it'll have to do.

THE IETV STUDIO SEEMS even more intimidating today than it did the last time I was here. After a quick instruction session in the orientation room to prep us for filming, I follow the instructions in my email to a massive hall that must be double the size of my whole house—at least. At the front of the of the hall is a raised platform with three armchairs lined up.

I look away from there as fast as I can. So far, I've tried to block out the idea of the competition. But this *is* a competition. Up there on those armchairs the judges will be sitting on their thrones watching us bake. Deciding our fate.

I try to rid myself of those thoughts and instead focus on the rest of the space around me, which is filled with different kitchen stations. There must be at least a dozen. There's probably one for each pair. Just one glance at the station tells me that this is the kind of kitchen I've only dreamed about having my entire life.

I want to rush up and start testing things out, but there are too many people hurrying about, trying to get things ready for the show. I see lighting and camera crew everywhere and try to ignore the anxiety gnawing a hole through my stomach.

Other contestants start trailing in as well. I note Kathleen Keogh arrive with her honey-blond hair up in a bun and her bright lipstick somehow brighter and redder than before. Today, she looks less like a flight attendant. Instead of her blazer, she's wearing a simple brown blouse with a floral pattern in gold, along with a plain blue knee-length skirt. She's in animated conversation with one of the crew members, paying so little attention to her surroundings that I have to duck out of her way as she approaches.

I definitely don't want to be the girl who gets run over by the show's host and camera crew before filming has even started. I was already the girl who almost fell flat on her face.

"You okay?" When I turn around, Chris is standing right behind me. I've been so focused on taking everything in that I didn't even notice her come in.

"I'm fine," I say, even though heat rises up my cheeks. She obviously saw my near collision with Kathleen.

"I don't mean about that," she says. Her voice is that controlled somber tone it has been for the past few weeks—since we broke up and a different Chris with a brand-new haircut emerged. I hate it, but I can't exactly do anything about it.

"What are you talking about?" I snap.

To my surprise, Chris reaches forward and grabs hold of my palms. I try to ignore the tingle it sends through me, the one that feels all too familiar. "Your hands," she says. "They're shaking."

It takes me a moment to realize that she's right. My hands are shaking. I pull them away from Chris, crossing them over my chest and sending a glare her way. I hate that she somehow knows my anxiety even better than I do.

"I'm *fine*." My voice comes out a little more high-pitched than I intended and definitely not fine. So I turn away and dash forward. I'm not really sure toward what or whom. I just know that I need to get away from Chris.

Behind me, I can hear her call out, "Are you really running away from me?" But I don't care. Thankfully, just at that moment, I notice Niamh and her partner enter the hall. They're in an animated conversation that doesn't exactly seem pleasant.

But I figure Niamh and I can help each other out.

"Hey!" I exclaim a little too loudly as I barge right into the middle of their heated conversation.

"Hi!" Niamh says, a smile lighting up her face. Séan, on the other hand, looks me over with distaste.

"You're another one of the contestants," he says, like this is the worst thing I could possibly be.

"Shireen!" I hold my hand out for him to shake, but he just looks at it with his nose turned up for a moment before turning back to Niamh.

"I'm going to go find our station," he says before swiftly walking off.

"That was a good first impression," I say.

"Don't take it personally," Niamh says. "During my short time knowing Séan, I've decided that the best descriptor for him is asshole."

I let out a giggle, and Niamh grins at me like making me laugh is her greatest achievement of the day. I try to ignore the fuzzy feelings that creates in my chest.

"Are you two going to be able to work together?" I ask.

"We'll figure it out. We have to," Niamh says, flicking a strand of red hair out of her eyes. "What about you and . . . your partner?" She nods at Chris in the distance. She's already at one of the kitchen stations, analyzing the equipment so closely that I'm pretty sure she's not analyzing it at all. I notice something that I hadn't before. Chris is wearing a soft pink lace cardigan over her all-black outfit of jeans and a T-shirt. It doesn't quite work. Usually, Chris wears hot pink T-shirts with funny sayings and pictures or crop tops. But I'm guessing Mrs. Huang didn't like the idea of Chris appearing on a nationally televised TV show wearing that.

I'm not sure exactly what it means that we're both wearing pink. That we both kept to our not-quite-an-agreement agreement.

"We'll figure it out. We have to," I repeat Niamh's words with a shrug.

"See you at the next round?" Niamh asks as Kathleen Keogh and the rest of the crew wave at us to get to our kitchen stations, where someone is waiting to get us mic'd up.

"See you at the next round," I say, even while my stomach is doing nervous flip-flops.

I make my way toward Chris and see that each of us have been assigned our own stations. Our names hang in gold-and-silver-lettered plaques in front of each station. I pass by Niamh and Séan's and right toward ours.

It feels strange to see our names lined up together: Christina Huang and Shireen Malik.

But it feels strangely right too.

One of the people from the crew carefully fits both me and Chris with our mics as soon as I arrive, and things start to feel a little too breathlessly real.

"Ready?" Chris asks. I wonder what she thinks of me and Niamh hanging out together. If she thinks anything about it at all.

"I'm nervous," I say, like it wasn't obvious from the incident earlier.

"You've never been nervous about anything to do with baking before," Chris says, her voice surprisingly reassuring. "And you don't have any reason to be now."

I want to believe her—obviously I do. Chris has always been the kind of person to dole out compliments—but none of them have ever been lies. She loved my baking. There was nothing

I made that I didn't save at least a little of for Chris, because I knew no matter how bad it was, Chris would know how to make me feel proud of myself.

But I don't know if I can believe her after everything that's happened. After how we broke up. *Why* we broke up. Even if she doesn't seem to understand it yet.

"This is different," I say, because I know hashing out our past is not a good idea at any point—and definitely not now. "There are going to be so many people watching this."

A hint of amusement flickers in Chris's eyes. Like she's trying to bite back a smile. "You know, there's only like five million people in Ireland, like seven million if you count Northern Ireland. Realistically, how many of them are going to be watching the *Junior Irish Baking Show* and won't just be binging *The Great British Bake Off* for the umpteenth time?"

"I guess," I say. That idea does make me feel better. How many people—exactly—might be interested in a junior baking show?

Chris parts her lips to say something more—but she's interrupted by the camera crews telling everyone to get into place. We exchange a quick glance before moving to our kitchen station.

We barely get to them when the doors to the hallway fling open.

And I realize just how wrong Chris is.

TEN

Batter Up!

"WELCOME TO THE FIRST-EVER *JUNIOR IRISH BAKING SHOW*!" Kathleen's voice rises, and her face relaxes into a smile that is so fake it looks absolutely real. Her teeth shine like pearls under the bright lights—looking even brighter and whiter against the stark red of her lipstick. "Where twenty-six junior bakers from all over Ireland will be competing for the chance to win ten *thousand* euros."

Chris stares at Kathleen intensely, but I can't take my eyes off the raised platform where the three judges sit: three people whose cookbooks I've thumbed through so many times that they're all but falling apart.

"Our judges." Kathleen walks past us and toward the raised platform. "First, we have Máire Cherry, the acclaimed Irish food writer and TV presenter."

Máire Cherry sits all prim and proper in her chair and gently waves at the camera. The string of pearls on her neck glints when they catch the light.

"Máire is the author of over fifty cookbooks and has hosted TV shows like *Máire Cherry's Cooking* and *Have a Cherrific Christmas*!"

"Hey, I know her," Chris whispers. "*I* know her." She seems a little dumbfounded at herself.

But of course Chris knows her. There are very few people who don't know exactly who Máire Cherry is.

"Our second judge is Galvin Cramsey," Kathleen continues, oblivious to the awe of all the contestants in the room. The camera crew zooms to the man sitting in the middle. He's in a tailored black suit and has a head of messy blond hair.

"He is a world-renowned food critic and restaurateur, with fifteen Michelin stars under his belt. And on top of that he's the TV presenter of the famous American show *MasterBaker* and the well-known British show *Cramsey's Kitchen Horrors*." As Kathleen finishes the introduction, Galvin flashes the camera a smile—his teeth as pearly white as, well, the pearls on Máire Cherry's neck.

"Shit," Chris says under her breath. She must recognize Galvin Cramsey too—I mean, how could anyone *not*?—because she looks adequately terrified about him being one of the judges. Galvin is not exactly known for his kind words and gentle demeanor.

"And our third and *final* judge hails all the way from India." I'm practically jumping from excitement as the camera crew closes in on the last judge. Máire Cherry and Galvin Cramsey might be world-renowned chefs, but it's this judge that I've looked up to and admired for years. Hers are the recipes that I've been trying to perfect for my entire life.

"Padma Bollywood." It doesn't surprise me that Kathleen somehow completely butchers her name, even though it's only two syllables. Still, Padma settles the camera with a polite nod and smile. "Her book *Great Rotis from Around the World* was named one of the top bread and pastry books of the decade. She's also known for her famous TV series *Padma Goes to Bollywood*, which follows Padma Bollywood's travels across India, learning about the country's culinary delights."

Chris looks at me with wide eyes. She might not recognize Padma Bollywood, but I've definitely spoken about her and her work enough that she knows who Padma is.

"Padma," Kathleen says slowly, like she's trying to build tension, "will you tell our young contestants what we have in store for them today?"

"Of course." Padma smiles at us this time, not to the camera. My heart nearly bursts out of my chest with excitement. All of the nerves from before have completely dissipated at the sight of these judges. Of course, now I know that this will be making a splash, but it's the idea of baking for Padma Bollywood that latches on to me.

The idea of her tasting something *I* make. Of her actually being impressed by it.

It's a dream come true.

"Today, you'll have one hour to create something that features chocolate," Padma says in the soothing voice that is all-too-familiar to me.

"Mm, chocolate." Kathleen speaks to the camera once more. "Seems like an easy enough task but at the end of today, half of the contestants will be eliminated. Contestants . . . are you ready?"

The cameras turn to us. Chris's expression changes into an

easy grin, but I'm barely paying attention to the camera. Chris and I had decided on making chocolate cake, but now it feels too basic. Too simple. Too safe. Now that I know Padma Bollywood is one of the judges, I want to make something that will really impress her.

"Put on your aprons, contestants!" Kathleen says from the front. She looks deliriously happy to be ordering us around.

I grab the apron with my name printed on it from the top of the counter before leaning closer to Chris.

"We have to change what we're making," I say, even though I haven't quite figured out what we should be making yet.

"What?" Chris stares at me like I've grown two heads, her hands hovering over the untied belt of her apron. "What are you talking about?"

"We can't make my chocolate cake. It's too boring. Unimaginative."

I'm all too aware that we have almost no time.

At the front of the room, Kathleen has moved from the judges' table to the ginormous digital clock flashing red numbers on the right of the room. Any minute now, our time is going to start.

"Shireen, is this your way of getting back at me or whatever? Because I don't think getting yourself kicked out of the competition is going to—"

"Do you trust me?"

Chris hesitates—and I try to ignore the fact that her hesitance is like a gut punch because of course she doesn't trust me. We've just had a horrible breakup, and we can barely go two minutes without sniping at each other. But after a moment, she nods.

Which is good, because just then Kathleen Keogh announces, "Your time starts now!" and the digital clock's giant red numbers begin to count down.

I take a deep breath. "You just have to follow my instructions. We're going to make chocolate lava cake. So basically our same idea, except a million times more impressive."

"Shireen, you know that I've never made chocolate lava cake, right?"

I can see the camera crew rotating toward the two of us. "Can you just trust me? That I know exactly what I'm doing?"

Chris doesn't look happy, but she nods her head anyway. "Okay, yeah. I trust—"

She's interrupted by Kathleen.

"Hello! Sharon and Christina! Our two bright bakers!"

"Shireen," I correct her.

"Chris," Chris adds.

Kathleen's smile flickers but doesn't go anywhere. I'm not sure if she's capable of being on camera and not smiling.

"What are you two making today?" she says in her strangely cheerful voice.

"We're going to be making a chocolate lava cake," I say.

"Wow, that is not an easy dessert to pull off. Do you think you can do it?"

"Yes!" I exclaim, shooting a smile at the cameras. Chris, on the other hand, doesn't look like she's thrilled about our change of plan.

Kathleen moves on to the next pair of contestants as Chris and I get down to work.

"You need to get all the ingredients and make the chocolate ganache," I say to Chris while searching through the many cupboards of our kitchen stations for the ramekins we need to make the chocolate lava cake.

"We haven't even discussed how we're going to do this," Chris says, just standing there. It's like she can't see the literal ticking clock in front of us, counting down our time. We've already lost time talking to Kathleen.

"Chris, we don't have time to discuss things. We have an hour to make something that is perfect for the judges!" I pull out the ramekins from the cupboard, a smile lighting up my face. And it's like seeing something go right pulls some kind of a trigger for Chris. She stomps off to the pantry to gather the ingredients we'll need.

"You need to make the chocolate ganache," I say again once Chris comes back.

"I've never done that before," Chris says, and it takes everything in me to not snap at her that if I had a partner with strong baking experience, we wouldn't be running into so many problems.

"Okay," I say, taking a deep breath, more to even out my simmering anger than because I actually want to do it. "I'll make the ganache. You need to prepare the ramekins and make the rest of the mixture."

"Got it," Chris says, though she doesn't sound totally sure about that. I don't have the time to hold her hand through this challenge, though. I glance at the glaring red numbers of the countdown timer for a quick moment, trying to tamp down my anxiety before looking away and grabbing what I need to make the ganache.

I've done this a million times before. Chocolate ganache fillings are always a major hit with customers at You Drive Me Glazy. But still, on my first try I overheat my cream by just a few seconds and mess it up. Chris glances at me as I toss the cream in the bin and start over. I can't read her expression, but I imagine she's also biting down her snarky comments. I know I would be if I were her.

I turn on the stove again and wait for it to simmer with watchful eyes. Chris is watching the pot as well, even while she's flouring the ramekins.

"What?" I ask. I'd much rather we just got our snarky comments out of the way.

"Nothing," Chris says. "Just try to forget about the competition." She says it like it's an easy thing to do. She says it like she knows my heart is going a million miles a minute, and I can feel sweat concentrated on my scalp and forehead. She says it like she knows me.

"Easier said than done," I mutter.

"I know, but you always do your best work when there's no pressure. So let me handle the pressure." She gives me a small smile that is so reminiscent of the old Chris—the one I fell in love with—that it tugs at my heart. But then she turns around and puts the floured ramekins to one side to start working on her part of the mixture.

I close my eyes and take a deep breath. Chris is right. I can't let the pressure get to me.

Once I stop focusing on the ticking clock counting us down—and Padma Bollywood—things don't seem so difficult. I mean, things aren't that difficult. I've made chocolate lava cake a million times before. And almost every single time it has been perfect. There's no reason why it shouldn't be perfect this time either.

At least, that's what I tell myself as I get down to work.

Once we get into the rhythm of things and forget about Kathleen, the judges, and the camera hovering around us, Chris and I get lost in our own little world. Even though baking is not Chris's favorite activity, she has enough experience with it that making this dish with her feels easy. We've baked together before, though it was only just for fun. We know each other's rhythms, and we never get in each other's way. I rattle off a task and Chris completes it with no questions asked—like she really does trust me.

I don't even pay attention to the other contestants and what they're doing.

Whenever Kathleen comes around with the cameras, Chris manages her with her easy grin. I continue working, like I'm not on a reality TV show at all.

I have never been so determined in my life. I'm working like my life depends on it. I feel like my life *does* depend on this.

Finally, with five minutes left, everything is coming together.

Chris pulls the rack with the ramekins out of the oven, and the chocolate lava cakes look absolutely perfect. And that sweet chocolaty smell is all around us in the air. I can't help my smile. I guess Chris can't help hers either because she's grinning from ear to ear.

"Maybe this was a good idea after all," she says.

"Let's see what the judges say first," I say, even though I know there is no way the judges aren't going to love this chocolate lava cake baked to perfection. I grab an empty plate and one of the ramekins because I know presentation is just as important as anything else. I tip the ramekin over and tap the bottom. But . . . nothing happens. The lava cake doesn't slowly and beautifully cascade onto the plate like it's supposed to. It doesn't even jiggle.

I tap it once more. A little harder this time, but nothing happens.

"You *did* put flour in these ramekins, right?" I ask.

"Of course I put flour in the ramekins," Chris says.

"And you weren't stingy with it?" I ask because the cake is still refusing to come out.

"I . . ." Chris trails off, and when I look at her she doesn't look very sure at all. Anxiety settles into my stomach. But I barely have time to think about that because Kathleen Keogh's voice echoes across the entire hallway.

"One minute left, bakers!"

ELEVEN

Not Exactly a Piece of Cake

"HOW MANY TIMES HAVE WE WATCHED EPISODES OF *NAILED IT!* where they forget to put enough flour in the pan and their cake falls apart?" I half scream at Chris while furiously going through the rest of the ramekins and trying to get one onto the plate.

But none of them budge, and beside me Chris is chewing on her lips in a way she only does in high-stress situations. If we were together—and we weren't on the *Junior Irish Baking Show*—I would accept this as one of Chris's adorable quirks. But right now, I hate her. I have never hated her more in life. Not even when—

"We get a knife and that'll help it slide out," Chris says.

"No, that'll help it come out all broken and disheveled and not presentable to the judges at all!" I cry, slamming down the last ramekin onto the counter. All our hard work ruined just like that. Because of one ridiculous mistake. A mistake that wouldn't have happened if I weren't paired up with Chris.

"Forty seconds!" Kathleen's voice has never grated on my nerves more before. But I'm spiraling. My breath is coming too fast and too shallow. I can't do this. But I can't lose. I can't get kicked off in the first episode. I can't, I can't. I know in the back of my head that this is just a spiral. It's not the worst one I've ever had, but it might be the one that costs me my dreams.

"Shireen." Suddenly, Chris is in front of me. Her fingers linked with mine and her brown eyes gazing into me. "It's going to be okay."

"I don't know how—"

"Just breathe," Chris says. And I know that doesn't fix anything, but somehow Chris's calmness helps me feel better.

I watch as she lets go of my hands, grabs a knife, and gently glides it along the edge of the ramekin.

I close my eyes. I can't watch this. Can't watch her butcher all our hard work.

"Twenty seconds! Make sure you get everything plated, bakers!" Kathleen's voice rings loud.

"It doesn't look so bad," Chris says, her voice sounding too quiet and meek right after Kathleen's.

I open my eyes, though I'm afraid to look and my breath is not quite back to normal yet.

The cake is on the plate. It hasn't split open. The chocolate ganache is surprisingly not spilling out everywhere.

But it's not perfect. The sides are jagged, and you can tell just from one glance that Chris had to cut this out of the ramekin with a knife.

"It'll have to do," I say, glancing up at the judges. No, glancing at Padma Bollywood—my hero and icon—sitting up there like she's royalty. To me, she is. And I need to impress her.

I take one deep breath and quickly dust powdered sugar on

top of the cake, just as the buzzer sounds loudly. Chris casts a forlorn glance at the chocolate syrup and strawberries sitting on the counter. If we had a minute more—even a few more seconds—Chris would have made the dish look like a marvel. Decoration was always her strong suit.

"Bakers, hands off your plates!" Kathleen says, and Chris and I back off, our hands in the air to show that we're not secretly trying to make our dish presentable at the last minute.

"It looks good," Chris says hesitantly. "Right?"

I nod, though I know *good* doesn't mean we're going to move onto the next round.

WE BARELY HAVE TIME to catch our breath before we roll right into the judging process.

"We'll start with Niamh and Séan," Kathleen says from the front of the room. "Can you please bring your dessert up to the judges?"

Niamh and Séan's station is right behind ours, so as they pass by I glance at them curiously. Neither of them look particularly pleased as they carry over their dish. I can make out at least three flavors of macarons on their plate, just from the different colors of the shells and fillings.

That makes my stomach sink. Macarons are technically difficult—more difficult than chocolate lava cake.

Máire Cherry's face lights up when she sees the macarons. "Wow, these look beautiful!" she says.

"Can you tell us what you've made?" Galvin Cramsey asks, his face grim as ever. He's already cutting into one of the macarons with a knife and fork.

"So, we made three different types of macarons, with three different types of chocolate," Séan says. And I can already see what Niamh meant about him, because there is no sense of nervousness in him. Even though he's face-to-face with some of the most famous people in the entire food industry. People that can make or break his entire career. Instead, Séan is wearing a smile that exudes absolute control and confidence, and his voice is more of a bored drawl than anything else.

Niamh, on the other hand, has a nervous waver in her voice as she explains the three flavors. "First, we have a raspberry and dark chocolate macaron, followed by a milk chocolate and hazelnut macaron. And lastly, a white chocolate and vanilla-flavored macaron."

As Niamh explains, the three judges carefully tear into the macarons with their knives. They each lift the smallest sections of them with their fork and take a bite. They chew slowly, almost like they're savoring more than just the flavors of the macarons. Like they're savoring the nervousness on Niamh's expression and how the entire room is breathless with anticipation.

"So," Galvin finally says, breaking the silence. His face betrays no emotion. "You two seemed to have had a few problems in the kitchen working together."

I exchange a glance with Chris. I had been so focused on

my own work that I hadn't paid attention to any of the other bakers—not even Niamh and Séan, who were directly within our earshot the entire time. Chris just shrugs, like she's not sure either.

"This is what this first challenge was supposed to test," Máire Cherry says. "Everybody has to learn how to work with others in a kitchen. Learning how to work in a team is necessary."

All the while that she speaks, Niamh is looking down at her feet, shuffling around. Like she's embarrassed about whatever happened between them during this challenge. Séan, though, doesn't seem bothered in the least. He's staring the judges face-on, with his chest puffed out.

I make a mental note to ask Niamh for all the details later.

"The good thing is your macarons didn't suffer. They're beautiful to look at, and I love the balance of flavors," Padma says with a nod.

I feel a tug of jealousy at hearing the compliments for their dish. Of course, I don't want Niamh to fail—but this is a competition. And after the last five minutes of the challenge, I'm not sure how confident I feel about our dish.

As if Chris can read my mind, she bumps me with her shoulder and whispers, "Ours is going to be better. Don't worry."

I don't get a chance to reply though, because as Niamh and Séan shuffle back to their station—and Niamh shoots me a fleeting smile that I hope Chris doesn't catch (or maybe I hope she does?)—Kathleen Keogh calls us up to the judges.

Chris trudges out of our station first, grabbing hold of our dish. I take a deep breath before following suit.

The walk up to the judges feels like the longest walk of my

life. And all the while, my throat feels parched. I can feel sweat pooling on my scalp once more.

I have to remind myself that no matter what, my chocolate lava cake is good. It's always good. The judges have to see that.

"Chocolate lava cake," Galvin says. He doesn't sound impressed.

"It's not always easy to make," Padma says. And I know that all too well. Chocolate lava cake is one of Padma's signature dishes. "And it seems you had a few difficulties."

"We had some problems getting the cake out of the ramekins," I say quickly. Galvin stares at me a little too long at that confession, and it feels like he can see right through me.

"That is a basic mistake that really nobody in this competition should be making," he says. I feel my face heat up. Is this it? Is this what's going to get us kicked out of the competition? Before it's even really begun?

"Galvin, don't be so harsh," Máire says, directing a smile toward me. I wonder if she can see that I'm on the verge of a panic attack. "The skill is in the fact that they managed to get the cake out unscathed. Structural integrity is pretty important for a chocolate lava cake, and that's been preserved."

"Which one of you forgot to flour the ramekins?" Galvin asks, glancing between me and Chris, as if Máire hasn't spoken at all.

I quickly share a glance with Chris. She looks about as panicked as I feel.

"We did flour the ramekins," I offer. "But . . . not enough, I guess."

"Which one of you?" Galvin asks us again.

Chris takes a breath. Parts her lips.

"It was both of our responsibilities." The words rush out of me so fast I'm not sure if it's even understandable. "I mean . . ." I slow down a little to say the rest. "We're a team, and this cake is our creation. It doesn't matter who made a mistake because the mistake is both of ours."

"Now that is good teamwork," Padma says with a smile directed right at me. And suddenly I feel like I'm floating on air. Because Padma Bollywood is smiling. *At me.*

It gets even better though because she leans forward and cuts into the cake. The ganache pools everywhere, just as it's supposed to. And it looks rich and creamy—but not too much. It looks perfect.

Padma takes a bite and closes her eyes. And even though I can tell she doesn't want her expression to give away what she thinks, I know she's impressed.

"This is . . . delicious." She meets my eyes with that smile on her lips once more. "The cake is just moist enough, and the ganache is absolutely perfect."

"It reminds me of your ganache, actually," Máire says after she's taken a bite of her own. "Just rich and creamy enough."

Even Galvin doesn't seem to have anything bad to say as he samples the cake. I'm so high on the buzz of Padma's compliments that his words don't even register. Though I smile and nod as politely as I can. Inside my head, there's only one thought running through on a loop: *Padma Bollywood likes my chocolate lava cake!*

"You should have let me take the blame," Chris whispers to me once we're back at our stations and the judges have moved on to another pair of contestants.

"Don't be a martyr," I say. "We would have probably both been eliminated if you took the blame."

"Well . . . thanks," Chris says after a moment, her eyes trained up ahead and not on me.

"For what?" I ask.

"Not letting me throw myself under the bus," Chris says.

"Well, then I guess I should say thank you too."

Now Chris does look at me, a question on her face. "Why?"

I shrug before turning away from her and toward the judges. "For trusting me."

We wait and watch as all the other contestants bring their dishes up to them. David and Ruby's peanut butter and chocolate cupcakes are a hit. The pair practically dances back to their station, and I can see them high-fiving like they've already made it through to the next round. But Eimear and Tricia's chocolate brownies are overdone, and they're pretty much in tears after they receive their feedback.

Even as all of this is going on around me, I'm not really paying attention. I'm just thinking about the fact that Chris and I *have* to get through to the next round. We will, right? There's no way we won't. Not after getting glowing compliments from all the judges.

Finally, the judging is finished and they disappear into a room at the back to decide who they're going to eliminate. Most of the cameras and—thankfully—Kathleen disappear along with them.

Niamh slips over to our stations almost as soon as they're gone. She leans on one of the counters with a grin directed right at me.

"So, looks like the two of us at least will be in the next round," she says. "They loved our macarons, and they loved your cake."

"Lava cake," Chris corrects. "And it's going to be four of us in the next round at least. I *am* Shireen's partner." If I'm not mistaken, there's a hint of annoyance in Chris's voice. Maybe even some jealousy?

"Who else do you think will make it?" Séan comes up right beside Niamh, throwing his arm around her like they're best friends. She edges away as far as she can, while still being at our station. Séan doesn't seem at all fazed by this. Instead, he's staring at Chris with a little too much interest.

"I think Bridget and Emily probably have a shot," Chris comments. "The judges seemed to like their triple chocolate cupcake. It's exactly what they wanted, isn't it? A lot of chocolate."

"Chocolate on top of chocolate on top of chocolate on top of chocolate?" Niamh scrunches up her face. "I don't know. I think David and Ruby probably have a far better chance at it. I mean, that peanut butter and chocolate cupcake with caramel sauce . . . I still want to eat it."

"It did look good," I admit. The more we talk about the

other dishes, the less nervous I feel. And the more convinced I am that Chris and I are making it to the second round. Cupcakes and macarons are good. They're even difficult to make. But the chocolate lava cake has a personal connection to Padma, and Chris and I showed teamwork on top of that. Isn't that why they paired us up in the first place?

"I'm Séan, by the way." Séan edges a little closer, even though Niamh glares daggers at him. He sticks out his hand toward me, though he's still looking at Chris.

"We already met this morning? I'm Shireen?" I take his hand for a brief shake, a little surprised at the sudden show of politeness that didn't seem to exist this morning.

He moves on to Chris, his smile widening.

"I'm Christina, but everyone calls me Chris." She doesn't lean forward or even acknowledge that he's given her a hand to shake.

Eventually—when it gets a little awkward and the silence between us stretches out a little too long—Séan withdraws his hand, though his smile remains.

"Well, Chris. I think you've got a pretty good shot at this thing. I saw the way you were hard at work. I can tell talent when I see it." His grin is almost wolfish, and he runs his fingers through his hair, like that's supposed to make him look attractive. To his side, Niamh rolls her eyes.

Chris barely looks at him as she says, "I'm a lesbian."

Séan blinks. His eyes take her in like it's the first time he's seen her. I have to stifle a laugh. I almost wish I could glance at Chris now. Like this could be an inside joke. Instead, the person who glances at me with a glint in her eyes is Niamh, and I try to ignore the fresh flurry of butterflies that sends through my stomach.

"You don't look like a lesbian," Séan finally says.

Chris cocks an eyebrow at Séan. Even though she's much shorter than he is, somehow she seems to tower over him in this stance. "And what does a lesbian look like?"

Thankfully for Séan, this is the moment Kathleen Keogh hurries back to the hall, a flurry of camera crew at her heels.

"Everybody back to your positions, please. We're about to start filming once more!" Kathleen says, waving everyone to their places.

"Good luck." Niamh reaches over the counter and gives my hands a squeeze before she and Séan shuffle back to their station.

When I turn to Chris, I know that she's seen the interaction because her expression is back to unreadable. All the good feelings between us from working together and getting praised for our dish seem to have disappeared into thin air.

I shouldn't be surprised. The goal was to get through this challenge with Chris in tow. Not anything else.

As the cameras begin to roll, the judges stroll back in.

"We've made a decision," Galvin announces somberly, his eyes roaming the room. "There was one dessert today that we enjoyed more than all the rest. One that had skill, presentation, and the perfect flavor. And those two contestants will have a major advantage in the next round of the competition."

An advantage? Nobody had mentioned having the best dish would mean some kind of an advantage.

"And the best dish from today was . . ." Padma Bollywood continues on from Galvin. She glances around the room, and I feel cold anxiety wash over me. For a moment, her eyes rest on me, and I feel a flicker of hope in my chest. Is it possible that Chris and I didn't just get through to the next round but that we were the best?

"Niamh and Séan!" Padma finishes, glancing away from me as a smile lights up her eyes.

The entire room bursts into reluctant applause. I applaud, too, glancing back at Niamh attempting to smile.

"I thought this challenge was supposed to be about teamwork," Chris whispers from beside me, clearly annoyed that two people who had done such a poor job of being a team ended up getting the advantage.

"Teamwork is about more than not arguing. It's about being able to get the job done," I say. And I don't mean it as a snarky comment on Chris messing up with the ramekins, but she must take it as one, because she bristles and steps away from me. Like putting distance between us will make things better. Like we're not already distant enough since our breakup.

"The next team through . . . Ruby and David," Máire Cherry says. I see Ruby and David cheering and can't help that gnawing jealousy in my stomach once more.

"Shireen and Christina," Galvin says, barely glancing at us as he announces our names.

I take a breath of relief, finally feeling the weight lift off my shoulders.

I glance at Chris with a grin, but she doesn't even look at me. She's smiling like she's happy, but I can tell her heart's not in it. It's just for show—for the cameras.

We may have gotten to the next round, but I guess Chris and I are back to where we were before this challenge.

TWELVE

Cruller Intentions

THE *JUNIOR IRISH BAKING SHOW*'S CONFESSIONAL BOOTH IS A LIT-tle room on the side of the hall where we shot the first episode. We have to wait around to shoot our confessionals, even though we're all tired and achy from a whole day of filming and baking. When it's finally my turn, it's a few hours later, and my eyes feel heavy with sleep. I don't think I've ever been so tired in my whole life.

But the confessional booth wakes me up. It's tiny, and the producers of the show have managed to squeeze a few too many things inside. There's a comfortable-looking armchair in the middle and cameras and lights set up all around. Right behind the armchair is a massive green screen.

"Shireen!" a man in suit and tie cries when he sees me. It's a little strange to be greeted so enthusiastically by someone you've literally never met before.

"Um, hi," I say.

"I'm Andrew McNamara, one of the producers of the show," he says, extending a hand. I take it, and he shakes it a little too firmly. "Why don't you take a seat and we'll get started."

"Okay." I slip onto the sofa, suddenly a little too aware of the conversation Fatima and I had before the meet and greet.

Fatima was right. Reality TV shows do have villains and heroes, and I have to remember that when I speak at this confessional. It's probably the most time I'll have speaking to a camera, and I have to make it count.

"So, Shireen, since this is going to be the first episode of the show, why don't you introduce yourself to everyone?" Andrew asks.

"Sure, well, I'm Shireen," I say.

"A little louder, love. And looking to the camera," Andrew says.

I glance up, meeting the camera lens with my gaze. It's a little unnerving. I've never been in the spotlight like this before. I blink a little too fast and take a deep breath, trying to settle my nerves.

"I'm Shireen," I say, a little louder now and with a bright smile. "And I love baking. I'm in fifth year, and I'll be going into my final year at school next year."

"And why did you apply to the show?" Andrew asks, waving his arms around in wild gestures and almost hitting one of the cameramen in the head.

I stifle a giggle and begin to speak again. "Well, I want to go to culinary school so one day I can open my own dessert shop. Right now, I work at my parents' donut shop called You Drive Me Glazy, but my dream is opening up my own shop where I can sell all kinds of desserts, especially Bengali ones. I hope this show can help me achieve that."

"Tell us about where you're from. You said you want to make Beng . . . Bang . . . Indian desserts?"

"Bengali desserts," I say, trying not to frown too hard. "I'm from here, from Dublin. I was born here, grew up here. But my parents immigrated here from Bangladesh right after they got married."

"And was it difficult to convince them to allow you to come on the show?" Andrew asks.

I shake my head slowly, but when Andrew gestures for me to speak I say, "No, not really. I mean, they're kind of big dreamers. They wouldn't have moved here and started a donut shop if they weren't. I love my parents! They want me to achieve my dreams, and they've always supported me."

Andrew frowns, like that's not quite what he was hoping for, but he swiftly moves on. "Can you tell us a little about your journey as a baker? How did you get started?"

"Oh, well, I've been baking for a long time," I say. "Food is a big part of my culture, especially sweet foods. When you're Bangladeshi, you're taught that any good news or celebration has to be accompanied with some sweet food. Every time you visit someone's house it's polite to bring a box of sweets. But in Ireland, there aren't really a lot of places where you can buy Bengali sweets, so when I was younger my mom started making them herself. She was really good at it, and I used to watch her. Sometimes I helped her out. As I got older, it just felt like second nature to start baking. For school bake sales, I would make my own cookies. For friends' birthdays, I would always bring along a cake I baked myself. I became the girl who bakes. And I loved being that girl. I guess baking is kind of in my blood."

"What a sweet story," Andrew says with a smile that doesn't quite reach his eyes. I have to stifle a giggle at his unwitting pun.

"Let's talk a little bit about the other contestants," he says. "What are your thoughts on them? Have you made any friends? Any enemies?"

"Um . . ." I try not to think about Chris. If I speak about her, they'll latch on to it. Having to compete with your ex-girlfriend is definitely reality TV show worthy. My stomach drops when I realize that Chris also had to do a confessional. What if she spoke about me? What if she told them everything? But Chris wouldn't do that. She's always been a private person. She's definitely not the type to divulge secrets on national TV.

"I like the other contestants," I say. "They seem nice. Dedicated to the craft." I smile a big grin.

"Your partner and you got along?" Andrew asks. "No problems with your baking?"

"It was a little difficult at times. It's always difficult to work with someone," I say. "But it turned out okay. We got to the next round. That's really all that matters."

Andrew sighs, like I'm definitely not giving him the kind of material he's looking for. "Tell us about Padma Bollywood. It seemed like you knew her."

"Of course I know her," I say with a laugh. "She's like world-famous." When Andrew gestures for me to continue, I take a breath and say, "I love Padma Bollywood's food. I've read all her cookbooks."

"How did you feel when you saw her on the judges' panel?"

"I was surprised," I say. "When I saw her here today, I knew I had to make something for her. Something she would appreciate. That's why we made chocolate lava cake. It's one of Padma's well-known recipes."

"Was your partner annoyed that you made something specifically to impress Padma?"

"No, she trusted my instincts," I say. "I would have trusted hers too." I add, even though it's a lie. I definitely would not have trusted Chris's instincts over mine in that situation.

"Well, Padma must mean a lot to you if you wanted to impress her so badly," Andrew says, swiftly changing the subject.

But gushing about Padma Bollywood is definitely something I can do. "I think Padma means a lot to a lot of people, especially to South Asians. There aren't a lot of brown cooks or bakers out there. The few that are . . . they don't really get the amount of praise and fame that they deserve," I say. "Food is this *huge* part of my Bengali culture. But there aren't really many South Asian chefs making it big. Our food is still considered . . . lesser? Not really appreciated. It means a lot to see Padma Bollywood making South Asian cuisine and sharing it with the world. It makes me think that maybe I can do it, but for Bengali food."

"Understood." Andrew nods. "One last question before we let you go. Do you think you can win this show, Shireen?"

The question takes me aback. After all the questions about the other contestants and the judges, I expected to be thrown some kind of a curveball. Not a simple question like this.

"I can definitely win this show," I say with a smile. "I'm talented and hardworking, and I make really good desserts."

THIRTEEN

A Valuable Friend-Chip

"PADMA BOLLYWOOD ACTUALLY KNOWS WHO I AM," I SAY TO FATIMA the next day. I'm still riding the high of filming the first episode while trying to pick out my outfit for our next episode's filming.

I got home so late last night—after the filming and all the interviews—that I didn't get a chance to talk to Fatima at all. So even though it's late in Dhaka right now, she snuck away to the balcony of their apartment to have this conversation.

"So is that like your dream made? Are you going to ask her to marry you?" Fatima asks. She clearly doesn't understand the gravity of the situation. Or that how I feel about Padma is completely different from a crush. It's pure admiration. It's having someone to look up to in a world where there's barely anybody like me *to* look up to. It's seeing a reflection of myself in Padma—even if we're probably completely different.

"I'm not attracted to her," I say, rolling my eyes even though Fatima can't see me. I have my back turned away from her.

"How about this?" I pull out a baby blue dress that comes down to my knees. It's simple—but with the apron tied around my waist, I'm realizing that what I wear is probably not the most important.

"I like it." Fatima nods her approval. I had wanted a little more than muted approval, but I guess it will have to do.

"So, the first episode is airing this Saturday, right? Because I am dying to see it, to see you get through the first round and brag all about it. I'm going to go on Twitter just so I can be #TeamShireen."

I let out a laugh as I turn back to Fatima on my screen. "Yeah, it's this Saturday . . ." Ever since filming the confessional, I'd been feeling a strange kind of worry in my gut. Now I'm not sure how to even tell Fatima about that.

"Shireen . . ."

"It's just . . . I'm going to be on TV," I say. "And there are going to be people watching me."

"You didn't know that when you applied for a reality TV show?" Fatima asks with a laugh. I crack a smile, too, though I don't quite feel like smiling.

"I don't know. It's different knowing it and *knowing* it," I say. "I mean, I don't even know what I'll look like. And what if people hate me?" I've never been hated before, but I know people get really emotionally invested in reality TV shows. How many times have I absolutely hated someone on my favorite show, even though I know nothing about them other than the persona they're putting on for TV? "What if people I know hate me? What if strangers hate me? I mean, I know what I said on TV." Though now that I think about it for longer than a second, I'm not sure if I do know what I let slip on TV. "But . . . but I can't control everyone else. What if Chris talked about me?

Or one of the other contestants? What if they said something bad and then—"

"Shireen." Fatima's voice stops me from going down into one of my spirals. She's not laughing anymore when I meet her eyes.

"I know it's scary, but it's going to be okay," Fatima says. "And nobody could hate you. You're like . . . the most lovable person on Planet Earth."

"People find a way," I say.

"I don't get it," she says after a moment. "You've been so excited about this. Where is all the worry coming from? Did someone say something?"

"No. I don't know," I say. "Maybe it's because of who the judges are? Maybe it's because I didn't think things through as well as I thought I did?"

"Well, you need to stop thinking things through that well then," Fatima says. "You know what'll make you feel better? Watch the first episode with your parents. They're like the most supportive people ever, and they'll probably feed you really good food. That'll solve all your problems."

"Yeah . . ." I'm unsure whether to mention the next part or not. "One of the other contestants, Niamh, invited me to a viewing party at her house." I try to say it as nonchalantly as I can. In fact, Niamh has kind of been inviting me to a lot of things for the past couple of days. But I've been declining them as politely as I can. My excuse? That I'm focused on the competition. But with nothing really happening with the competition until our next filming date, it's not like I have anything to focus on anyway, so I'm pretty sure Niamh sees right through me.

"Niamh, as in the girl who got best dish, along with that guy?" Fatima asks.

"Yeah, exactly," I say.

"And how do you know her?" Fatima narrows her eyes, like she can see right through my nonchalant facade.

"Um, through the competition, obviously," I say. "She's just one of the contestants. Like I said."

"Shireen." Fatima says my name like she knows. We've never been able to keep secrets from one another.

"Okay, we got coffee together like once," I admit. "But that's it. And *everybody's* going to be at this party. All the other contestants. So it would be weird if I didn't go, right?"

Fatima heaves a sigh, like she doesn't really believe what I'm saying but she's willing to entertain it—at least for a little bit. "So, you said that because she got best dish, she gets an advantage. Right?"

"Right." I nod.

"So maybe she'll tell you what her advantage is," Fatima says.

I have to stop for a moment, because I hadn't really thought about asking Niamh about that. I had just thought about how things seemed a little too much the last time we got coffee—and I definitely was not ready for something like that. But maybe Fatima is on to something. Though it does feel a little weird.

"I don't know," I say, shaking my head. "Niamh seems kind of competitive. She wouldn't even tell me what she and Séan decided to make for the first round. I don't think she would tell me anything."

"And it is a bit sleazy," Fatima adds.

"Just a little," I say. I don't really want to talk about Niamh anymore though, so I decide to change the subject. "Tell me about you. What exciting news from Bangladesh do you have?"

Fatima tosses back some locks of her hair and takes a deep breath. "Oh you know, nothing, except, Sabir, who is my oldest chachato bhai, is taking us on a trip. We have to decide where we're going to go though."

"What are the options?" The most I've traveled in Bangladesh is from the house of one relative to the next.

"Well, we're going to go outside Dhaka. So we can go to the tea gardens in Sri Mongol, and then onto Sylhet. Or we can go to Cox's Bazar, or maybe Jaflong. We're all going to have a vote and then on Friday, we're going to go." The smile on her face is contagious. I don't think I've seen Fatima this excited about anything in a long time. I definitely didn't think I would see her this excited about traveling around Bangladesh, considering she didn't even want to go there in the first place.

"You know, I'm glad you're having a good time there," I say. "Even if I miss you like mad."

"I miss you like mad too," Fatima says. "This would be so much better if you were here. But it is nice to get to know my cousins. And you know, my Bengali is getting better. Next time you see me, I'll probably only speak Bengali to you."

"As long as you don't use any big, complicated words, I should be good."

The sound of the night guard's whistle pierces the air—as if I'm in Bangladesh right now too. It makes both Fatima and me wince.

"I should probably go to sleep. It's really late," she says. "But look. Wherever I am on Saturday, Dhaka or in the middle of a bloody tea garden, I'll find a way to watch the episode."

"And you'll find a way to tweet out #TeamShireen?"

Fatima grins. "Definitely. Good night."

BETWEEN THE FIRST DAY of filming and the day the first episode is supposed to air, I see at least two dozen advertisements for the show. It seems that wherever I go, there is a new ad for it. On the TV, Ammu and Abbu see a brief ad with a flickering image of Chris and me hard at work, and their faces light up with excitement.

"That's the Huangs' daughter, right?" Ammu even asks, though she doesn't seem as put off by it as I would have thought.

"She was my partner," I say, like partnering with my parents' sworn enemies' daughter is no big deal at all. Ammu and Abbu exchange a glance, but as always, I don't really have a clue what it means. They don't say anything else about Chris or the Huangs or the feud that's existed between our families since we opened up You Drive Me Glazy right across from the Huangs' donut shop, so I decide not to press any further.

Then there are the ads I see that Ammu and Abbu obviously miss. Like when I scroll through my Instagram or Twitter and the new *Junior Irish Baking Show* just happens to pop up on my feed. Anxiety floods me every time I see one of those ads, and I feel a little rush of relief when they don't feature me. I'm not sure if I'm ready to see myself as a contestant on a reality show yet.

It seems like the show will have a proper audience and not just a group of our relatives crowded around their TVs being impressed because of the sheer idea that someone they know is on the telly.

The day before the show is supposed to air, my phone lights up with notifications. At first, it's just a few friends and acquaintances from school asking if they really did see me on an ad for the *Junior Irish Baking Show* or if they'd just mistaken someone else for me. But by early afternoon, I'm getting Instagram DMs from almost everyone in our school year asking if it's really true that I'm competing on the show.

I have no idea how to respond to them. I have no idea if I even want to respond to them. Most of these girls are people I haven't spoken two words to. When I go on my blog to post a new recipe like I do every other week, I notice that suddenly I have views that aren't just me hitting refresh over and over again. I've even gained a few followers. It takes me way longer than usual to type up my new post—a recipe for lavender and honey macarons—because I have no idea how this sudden influx of followers will react to this new post. Because maybe they just want gossip about the show and aren't interested in my recipes at all.

Fatima sends me a message in the late afternoon that just says, Check Facebook!

Now, I've had a Facebook account since I was thirteen, solely because it's the only way to keep up with the lives and goings-on of most of my Bangladeshi relatives. But it's been a few months since I've logged on. And it takes me a few attempts to remember my password.

When I finally get through, the first thing I see is a post from our school's Facebook Page:

We're so proud of one of St. Ida's secondary school's talented students! Shireen Malik will be competing in the *Junior Irish Baking Show*, the first episode of which will be airing this Saturday at 6:00 P.M. on IETV! Make sure you tune in to watch our talented student baking her heart out.

The post has been liked by a few hundred people already. And it seems that everyone on my Friends list has already liked it, and some of them have even shared it to their own pages.

Instead of feeling excited, though, a slow sense of dread creeps up on me. Sure, I've managed to get to the second round of the competition, but who knows what's going to happen during the second challenge? Now, on top of the challenge itself and everything to do with Chris, almost everyone I know will be watching this show. Even girls in school who I barely know—or like. People who might just be looking for a chance to take me down a peg.

I know I *should* feel excited that so many people are willing to support me. That's probably why Fatima even told me to look on Facebook. But really, I just feel a bit sick at the thought of it all. Who knows how the show will portray me tomorrow? And what kind of judgments people will make about me? Not just the people I know but strangers too.

I can't help but glance down at myself. Today, I'm wearing a multicolored rainbow-striped summer dress, even though it's kind of gloomy outside. The bright clothes help me feel better about the depressing weather. But I know that that's not what people are going to think if they see me wearing this on TV. I've heard the comments my entire life. Why would a fat, dark-skinned girl like me wear such "unflattering" clothes? Such bright clothes? The kind of clothes that draw attention to me? It's one thing to hear that in person but another to not even know what strangers are saying about you after watching a clip of you on TV—without knowing anything about who you are.

I pick up my phone and open my text chain with Chris. She's the person I've spoken to most about this. And even though she doesn't get it, she gets it—more than most other people. But we're not together anymore. We're not even friends anymore.

And I know I shouldn't even want to text her. Not after what she did to me.

Me: Is it bad that I feel sick at the idea of people watching me on TV?

I send the text off to Niamh before I can do any of my regular overthinking. The three dots that indicate Niamh is typing show up almost immediately. Almost like she's been waiting for me to text her.

Niamh: Is it bad that I can totally relate?

Despite my anxiety, a smile tugs at my lips. Maybe Chris doesn't have to be the only person who gets it—who gets me. Before I can reply, Niamh sends two more texts.

Niamh: We'll probably feel better about it once the first episode has aired, right?
Niamh: Are you coming to my viewing party btw? It wouldn't really be the same without you . . .

I don't have to think for long before I text back: I'll be there.

FOURTEEN

Don't Sweet the Small Stuff

NIAMH'S AUNT'S HOUSE IS IN A LITTLE APARTMENT COMPLEX JUST off the main street in Dún Laoghaire.

"You're here!" Niamh exclaims as soon as she opens the door. She flings her arms around me, and I get a whiff of her flowery perfume. She smells as sweet as the macarons she baked for the first challenge and—though it's a very different smell from Chris's citrus-fresh, just-stepped-out-the-shower scent—I can't say I dislike it.

"I did tell you I would be here," I say when Niamh finally lets go of me. Out of the corner of my eye, I notice Chris deep in conversation with one of her friends from school. She's white and half a head taller than Chris, with chestnut brown hair. I'm pretty sure her name begins with an *a* or an *o*—maybe Orla, Alanna? But clearly, she wasn't close enough friends with Chris for me to have been properly introduced during the time we were together.

"I know," Niamh says. "But you haven't really been . . ." She shakes her head, like it doesn't really matter what I haven't been. "You're here now. Just in time for the episode to air."

Niamh pulls us past Chris and her friend—neither of them spare us a glance, though I know Chris is trying not to look at me from her tunnel vision focus on the girl with her—and into the sitting room. It's filled with people. There's a single couch opposite the TV where five people are sitting, basically on top of each other. And the floor surrounding the screen is littered with people sitting with their legs crossed, eyes trained on the bright screen in front of them.

"There are a lot of people here," I say, taking the room in. I'm not sure who half of these people are. I had expected this party would just be the twelve contestants left on the show after that first episode.

Niamh shrugs. "People brought friends."

I note the other contestants from the show gathered in all corners of the room. Bridget and Emily seem deep in conversation by the TV screen, while David and Ruby are speaking to none other than Séan in the farthest corner from us.

"I didn't think you'd invite him," I say, watching how Séan acts like he own this whole house.

"I didn't think I would either, but I wanted to invite everyone so . . ." Niamh just shrugs again.

She links our fingers together and pulls me toward the only empty space in the room: a solitary armchair that I guess has been left empty for Niamh. It is her party and her house, so it makes sense for her to have first dibs. Though in my Bengali household, there would never be a time where the host sits on a chair and the guests sit on the floor. White people must do it different.

Niamh pulls us both down into the armchair and though it's pretty big, we're a little too snug against each other. Niamh doesn't seem to mind, but I feel warmth creep up my neck and toward my cheek. Shifting position doesn't put much distance between us, so I climb up onto the armrest instead, precariously balancing myself on it. Which is difficult enough when you're waif thin like Niamh (I imagine, having never been waif thin) and basically an extreme sport when you're the same size as me.

Niamh raises a questioning eyebrow. "It's more comfortable here," I lie.

Thankfully, she doesn't ask any more questions. I see Chris and her friend stroll into the room and hover by the edge. They're a little bit too close for comfort, but I try to ignore them and focus on the screen in front of me.

I'm not here for Chris. I'm here to see the first episode of the show.

That's what I tell myself anyway as the TV lights up with the logo for the *Junior Irish Baking Show* and plays a quirky upbeat jingle that fills the whole room. Everyone goes silent as the screen shifts to Kathleen Keogh on the screen, her brilliant white smile seeming to take up almost too much space.

"Welcome to the first-ever *Junior Irish Baking Show*," Kathleen says. Behind her, I can make out the faded view of the studio and all of our kitchen stations. "Where twenty-six junior Irish bakers from all over Ireland will be competing for the chance to win ten thousand euros. But they'll have to impress a few people before they manage to get their hands on the grand prize." Kathleen walks up toward the judges, her heels clicking loudly against the floor. "Like our three judges."

On-screen, they are slowly introduced before the camera

cuts to a video of Chris in the confessional booth. The background has a logo of the *Junior Irish Baking Show* and an even bigger IETV logo on top. Chris smiles into the camera, but there's something in her expression that's a bit blank. That's not quite Chris. Then again, I'm not sure who Chris is nowadays.

"There's Chris," one of the girls from Chris's school exclaims to the sound of a few cheers. Some of the people standing around Chris give her a pat on the back, and she responds with a half-hearted smile.

The Chris on the screen begins to speak. "I'm Christina Huang, but most people know me as Chris. I've just finished up my fifth year at school and when I'm not there, well, I'm usually working at my parents' donut and bubble tea shop. It's called the Baker's Dozen."

The screen cuts to a shot of me and Chris at our station. I'm busy mixing everything together, and my hair is sticking up every which way. Definitely not a flattering introduction to me. I try not to think too much about that.

Chris, on the other hand, is the picture of calm and collected as Kathleen approaches us.

"What are you making today?" Kathleen's sugary sweet voice asks.

"We're making a chocolate lava cake. Very classic, but we're hoping it'll catch the judges' attention."

"Has it been difficult working with a partner?" Kathleen's expression shifts to something resembling sympathy. Chris glances over at me—her face softening. A familiar feeling tugs at my heart, something warm and soft and wonderful. Something

I've felt a million times before. I glance over at the real Chris, but she's staring at the TV screen with a frown.

"Shireen is really good at what she does," the Chris on-screen says. "We're working together pretty well, actually. I'm pretty confident, because I'm working with Shireen."

The shot on-screen cuts once more. This time, I'm the one in the confessional booth.

"I'm Shireen," I say into the camera with a smile so wide that it seems to take up my entire face. I try not to cringe seeing myself. "And I . . . love baking. I'll be going into my final year at school. I want to go to culinary school so one day I can open my own dessert shop. Right now, I work at my parents' donut shop called You Drive Me Glazy, but my dream is opening up my own shop where I can sell all kinds of desserts, especially Bengali ones." The camera cuts to a shot of me watching Padma Bollywood with wide eyes. I feel a bloom of warmth in my cheeks. I basically look like a complete fangirl.

"I love Padma Bollywood's food," I say in the confessional box. "I've read all her cookbooks. When I saw her here today, I knew I had to make something for her. Something she would appreciate."

"Oooh," someone in the sitting room says. I just roll my eyes. But my cheeks are still warm. I'm kind of regretting the decision to come here now. I'm even regretting my decision to talk about Padma Bollywood at all in my confessional. I'm hoping they'll quickly move on to one of the other contestants. Instead, after a few clips of all of us hard at work and Niamh and Séan bickering over macaron flavors, we come back to my confessional.

"There aren't a lot of brown cooks or bakers out there. The few that are . . . they don't really get the amount of praise and fame that they deserve," I say. "Food is this *huge* part of Bengali culture." I hold my arms wide apart as if to show exactly how huge a part it is. "But there aren't really many South Asian chefs making it big. Our food is still considered . . . lesser? Not really appreciated. It means a lot to see Padma Bollywood making South Asian cuisine and sharing it with the world. It makes me think that maybe I can do it, but for Bengali food."

The screen cuts once more. This time David and Ruby are on-screen filling Kathleen in on their plans to make cupcakes and why they chose that. Everyone else seems to have moved on from my confessional. But Niamh nudges my hands with hers.

"You know, I bet Padma watched that and was impressed by you," she whispers in a voice so low that only I can hear. "You should feel happy."

And I should feel happy. I know that. But it still feels like a lot—like I'm baring vulnerable parts of myself to the whole world. When even the person I loved couldn't support those vulnerable parts of me.

At the thought of that, I turn my head to the back corner of the room. Chris isn't deep in conversation with the girl from before anymore. Instead, she's looking right at me, and I'm not sure what to make of the expression on her face.

I glance away as fast as I can, back to Niamh, who I guess caught my glance. But she doesn't say anything about it.

Instead, she says, "I know it's weird to see yourself on the telly, but you're already doing it, you know. What you said in your confessional . . . I bet in the same way that you look up to Padma, someone is watching this and looking up to you."

That seems like a stretch, but for a moment I can almost imagine it. And it's a pretty nice feeling.

FIFTEEN

Twitter and Sweet

THANKFULLY, AFTER MY CONFESSIONAL, THE SHOW MORE OR LESS forgets about me, other than a few shots of Chris and me hard at work. We watch Bridget and Emily argue over exactly how much chocolate is too much chocolate, while in the next scene Ruby and David are so in sync it's like they've been baking together their whole lives. But the camera and Kathleen mostly focus on Séan and Niamh—to Niamh's great distaste. She sits watching with her lips pursed as the Séan and Niamh on-screen bicker about a fourth macaron flavor. The batter is all done in the bowl in front of them, but according to Niamh, it's not going to turn out well because it's way too thick. According to Séan, Niamh is overthinking everything.

They're bickering so much that I have to wonder for a moment how Chris and I missed all of this.

"We're wasting our time making four ridiculous flavors!" Niamh exclaims, throwing her arms up. "Quality over quantity, Séan." She's speaking through gritted teeth as if she wants to call Séan something that is very much not his name. Séan just sighs, pouring the batter out onto a baking sheet anyway. As if Niamh hasn't said anything at all. She makes a guttural sound before stalking off as far away from Séan as possible. Which isn't very far considering our kitchen stations are not exactly massive.

Beside me, the real Niamh shoots daggers at the real Séan sitting on the other side of the room. He's grinning sheepishly at the screen—even when the macarons come out misshapen and hard, and Niamh tosses them into the bin with a murderous glare directed at him.

"Don't worry," I whisper. "Next challenge, he'll be all on his own." *That* gets a satisfied grin out of Niamh.

Finally, we move on to the judging. A rousing orchestra plays as Padma Bollywood compliments our cake. The camera closes in on my face, and I feel my cheeks warm once more. But the show moves quickly through the rest of the judging.

The whole room seems to grow uncomfortable as the judges call out the bakers who have made it through to the next round. Because alongside our own bright, happy faces, we can see the disappointment of everyone who has just been eliminated. We all know that our feeling of accomplishment—our celebration—is temporary.

In just a few days, we'll be facing another challenge.

And we'll be on the chopping block once more.

WHEN THE SHOW FINALLY ends, there's a round of applause throughout the room—though the sense of discomfort remains.

"Can we order some pizza?" a guy that I don't recognize asks Niamh. She nods, and then someone pulls up the Domino's website on their phone. Soon questions about what pizza toppings to get are floating around the room, and everyone's pooling their money. A few people filter out of the sitting room and into other places in the house.

I come to a stop and glance around the room. I tell myself I'm not looking for Chris, but I know that really I am. But she's not in the spot she had been standing before. In fact, she's not anywhere in the room.

"There's drinks in the kitchen!" Niamh's cheerful voice pulls me out of my search for Chris. "I can grab you something if you want?"

"I'm alright. I should probably get going."

Niamh's expression shifts ever so slightly. "So, you just came to watch this. It's supposed to be a viewing *party*."

"I know, but it's getting late and—"

"Come on." Niamh reaches forward and pulls my fingers into her own. I try to ignore the jolt of electricity it sends through me. "In just a few days, we're going to be back in there, and one of us might not make it to the final. You can have fun for like one day before you go back to preparing for the show or whatever."

Against my better judgment, I nod. "I guess you're right." I don't really want to leave this party. I know that once I get back home, I'll probably spend a little too much time overanalyzing everything. From the entire episode of the show to everything about Chris's behavior tonight.

Niamh's grin at my response is contagious. And pretty soon, we're both smiling from ear to ear as she leads me out of the sitting room and into the kitchen. I'm trying to not think about our hands still joined together and what that means.

"I think the first challenge was way too easy," one of the other contestants from the show—Anna—is saying in the kitchen. "The next round is definitely going to be way more difficult."

"I don't know," David says. "I mean, the thing about the last round was there was so much left up to us. We could have made anything with chocolate. I think the next challenge is just going to be more specific."

"You know what it is, don't you?" Ruby asks. For a moment, I think she's talking to me. Then I see Niamh shaking her head beside me.

"Of course not," she says.

"That wasn't what your big advantage was?" Ruby presses. Even David and Emily glance over at Niamh questioningly.

"It wouldn't be much of an advantage if we told you what it was. And I don't see anyone bothering Séan about it," Niamh says.

"Yeah, because Séan's an asshole who wouldn't help us out even if our lives depended on it," David says. I'm glad that we're all at least agreed on that.

"Well, I would help you out if your lives depended on it," Niamh says. "But I'm definitely not going to tell you what the advantage Séan and I got is." She pulls me away from them.

"God, can you believe them?" Niamh asks as she grabs two

plastic cups and pours us both some club orange, the only drink within reach.

"I guess they just thought they would try their luck," I say. I can't exactly blame them. I'd be lying if I said I hadn't thought about asking Niamh the same question.

She looks at me, and the expression on her face is not so pleasant anymore. She looks colder somehow.

"Not you too," she says. "I thought we were friends."

"We *are* friends. But I'm just saying. I understand why they're asking."

Niamh sighs. "This is the *Junior Irish Baking Show*, Shireen. Not the *Junior Irish Best Friend* show. We all have to make the most of our advantages . . ." I can tell she wants to say more, but we're interrupted by Séan's voice reverberating around the room.

"Did you know we're trending on Twitter?" he's saying, waving his phone around. Even from this distance, I can make out that #JIBS is the top trending hashtag on Irish Twitter.

Suddenly, everyone pulls out their phones, and I do too.

Don't know what that ginger girl's problem was. The macaron would have been fine if she'd just stopped nagging. Séan reads this out with a grin, looking up to catch Niamh's eye as if to say, *See?*

Niamh doesn't bother to give him a second glance. Instead she narrows her eyes at her screen and reads out loud too. Good thing Niamh was there to pull Séan's head out his feckin' ass, otherwise he definitely would NOT not have gone on to the next round. Niamh looks up at Séan, as if she's issuing a challenge.

Shaking my head, I scroll through the rest of the hashtag.

There are hundreds of tweets from all over the island. It's strange to think that this many people were just watching *us* on their tellies—especially when I'd think most people would rather binge-watch something on Netflix.

> Those double chocolate cupcakes looked delish. Would like a million of those thnx #JIBS
>
> Niamh was obviously CORRECT about the macarons #JIBS

Obviously, Niamh and Séan's bickering has started a whole conversation on Twitter. Alongside the tweets, there are pictures and clips circulating from the show. There's a clip where Bridget accidentally gets chocolate frosting on her perfect blond locks, making them . . . not so perfect. I have to stifle a giggle as I continue to scroll.

> Can't believe Jennifer and Emma didn't make it in!!! Their double chocolate brownies looked DIVINE #JIBS
>
> Thought this was the junior IRISH baking show, since when was Ireland in Asia? #JIBS

That last one makes my stomach drop. Not because I haven't heard comments like that before but because all of the other tweets are about who was right, Séan or Niamh. Or about how delicious everything looked. I take a deep breath. *There are always one or two assholes*, I remind myself. I keep scrolling, trying to wipe that tweet from my memory.

But . . . that's not the only tweet.

IETV is really trying some propaganda with this #JIBS how can two asians b IRISH they're ASIAN not Irish!!

"Diversity" is really killing Irish media #JIBS

I close out of Twitter, feeling my breath coming in sharp. There are so many of them. Tweets that are racist, fatphobic . . . horrible.

But everyone around me is still scrolling, amusement visible in their eyes. Have they not seen those tweets? Do they not care? Or are they laughing at them?

"Hey, these are just eejits," Niamh says from beside me. "Ignore it. You know how people get."

"Right," I say, though I *don't* know how people get. I've never had so much vitriol directed at me all at once before.

"Look, there are so many tweets calling me a ginger. I mean, come on." Niamh goes back to scrolling through the tweets. There's still that smile lighting up her face.

I nod, blinking back the tears prickling my eyes. I stuff my phone back into my pocket and look around. This time, I'm not pretending to not look for Chris. I need to find her. She's the only one here who would understand this. She's the only who is being attacked the same as me. But there's no trace of her in the kitchen.

"I'll be right back. Bathroom," I manage to get out to Niamh before slipping out of the kitchen. I walk around the entire house—find stragglers here and there, laughing and drinking, taking screenshots from Twitter. But there's no sign of Chris anywhere.

Did she go home? Did she have enough of the party? I wouldn't blame her.

The bell rings, shrill and sharp, breaking through my thoughts.

I don't know why, but I rush forward and fling the door open, hoping that it's Chris on the other side. But of course it's not. It's a lanky boy with freckles all over his cheeks holding a tower of pizza boxes.

"Hi, pizza for—" I push past him, into the surprisingly cold evening. It's been warm for most of the summer, but now the air feels biting. I don't know if it's because I suddenly feel untethered or because the temperature has actually dropped. It could be either, really—considering it's Ireland.

I start walking, not really sure where I'm going. It's only when I've left the noise of the party behind that I realize I probably should have said something to Niamh before I left. But it's a bit too late for that now.

Instead, I dig my phone out of my pocket and text Chris.

Me: Where are you???
Me: Did you leave the party???
Me: I need to talk to you!!

My hands are shaking, but I don't put the phone back. I watch the screen glaring back at me, waiting for an answer. But there's nothing. I don't even know if she's received my messages.

I take a deep breath and dial her number instead. It immediately goes to voice mail.

"Hi, it's Chris." Chris's voice sounds strange over the phone. Deeper and more posh somehow. "I can't come to the phone right now, so leave me a message . . . or probably better if you send me a text."

I bite my lip, not sure what to do. I could walk around here, waiting for Chris to answer her phone or reply to my texts. Or I could go home.

I *should* go home. I don't know how long I can roam around in the middle of Dún Laoghaire. The sun is lighting up with the colors of the sunset, and soon it'll be dark.

I take a turn toward the bus stop and toward the smell of the ocean air. The sea stretches out in front of me, dipped in shades of faded red and pink from the sun and sky. Finally, at the edge of the pier, I see what I've been searching for.

Chris.

SIXTEEN

I Tirra-Miss-You

CHRIS IS SITTING WITH HER SHOES OFF, HER LEGS SWINGING BACK and forth over the seawater. In front of her, the boats and yachts of the pier stretch out all the way to the lighthouse. But she doesn't seem bothered by the fact that her view is blocked. She looks out on the horizon, and her lips are set in a thin line. She looks . . . contemplative. Deep in thought.

I pause behind her, wondering if I should go up to her at all. I've trekked all the way here. I *want* to talk to her. I kind of need to talk to her. But she obviously came here to get away from the party and its people. I'm probably the last person she wants to see. And I know she should be the last person I want to see.

"How long exactly are you going to stand there?"

I freeze, halfway between turning and not. "How did you know I was here?"

Chris finally turns—ever so slightly—to glimpse at me. "I saw you coming. There aren't exactly a lot of people here. Do you want to sit? Or were you leaving?"

"Do you want me to leave?" I ask.

She sidles to the right, like she's making space for me. A space to sit. I stare at the empty spot for a moment before moving toward it. Slipping my black flats off, I settle down beside her, my bare legs dangling below me.

"How come you left the party?" I ask after a moment.

Chris just shrugs, her focus in front of us once more, where the ocean meets the sky. It's already gotten darker. In a few minutes, it'll be nighttime.

"Did you see . . . ," I begin hesitantly, not sure if I really want to be the one to introduce Chris to the horrible tweets if she hasn't already seen them. If I could go back in time, I would stop myself from looking at them.

Chris leans her head back and closes her eyes, like she doesn't really want to talk about this. Even though I haven't said what I wanted to yet. "How could I have missed it?"

She's right. How could she have missed it? That must be why she came out here in the first place. Away from all the people who are excitedly going through Twitter, pretending not to see all the awful things being said about the two of us.

"They're horrible," I say. "The rest of them . . . they don't care."

"They won't get it." Chris opens her eyes and turns toward me. "They haven't exactly experienced this place like we have."

"Niamh said just to ignore it," I mumble.

Chris meets my eyes now—for the first time today. She doesn't look happy. "That's easy for her to say. Everyone loved the whole shtick with her and Séan, didn't they?"

"It's not like they put it on," I say, and I don't know why my voice comes out defensive. What Niamh said made my stomach sink with dread. "I mean, you've met Séan."

Chris sighs. "We got to the next round of the challenge. We did well. All the judges loved our dessert. We shouldn't feel like shit, right?"

"You feel like shit?" I ask. Mostly because I guess I feel like shit too. Even more like shit since Niamh tried to equate the bigoted tweets to someone calling her a ginger.

"Really, really shit," Chris says, and turns back around to face in front of her. She reaches out to tug at the ends of her hair, something she always did when she was feeling nervous or anxious. One of those small details you pick up on when you know someone intimately. But when she realizes the length is gone, her fingers hover in the air for a moment, like she's not sure what she's supposed to do now. "Did you see that one tweet where they called us both slurs?"

I wince. I can just imagine what those slurs were. Neither Chris nor I are alien to the awful things that people call East Asians and South Asians.

"Did you see the one where they said it would be racist if we *hadn't* gotten through to the next round?" I ask.

Chris laughs, and there's a bitterness to it. "People. Are. The worst."

"I don't know why but I thought this would be easier," I say. "Like we would have to worry about the same things the rest of them did. Did we pick the right outfit? Did we say the right things? Did we bake the best dish?"

Chris smiles, and even though she doesn't look at me, it makes me feel better somehow. She's always had a kind of smile that can light up a room.

"That's what I always liked about you, you know," she says finally.

"That I worry about the same things as everyone else?"

"No." She chuckles. "That sometimes you live in a fantasy world. And you see the best in everything. In people. In the world. In all of it. And somehow it actually makes things . . . less shit."

"I came here looking for you because of the whole thing on Twitter. Not because I saw the best in that or the people who were saying all of that."

"No, but it's the fact that none of it is going to deter you," Chris says.

"Well, it shouldn't deter either of us!" I say, probably a little too loud from the way my words echo around us. "I just mean . . . we have to go into the next challenge and make the best dishes, and beat everyone, and get to the final and . . . one of us . . . has to win. Because that'll show them. The winner of the *Junior Irish Baking Show* being ethnically Asian is going to make them rage, especially when we walk away with all that sweet, sweet cash."

Chris finally turns to me, and there's amusement flickering behind her eyes. "You wouldn't be mad if I won?"

"Not if we can stick it to the racists," I say. She holds my gaze for another moment before turning her body all the way away from the water and facing me entirely.

"Shireen . . ." The sound of my name on her lips is feather-light but somehow feels as heavy as a stone. "I'm really sorry."

"Racists will be racist," I say.

But Chris shakes her head. "I mean, yeah, but I'm sorry for . . . I don't know. All of the stuff between us." Her fingers trace a shape I can't make out on the gravel between us. "I was being a horrible girlfriend when I asked you to not apply for the show because I wanted to win it. You were right about that."

There's a lump forming in my throat, and my mouth is dry. I can't think of any words to say to that. It was one of the worst days of my life.

It was our anniversary. That had made it all the worse. A day Chris and I had been planning for weeks. It was meant to be perfect.

I remember I had managed to usher Ammu and Abbu out of the house for most of the day, so I could make Chris the perfect anniversary dinner—even if it was a little early in the evening. I had made classic Bengali food: polau and roast chicken, along with the perfect rainbow confetti cake, and I had even attempted to make sesame balls with red bean paste filling—Chris's favorite.

When Chris arrived, she was more than impressed with the food. She inhaled it all down like she hadn't eaten in a million years. It's not like she gets to eat a lot of Bengali food in her Taiwanese household. Though Taiwanese food is nothing to sneeze at either. In-between the bubble tea from her parents' restaurant, there were all the times Chris had snuck in the most amazing things her parents cooked—flaky pineapple cakes and soft, silky douhua. Food that I couldn't get enough of.

"I have something to tell you," I said once our dinner was over. "Ammu and Abbu told me about this competition that's starting here. The *Junior Irish Baking Show*. They heard about it from one of their friends and they thought, you know, I'd want to apply!"

To my surprise, Chris didn't say anything. She wouldn't even meet my eye.

"Well?" I asked when the pause between us had stretched long enough to make things awkward.

"That sounds really great," she said, though her voice didn't betray any emotion—definitely no joy. "I . . . actually heard about the show already."

"You did? And you didn't tell me?"

"Well, I heard about it from my parents." Chris looked down at her lap, like that was somehow more interesting than our conversation. "They got me to audition for the show."

It took me a moment to digest that information. "They . . . *got* you to audition. So, you already sent in audition tapes and your forms?"

"Yes." Chris looked up and met my gaze, seeming slightly ashamed to admit this.

"Why did you keep it from me?" I couldn't help feeling hurt. I had thought we were killing it at the whole relationship thing, but apparently we kept big secrets like this from each other. "You didn't think I would want you to compete with me? Because I don't care. It could even be fun to do it together."

"No, I knew you'd be okay competing with me," she said. She tucked a strand of hair away from her face. "I don't want to compete with you. I was hoping . . . you wouldn't hear about it."

It felt a little like I'd stepped into an alternate reality where my girlfriend who loves and supports me through everything is someone I barely knew—someone who acted completely different from the Chris *I* knew and loved.

"So, you wanted me to not compete? And what were you going to do when I inevitably found out *you* were competing?"

"I obviously didn't think it through very well," Chris mumbled.

I didn't even feel angry, just an overwhelming sense of sadness. I took a deep breath and met Chris's gaze. I tried to give her a smile, though I'm not sure if it quite looked like one.

"Well. We're here now, and we're both going to be competing so . . . it'll be okay. It can be fun, you know." I was saying the words hoping that I believed it as much as Chris did. Because the feeling of hurt, betrayal, and sadness all tangled up was still growing inside me.

"Right," Chris said to the table—not to me. Then, she looked up and said, "Can I ask you for a favor?"

Even then, I had a feeling that I wouldn't like whatever Chris had to say, but I still hoped it would be something that would make everything make sense. Like she'd ask, *Can we put this behind us? Can we forget I tried to keep you from entering this show?*

So against my better judgment, I asked, "What kind of a favor?"

Chris took a deep breath before she answered. "Can I ask that . . . that you . . . *don't* enter the show? I just mean because . . ." She dropped her gaze to the table once more. "There is no way that I have a shot with you in the running, and"—she took another breath—"and I really need to win."

I just shook my head because my mouth had dried up. I didn't even know how to answer Chris. Never in a million years would I have thought that she would ask me for a favor like that. Instead, I gulped down my tears, pushed back my chair, and came to a stand.

"Let me get this straight." Turning away from Chris, I leaned my back against the chair and closed my eyes. It was easier to do this when I couldn't see her in front of me. When I could just imagine this wasn't even a real conversation—just one of those imaginary conversations you have in your head hours after the real conversation has passed. Because there was no way this was real. It had to be a dream—right?

"You know that all I've ever wanted in my life is to go on shows like *The Great British Bake Off* and win and prove to everyone what I'm capable of and to make use of all of the opportunities that come with something like that and open up my own dessert shop. You know all of this because I tell you. Almost every day. And you're still asking me to give up on my dreams because you want to win?"

"I'm not asking you to give up your dream, Shireen. I would never ask you to do that. But you don't need to win this show. It's a tiny show that's only being broadcast in Ireland. You're meant for bigger and better things, and when you have them of course I'm going to support you. You know that. I just . . . I just need you to do me this one favor. Please?" She was pleading but the sound of her voice only grated on me. I couldn't make sense of any of it.

When I opened my eyes, Chris was standing right in front

of me. Those warm brown eyes of hers boring into me. She stretched out her hands and linked her fingers with mine. The feeling of her touch almost pushed the whole horrible night away.

"Please, Shireen." Chris stepped closer.

But nothing could really push it away. Not her touch or the sound of her voice. I pulled my hands away and put as much distance between us as I could.

"I think you should leave," I said.

"Shireen." Chris furrowed her eyebrows. "Come on. It's our anniversary. We haven't even finished our cake. We've barely even celebrated. We—"

"You should go." My voice was wavering, and I could feel the tears I was holding back threatening to spill out.

"Shireen, I—"

"Chris. Please go."

She gave me one last look before striding out the door.

Now, with Chris's apology right there, I'm wishing I could go back to that night. Do things differently. I wish we had both done things differently. I wish she had said all of this during our anniversary dinner and later over the phone—hell, even in a text—during all of those hours when I felt like my thoughts were a jumble trying to figure out what the two of us were to each other anymore. Trying to figure out who she was if she could try and put a stop to my dreams so easily. I wish she had said it the next day when I had ended things, and the two of us became history.

She didn't say it any of those times.

But she's saying it now.

And it's too late.

She looks up again when the silence between us stretches out for a little too long. I'm not sure what she sees in my expression, but she pushes on.

"You don't have to say anything. You don't have to . . . accept my apology. I know everything is all fucked up. Just, things have been hard, you know."

"They have?" I somehow manage to croak out.

She nods. "The donut business in Dublin is not exactly booming."

"Yeah, my parents say that too. I guess I haven't really given it a ton of thought."

"My parents have talked to me about it a little. I mean, things were not great, but I guess I thought I could help through this show, because I always felt like I was letting them down somehow by not wanting to take over the shop and not being there enough to help out with the baking. Not the way you help out your parents." She shakes her head. "It doesn't matter. It's not important. It's not exactly . . . I just wanted to say that to you. To say I'm sorry."

Even though there's still a lump lodged tight in my throat, I manage to blink away my tears and nod. I always knew Chris felt a certain burden because baking wasn't what she wanted to do, even though it's what her parents wanted for her. She wanted to explore her creative side, go into video game development and work on her art that way. It was creative but also practical. But it wasn't following in her parents' footsteps. I had never quite understood how she felt about it all. I'm not sure if I ever could.

"I guess I was being kind of a bitch too," I admit. "I mean . . . your hair." I reach forward, touching a strand of her hair with the ends of my fingers. It's only a moment before I pull away—realizing maybe it's too intimate for two people who haven't really even been talking for the past few weeks. "It looks nice. Your hair always looks nice."

Chris's eyes meet mine. There's something familiar in her gaze. But in the moment it takes me to realize what that is, she's already leaning forward. In one swift move she closes the space between us.

For a moment, I'm caught up in the familiarity of all of this. Of the taste of her lips, the feel of them against mine. Of the smell of her mixed with the fresh scent of the ocean all around us. The warmth of her spreading through me. The feel of her fingers threaded through my hair.

But then it comes crashing down. Because one sorry doesn't erase the last few weeks. One apology doesn't take away the fact that for weeks Chris must have believed she did the right thing: that there was no problem in crushing my dreams if it meant she could win this show.

So I give her the gentlest push I can and disentangle myself from her.

Chris blinks at me, a soft flush creeping up her cheeks. I realize that the sun has set sometime during our conversation and our kiss because we're plunged in darkness. And even in the glint of moonlight, I can make out Chris's blush, which looks even pinker than usual. "Sorry," Chris says, looking away from me. Her voice is soft—and maybe if we were anywhere other than this deathly quiet pier, I wouldn't even hear it. "I thought . . . I guess . . . I miss you."

I gulp down the same words. Because obviously I miss her too. How can I not? I might pretend that I don't—that all my feelings for her have vanished into thin air. But Chris isn't exactly easy to forget. She isn't easy to get over.

But neither is the fact that I can't trust her anymore. That she's let me down. And I don't know how to forget that.

When I don't reply for a breath too long, she glances at me, the blush still visible on her cheeks. "I fucked up again, didn't I?"

I shake my head, even though she's kind of right. "Just . . . I can't really . . . I mean . . ." I don't know how to form the words. My head is still a jumble, and I'm still stuck on her kiss and her apology. "We're still competing and you still . . . you know."

"Asked you to not compete for my sake?" Chris finishes for me.

I nod slowly. A moment later, she does too.

Taking a deep breath, she asks, "So, if we're not going to be together, can we maybe be friends?" There's a strange kind of hope laced in her words. Strange because Chris is usually not the one with bashful hope in her voice. "I mean, losing a girlfriend sucks but it's been harder losing one of my best friends." Her gaze darts between the ocean in front of us and me, like she doesn't dare look at me with that hope in her eyes for too long.

"We can . . . try that. I mean, we need each other in this competition clearly," I say. "Because people suck."

"They're the worst," Chris agrees. "It must be harder for you. I saw some of the fatphobic stuff too."

"I'm used to it," I say. Considering I have dealt with it my entire life, it doesn't bother me so much.

"I wish you weren't," Chris says softly.

For a moment, we sit there in silence. Neither of us really looking at each other. Then, Chris asks, "So, are you and Niamh . . . a thing?"

I should have guessed the question was coming. Chris saw the two of us at the party, and Niamh hasn't exactly been discreet about, well, anything. But the question still takes me aback.

"Is that why you don't want to . . . I mean, not that you owe me anything. Or that it's any of my business. I just thought—"

"We're not." I wish more than anything that we weren't having this conversation. "We're friends."

Chris finally looks up at me. "You know she likes you, right?"

I shrug, hoping she takes from it what she wants to take from it. And even though she doesn't quite look satisfied by my answer, she nods firmly.

I don't give her a chance to ask any more questions. Instead, I hop on my feet and slide into the black flats I had just discarded.

"It's late," I say as a way of explanation when Chris looks at me questioningly.

I extend a hand to her—since we're friends now. *Friends*. I have to remind myself when she actually takes my hand and I pull her up. Because everything about her is still too familiar. In my mind, she's still the girl I love—loved.

And when she lets go of my hand to pull on her runners, when we part ways at the bus stop to get on our respective buses, I have to keep reminding myself that what we were is in the past now. And I have to get on board with this new version of me and Chris. Even if it fills me with a strange kind of emptiness.

SEVENTEEN

Don't Dessert Me

ON THE WAY TO YOU DRIVE ME GLAZY THE NEXT MORNING FOR MY 7:30 A.M. shift, I can't help but look for Chris. I know it's probably not a good idea, but I'm so busy trying to peek through the window of the Baker's Dozen for a glimpse of her that I run right into a stranger in front of me.

"I'm so sorry!" I say, leaping away from a girl who has a frown plastered on her face.

"It's fine," she says in a voice that doesn't sound like it's fine at all. She adjusts the bag that had slipped off her shoulder when I bumped into her and then does a double take as she finally properly looks at me.

"Hey, you're, I recognize you," she says.

"Me?" I look around, like there's someone else she could be speaking to.

"You were on that show. You work here, right?" She glances up at the window of You Drive Me Glazy, and it's only then that I realize this girl is not just a stranger I bumped into. She's a customer. And she's standing in line for our shop. There are people in front of her, checking their phones and sighing with frustration at being held up for so long just to get a donut.

"Um, yes. Excuse me," I say, pushing past her and the rest of the customers and through the front door. There is a group of people huddled around the corner with the Post-it notes, camera flashes going off every few minutes. There's another crowd hovering by the display counter and a final group on the other side of the register, looking a little fed up with our wait times.

"Shireen, finally!" Abbu exclaims, waving me over. "Get on your apron and start serving customers."

"What's going on?" I ask.

"Less questions, more work!" He turns to a customer with his customer service smile and starts taking orders. I slip behind the counter and put on my apron with one hand and grab a box for the customer's donuts with the other.

"You're Shireen, right?" one of them asks. "We watched you on the show yesterday. You were pretty good."

"Um, thanks," I respond, not really sure what else I'm supposed to say. For a moment, I wonder if any of these people are the same ones who were on Twitter, saying horrible stuff about me. But I shake that off. No way would any of them make the effort to trudge all the way out here to try one of our donuts. No, these must be people who actually liked me—or at least were interested enough to give us a try.

"It's kind of like being a part of the show, isn't it?" the same customer asks. She has a head of black curls and a red-lipsticked smile. "Trying one of the donuts you've made?"

"I suppose so," I say with my best smile. Though mostly I'm hoping nobody starts critiquing me like the judges. The customer pays up and slips out of the shop, allowing for a new wave of people to pour in. And I settle in for what's probably going to be one of our busiest days in the shop.

The rush dies down around 9:30 A.M. to a trickle of customers. Abbu still seems happy though.

I don't want to burst his bubble, but I know he's going to find out about the Huangs' new donut sooner or later. Better it comes from me than someone else.

"Baker's Dozen stole our blueberry donut idea," I say to him between customers as he refills our display case. I saw the new selection of summer donuts on their website last night. Our blueberry donut is called the Drew BlueBarrymore. Theirs is just called a blueberry donut. So uncreative.

"How do you know?" Abbu asks, barely glancing up at me. I would have expected a bigger reaction. Usually, when the Huangs steal one of our ideas, Abbu is furious. And then he steals one of their ideas. And we go back and forth. Chris and I have had to entertain their rivalry for the past year, all the while pretending we didn't like each other for the sake of our parents.

"I saw it on their website," I say. I pull out my phone and wave the advertisement for it in Abbu's face.

"Hmm." He considers the picture for a moment, a small frown highlighting the wrinkles on his face. Then, he nonchalantly goes back to adding freshly baked donuts to the case.

"You're not angry?" I ask. "You're not going to retaliate?" In the last year, my parents have taken every opportunity they can to one-up the Huangs: stealing their bubble tea, their promotional ideas, their website design, anything to get at them really. Once, Abbu even made me sneak in to the Baker's Dozen in disguise to drop chili powder into their donut batter. It didn't work—mainly because I got "caught" by Chris as soon as I entered their shop. But Abbu was willing to try it is the point.

Abbu's frown deepens, but he doesn't look away from his work. For a minute, he's silent.

"I think the biggest retaliation right now will probably be you winning that competition. It's already helping us," Abbu says. "Their daughter is in it too." He says it like I've forgotten. Like I could forget. "And she's doing quite well. But if you beat her . . ." Abbu finally looks up and catches my eye, a smile dancing on his lips. "Well, there won't be a bigger blow to the Huangs than that."

"Right," I mumble. I hadn't considered that even though my parents were worried about me entering the show, it would mean a lot to them if I win it. It will mean a lot to this place. This is the busiest it's been since opening week. If I win, is this what it'll always be like? What will that mean for us all?

I look around the small space that is You Drive Me Glazy and feel warmth bubble up my chest. Despite all the strangers who are our customers, despite the rivalry between my parents and the Huangs, this place is my second home. Some days we spend more time here than at home.

I look out our window for a moment, at the Baker's Dozen, remembering how I had met Chris. Glancing out the window, seeing her in that ridiculous pink donut costume, the one that was exactly like the ridiculous pink donut costume Ammu made me wear. I had marched outside, ready to talk Chris's ear off. To tell her to back the hell off and stop copying my parents' business.

"Hey!" Chris's eyes snapped toward me at my call. My wedges sounded oddly loud against the footpath as I stomped toward her. "First, you steal our donuts! Now, you steal my donut costume?" My voice came out more like a banshee's screech than anything else.

Still, Chris wasn't fazed. Her lips even curled slightly at the edges, like she was trying very hard to not smile.

"I didn't realize you were the only person in the world allowed to wear a donut costume," she said.

"You saw me wearing it the other day, and you stole our idea!" I exclaimed.

"You stole our bubble tea!" Her voice finally rose a little, like I was getting under skin at least a little bit.

"Because you stole our donut recipes!"

Chris paused to take me in for a moment. I don't know what she saw—probably someone who looked a bit wild and haggard with all the screaming. Instead of screaming back though, she took a step away from me and said, "My parents made me put this on," the fight in her gone once more.

I looked at her with narrowed eyes, trying to figure out exactly game she was playing.

"Well, the bubble tea thing was my idea. We weren't just going to let you take our menu lying down. My parents worked hard on their recipes."

"I know," Chris said. "Your spice chai donut is divine. Way better than my mom's." Her eyes widened as soon as the words were out of her mouth and she snuck a quick glance inside the Baker's Dozen, like she was afraid her parents had overheard her complimenting the competition. "Don't tell her I said that," she added in a quiet rush.

"Don't worry. Not planning to sit down to tea with your parents anytime soon."

Then, Chris actually *did* smile and I noticed that she had perfect teeth—because of course she did.

"We should probably leave this stuff to our parents, right?" she asked, looking down at her donut costume with a dejected sigh. "Personally, I couldn't care less about all of this donut business."

"Well, I care about my parents," I said.

"I mean, me too," she said. "My parents. Not your parents," she added. "I mean . . ." She tucked back a lock of hair, a slight flush rising in her cheeks. "I'm sure your parents are great, but I mean—"

"You want to put this rivalry on the back burner and be friends?" I interrupted. I wasn't sure yet if I was entertaining the possibility, but with each passing moment, I was becoming more and more aware of just how cute Chris was, so I was definitely not *not* entertaining the possibility.

Chris, though, was always a little braver than me. She bit her lip, then said, "How about I get out of this donut costume and we go to a movie?"

It was the strangest request she could have made at that moment. I hadn't expected it at all. Maybe that's why I agreed.

The rest was history.

I shrug the memory off as a new customer steps into the shop. But all the while I'm thinking about how some of the best things in my life happened because of this place. I can't let it fail. I can't let my parents' dreams go to waste.

"YOU'RE AN EEJIT." FATIMA has never been one to hold back on her opinions, but after I fill her in on everything that happened at the party—and afterward—she seems especially reluctant to hold back her opinions this time.

"Wow, thank you," I deadpan, flipping to the next page of the Bengali cookbook with Ammu's translations penciled in. "No need to go easy on me, after all the Irish right-wingers have decided to come down on me."

"Okay, don't use that to garner sympathy."

"I'm not—"

"I just don't understand you!" Fatima exclaims, cutting me off. "Why would you agree to be friends with Chris? You either get back with her or you . . . you—"

"Declare her enemy number one?"

Fatima sighs. "You know I love Chris, but I don't get what you're trying to do here." If I'm being honest with myself, I don't get it either. I just know that I can't get back together with Chris—not after everything that's happened. I feel like I can't trust her anymore. But I don't want to lose her either. The few weeks after our breakup were agony, and I'm not sure I can deal with that again. The idea of not having Chris in my life again? This time, maybe for good? It might be the worst thought in the whole entire world.

"Don't tell me it's because of that white girl," Fatima says, interrupting my thoughts.

"I don't know what you're talking about," I say, glancing back down at my book. Even though I'm not registering anything on the page anymore—not Ammu's translation or any of the delicious pictures.

"You realize that I know you, right?" Fatima asks. "I've been wondering for a while, but when I watched the episode and then heard your whole story about last night, it became pretty clear."

"Niamh and I weren't even in the episode together," I say, my cheeks warming. Niamh had texted me last night—and again this morning—asking where I went off to last night and if I was okay. But I'm not sure if I am okay—and I don't know how to respond to her. So I just haven't.

"You were in it together for long enough," Fatima says matter-of-factly. And I don't correct her because I know Fatima too. And I know how well she knows me.

"I barely know her," I say.

"You're not saying it's not because of her." When I glance up, Fatima is looking at me with disapproval. Instead of making me want to set her right though, it just sends a tingle of irritation through me.

"I don't know why you're so bothered about it." My words

come out with a rough edge around them. I don't know why, but after spending hours telling Fatima about the racist and fatphobic tweets—and having to turn down Chris—I expected at least an inkling of sympathy. But instead, I'm getting accused—as if the idea of me being with someone else is preposterous. Like my love life is any of Fatima's business anyway.

"Because you're being ridiculous and irrational." Fatima's voice rises, and she even repositions herself. Like we're about to have a long, really serious conversation, and she needs to move into the optimal position. "First of all, she's your competition. Second, you're clearly still not over Chris. And being friends with her is just going to make things harder. Shireen, I just don't want you to get hurt. You've barely even dealt with your breakup with Chris, and now you're tumbling headfirst into this apparent friendship with Chris and potentially a new relationship and—"

"I'm not," I interrupt.

Fatima pauses and meets my gaze. "You're not?"

"Getting into a new relationship," I explain. "You don't have to worry about that."

Fatima doesn't look like she quite believes me but before she can get all impassioned again, I keep going. "I can't just cut Chris out of my life. She's important to me."

"Shireen." Fatima doesn't sound impressed at all, so I look away from my screen and back to the cookbook.

"She's been a part of my life for such a long time now," I explain, while tracing a picture of the shondesh in Ammu's cookbook. "I would rather get hurt than lose her forever."

"You remember last week, when you couldn't even have a conversation with her without getting into a fight?"

"I know." But what I don't know is how to explain to Fatima that even with the fighting, the tension, the anger—Chris was still a part of my life. And that was important. It was something that I knew. Something I've known all summer, since the moment of our breakup. Maybe it wasn't that I was dreading seeing Chris at the *Junior Irish Baking Show*. Maybe along with the dread, I was longing for it.

When I glance up once more, Fatima is rubbing the bridge of her nose, like I've given her a headache. I would probably have a headache, too, if I was in her shoes, so I can't blame her.

"I should go," Fatima finally says, even though our conversation doesn't really feel like it's over.

"I want to hear about your trip," I say.

"Next time," Fatima promises. "I'll talk to you later, okay?"

"Okay," I say. "Bye, Fa—" The screen goes blank before I can finish.

For the first time in maybe my entire life, I actually feel worse off after talking to Fatima.

MY PHONE BUZZES QUITE a bit over the few days after the episode airs. Old friends and classmates are still trying to get in touch and ask about the show, but most of the notifications come from comments and followers on my blog. People don't just comment about the new recipe I posted a few days ago. They're even requesting recipes. Specifically, requesting the chocolate lava cake recipe Chris and I made for the show.

When my phone buzzes the night before filming our second episode, I expect another blog comment. Instead, I'm surprised to find a text from Chris.

Chris: Are you nervous about tomorrow?

I remind myself: we're friends now. It's normal for friends to ask each other these things. Right?

Me: No . . . yes . . . I don't know.
Chris: it'll be weird not having you there working with me.

I try to tamp down the smile that's tugging at me. Because seeing Chris's texts should not be making me smile. They shouldn't make me feel anything.

My phone vibrates again before I can type back a reply to Chris. But this time it's not a message from her. It's Niamh, who I haven't seen since the party a few days ago.

Niamh: Hey . . . I'm really sorry about what happened at the party. I know it must have been upsetting, seeing all of those things people were saying about you. I figure that's why you've been ignoring me, but I wanted to say I'm sorry.

I almost feel bad now for putting off replying to Niamh for so long. The thing is that I don't know what felt worse. The abusive tweets coming from strangers or the fact that nobody seemed to care about them. That even Niamh didn't seem to care about them.

> Me: I guess I hadn't really expected that kind of reaction.
> Niamh: why would you?? You were amazing on the show. I don't know how anyone could write the things they did. Not after seeing how talented you are.
> Niamh: They'll be eating their words after tomorrow's filming. I know that.

I feel a strange swell of warmth in my chest at the fact that Niamh has such confidence in me, even though we barely know each other.

> Me: I'm sorry I was ignoring your texts.
> Niamh: I get it.
> Me: See you tomorrow?
> Niamh: See you tomorrow.

I lay back in my bed and take a deep breath. Trying not to smile too hard at that text exchange with Niamh. Or at the message from Chris, still waiting for my reply. I definitely shouldn't be smiling at either of their texts.

I think I'm starting to understand why Fatima called me an eejit.

EIGHTEEN

Flourting with Disaster

SOMEHOW THE SET WHERE WE FILM THE SHOW LOOKS EVEN MORE intimidating today than it did the last time I was here. Probably because it's completely unchanged but with only half the people.

The kitchen stations have been shifted because there are only twelve of us left now. And we're not going to be partnering up anymore.

I walk toward my station, and it's like fate has decided it truly hates me. Because in front of me and right across from the judges table is none other than Chris. She's wearing a blue-and-white-striped T-shirt and a pair of jeans. A pretty basic Chris outfit—which shouldn't make her look as good as it does.

Worse than that, the station right behind me belongs to none other than Niamh. And while Chris plays it cool when she spots me walking up, Niamh . . . doesn't. She rushes toward the small gap between our stations, a grin breaking out on her face.

"Hey!" she exclaims, her voice a little too excited, considering we're about to start shooting the second episode of the show. Then I remember that Niamh has an advantage, so she's probably not as nervous as the rest of us. "You're not still mad, right?" she asks after a moment, her voice lower now. Some of the excitement is gone from her face.

"No, I'm just a little nervous I guess." About more than the competition, but Niamh doesn't have to know about that.

I pull on the apron over my red-and-green watermelon dress, just as Kathleen Keogh struts into the room. Unlike me, she seems to be getting less and less colorful every time I see her. Today, she wears a plain black dress that stops just above her knees. But of course she wouldn't be Kathleen Keogh without her signature red lipstick.

"I know what the challenge today is," Niamh whispers before I can charge into my station.

"You do?" I ask. Though I shouldn't be surprised. Anybody could have guessed that's what Niamh and Séan's advantage was. While the rest of us have to think up what we want to make on the spot, Niamh and Séan have had the luxury of spending the last few days perfecting their ideas and recipes.

"And you're going to nail it," she says. "So you don't have to be nervous."

I want to ask her how she knows. It's not like Niamh and I have spoken at length about baking—especially with me barely speaking to her over the last few days. But I don't have the chance to ask her any more questions.

The next moment, the producers are yelling at all of us to get into place as the lights come on and the cameras start rolling.

"Welcome to another episode of the *Junior Irish Baking Show* . . . ," Kathleen Keogh starts off.

I close my eyes for just a moment and take a deep breath.

I can do this, I remind myself. Not just for me but also for

Ammu and Abbu—and You Drive Me Glazy. And for my dreams, and for their dreams too.

After all the judges are introduced, the cameras turn to Padma Bollywood to tell us about our challenge for today. She wears a black-and-white-patterned kurta with jeans that somehow makes her brown skin glow. A perfect combination of South Asian and Western.

She smiles at the camera and begins to explain the challenge in her deep and compelling voice. "The challenge today is pretty simple, and it's one designed after my own heart. Today you'll have to make one of the most technically difficult things for a baker: bread."

Bread. Of course! Padma Bollywood is famous for her cookbook of breads from all around the world. A cookbook that I've read from cover to cover time and again. That must be why Niamh said I'd be fine. I had no reason to be nervous. Because she knows how big a fan I am of Padma's.

But that doesn't exactly make things easy. Bread has never been my forte, even if I am the biggest Padma Bollywood fan in the world.

"You'll have two hours to complete this challenge," Máire Cherry chimes in. "And if you get anything wrong, Padma is an expert among us. She *will* know." Before she's even finished talking, I can see everyone's expressions shift, like they're trying to think up everything they know about baking bread. Except Niamh, and in the station next to her, Séan.

I don't have time to focus on them, though. My mind is

151

running through a list of all the different kinds of bread I know. Two hours is barely enough time, considering how long it usually takes for the dough to rise. But we'll have to make do. I'm running through Padma Bollywood's entire recipe list, when I remember the cookbook I had asked Ammu to translate for me.

She had only done a few recipes, and most of them were just mishtis. But suddenly, I know exactly what I have to make for this challenge. Something even Padma Bollywood didn't include in her book.

"Contestants, are you ready?" By the time Kathleen steps beside the giant clock with its glaring red numbers, I actually *am* ready. If a little nervous. "Your time starts . . . now!" And the digital clock begins to count down.

BY THE TIME KATHLEEN Keogh arrives at my kitchen station with a big smile, it's already fifteen minutes into the challenge. In that time, I've gathered all of my ingredients and—because what I'm making is Bengali—have even had to improvise on some things. I'm hoping against hope that I'm remembering the recipe correctly and that my improvisation won't actually be the end of me.

"Shireen!" Kathleen exclaims as she comes up to my station. I've kneaded my dough and start wrapping it up with cling film as I glance up at her.

"Hey, Kathleen," I say, trying to sound like it's not super

irritating that she's breaking my baking flow. Out of the corner of my eye, I see Chris glance over. Almost like she's worried about me. After all, Chris was the one who handled Kathleen during the last challenge.

"I see you're hard at work," Kathleen says, peering at the dough that I'm putting away. "Now, what do you think is the hardest thing about making bread?"

"Definitely the dough rising," I say. "If your dough doesn't rise, then your bread won't come out right."

"Hm, definitely something to be careful of," Kathleen says with a somber nod to the camera. "And what kind of bread are you making today?"

I pause in my work for a moment and glance up at the camera to give it my full attention. "It's actually a type of sweet bread from my home country."

"India," Kathleen says with a little too much confidence.

"*Bangladesh*," I correct with the kindest smile I can muster while my teeth are gritted. "And it's a special bread that I've only ever had in my region of Bangladesh, Sylhet."

"Oh? I've never heard of Seal-het before," Kathleen says with an appreciative nod.

"*Sill-et*." I correct her pronunciation. "It's called bakhorkhani." I don't even give her a chance to mess up the pronunciation before going into its description. "It's kind of like a porota, but it's sweeter."

"Like a paratha?" Kathleen asks, using the Hindi word, with an impressed nod toward the camera. Like knowing how to say *paratha* makes her worldly.

"Yes." I try not to roll my eyes on camera. Considering how quickly the world villainized me and Chris after the last episode, I wouldn't be surprised if the producers of the show are looking for more ways to make us out to be villains. I've watched enough reality TV to know how these things go, and I'm definitely not falling prey to that.

"Padma Bollywood must know about this one," Kathleen says, as if Padma being Indian means she must know about all of the food in the entirety of South Asia.

"Maybe," I say before turning away from the camera and back to my work. "She hasn't written about it in any of her cookbooks yet." *But maybe she would after tasting my bakhorkhani*, I think with a small smile.

NINETEEN

A Slice of the Action

WE'RE HALFWAY INTO THE CHALLENGE WHEN I GLANCE AT THE stations around me. Chris already has something in the oven. She's bent down low staring at it, as if that will somehow make the dough rise faster. From the way she's chewing at her lips, I can tell she's nervous.

But what's going on behind me is the real reason I became distracted from my work. Niamh and Séan are arguing back and forth, and for a moment I'm not sure if it's for show or not. After all, in the last episode their antics got them a lot of notice.

"You stole my recipe!" Niamh shouts, so loud now that even Chris—who was too focused on her work—glances back.

"How can I steal your recipe when I didn't even know what you were making?" Séan asks. Unlike Niamh, his voice is low— soft. Almost like he's appeasing Niamh. It seems to be making her even more furious, to the point where her face is flushed red.

"You obviously found a way to figure out what I was making!" Niamh exclaims, throwing her arms up.

"Wow, these are some wild accusations," Séan says in his infuriatingly quiet voice. And then—as if everybody else is in on it—he turns to one of the cameras hovering around him and rolls his eyes. Like this is all one huge joke.

I can see Niamh's balled-up fists, like she's about to explode from anger, and even the judges at the front of the room seem to be looking at her with some kind of apprehension.

I step forward. I know I have my own work to get to, but nobody deserves to be ridiculed on TV like this.

"Niamh. Forget about him. He's just trying to get a rise out of you."

Niamh glances at me, and her face seems to soften. Some of the rage gone from her now.

"But he's . . . he's . . ."

"Taken your recipe, I know," I say in the most reassuring voice I can. "It doesn't matter. You can't do anything about it now. But if you don't get back to work, you might not even have something to present to the judges." I point to the looming clock at the front of the room, and the numbers seem to be dropping almost a little too fast. There's less than an hour left, and all of us have a lot of work to do.

"Hey, I *didn't* steal her recipe," Séan says from the front of his station. Some of his enraging calm has worn away, and he narrows his eyes at me. Like he hadn't expected anyone to come to Niamh's defense.

"Ignore him," I say. "Just focus on your own work."

Niamh doesn't look happy, but she still nods her head.

"I didn't steal her recipe!" Séan says louder this time, calling to me rather than to Niamh. "I'm not going to stand by while she makes ridiculous accusations against me and tries to make me out to be the bad guy!"

"Okay," I say, not even sparing him a glance. Instead, I go back to my own station and get out my dough. Thankfully, it seems to have risen just the perfect amount. I stifle a smile as I take it out and begin to roll it into a ball. I just need to roll it out flat, like a ruti—which I've done a million times before. Fry it, dip it in syrup—and hopefully the bakhorkhani will taste the way that I want it to.

I wrap up the dough in cling film and finish making my syrup. I'm going through all the steps left to do in my head when something comes hurling my way.

I duck almost instinctively. And when I glance down, I realize that someone has thrown a piece of rolled dough my way. Like it was a snowball fight. I barely have the chance to register this before all hell breaks loose in the room.

"What the hell?" someone says.

"Hey!" Chris's familiar voice yells.

When I look up, there's food flying every which way. I'm not sure who's doing the throwing and who's actually getting hit, but it's like an all-out war.

All I know is that I have to protect my bakhorkhani.

I grab hold of my bowl of rolled-up dough and my bowl of syrup and duck back down. I crawl under the little space beneath my kitchen station, watching everything unfold with my dish safe and sound with me.

I really have no clue what is going on above. I can hear people shouting, people getting hit. There's flour flying along with the dough—and who knows what else. I can make out Kathleen

Keogh hiding in a corner of the room, too, though I don't know what she has to hide from. She's probably trying to protect her expensive clothes and that bright red lipstick of hers.

"Hey." I nearly jump out of my skin at Chris's voice.

"What are you doing here?" I ask in a whisper. She crawls into the space below my kitchen station, squeezing herself in beside me.

"Safety in numbers?" she says. "Who started this?"

"Séan?" I ask. He seems like the type of person who would get angry enough to start a food fight in the middle of a challenge.

"Or Niamh," Chris suggests.

"No way it was Niamh," I say, and I hate that my voice sounds so defensive.

Chris glances at me quickly, and I'm not sure what she's thinking. "She just seemed pretty angry a few minutes ago."

"So did Séan," I say. "And you've seen him, you've heard the way he talks, he—"

Chris intercepts a flying ball of dough from in front of my face. "I don't think you were the target for that," she says, shaking out her hand and pulling dough off of it with a disgusted look on her face.

"How did you do that?" I can only blink at Chris with wide eyes. I've never seen such quick reflexes.

"I think it's probably from years of playing too many video games?" Chris says. I guess I shouldn't be that surprised. In the year that I've known Chris, she's never been a klutz like me. She's always the one pulling me out of the way of oncoming bicycles in the park or streets and catching me before I can fall flat on my face. It's not so bad being the ungraceful one when you have a girlfriend like Chris to catch you last minute and save you from making a total fool of yourself. It's actually kind of romantic.

"How much longer do you think they'll go on for?" Chris asks after a moment.

"Hopefully not long," I mumble, glancing at my bowl of dough and syrup. I don't know how much longer we have left, but I do know that if the food fight doesn't stop soon, I might not even have anything to show the judges.

Finally, after what feels like way too long, the flying dough and flour seem to stop. For once, it's not Kathleen Keogh who turns toward the cameras but Galvin Cramsey. Everyone watches with bated breath as he approaches the front of the room, his forehead crinkled from the severe frown he's sporting.

"Never in my life have I ever been in a kitchen like this before," Galvin says. His voice is low and soft, but it carries over the whole room. It has this strange sort of authority that makes it scary. "In a professional kitchen, this kind of behavior would never be tolerated," Galvin continues. "And trust me when I say the judges and I will figure out who perpetrated this and who participated to make it worse. And there will be consequences for everyone involved."

Chris and I exchange a glance. I had ducked out of sight as soon as the first piece of dough was thrown, but who knows what Galvin and the judges will think of as participation.

"Now there's only thirty minutes left of your challenge," Galvin says, pointing to the red countdown clock. "And I don't care if someone's ruined your dish or if you haven't got enough time because of . . . all of this." He waves his hand around the room, which is a big floury mess. "But what I do know is that when time is up, we want to see your dishes. And then, we will investigate."

With that, Galvin turns around and marches away. Not to the judges table but right outside the set. I can't blame him. Even I can see that neither the judges nor anybody on the crew has managed to keep clean during all of this. I can't imagine what the rest of them are thinking.

"Do you think he'll come back?" Chris asks in a whisper as the two of us climb up to our stations once more.

"He has to," I say, though really, he doesn't. I glance around the room properly now, and it's even worse than I could have imagined. My entire station is a mess. I'm glad I managed to find a hiding place when I did because I definitely would not have survived this.

"Oh, shit!" Chris suddenly exclaims from beside me. Before I have the chance to ask her what's going on, she rushes toward her station and opens the oven door. A puff of smoke escapes from it, and Chris tries to wave it off while coughing.

From the look on her face, I'm pretty sure her bread is burnt.

I watch in sympathy for a moment before picking up my own things and putting out a pan to start frying my bakhor-khani. There's not long left in the challenge, and I have to make sure that this food fight didn't ruin my chances in this competition.

"AND TIME'S UP!" WE all put our hands up and step away from our dishes as the buzzer sounds and Kathleen announces the end of the round.

I glance around. Not at the judges but at my fellow competitors. Everybody is grim faced. There's none of the excitement—or even the anxiety—from the first challenge. It's like everybody is afraid of what Galvin said—afraid of the consequences he mentioned. Maybe they shouldn't have gotten into a food fight, which I didn't even think was something that happened in real life.

Kathleen glances at the door that Galvin disappeared through, obviously wondering if he's planning on coming back. She turns to the rest of us with only the ghost of the bright white smile she usually wears. "Let's give the crew a chance to clean all this up before we shoot the judging," she says.

With that, the twelve of us are ushered into the back of the studio as everybody begins to clean up.

"Do you think they'll send home whoever started it?" Bridget asks. She tugs at the ends of her blond hair, while her eyes dart around at each of us. Like she's expecting someone to confess.

"Who *did* start it?" Séan asks. He surveys us all, his arms crossed.

"Probably you," says Niamh. "You were the one getting annoyed because Shireen told me to ignore you and pay attention to my own work."

"You were the one who was actually angry. I wouldn't be surprised if you started it to distract from the fact that my dish will be so superior to yours," Séan says.

"You were the one who—"

"Stop." Chris's voice is not loud. She doesn't shout. But somehow it holds the same power that Galvin's does. Same power that makes people listen. "Your arguing is what got us here in the first place, so you need to stop."

Séan looks like he's about to say something more, but Niamh nods.

"Come on, Shireen," she says, grabbing hold of my hand and pulling me away. From the annoyed look on Chris's face, this is not what she wanted when she told the two of them to stop arguing. Still, I let Niamh pull me along to the farthest corner of the room—as far away from Séan as we can get. The other contestants also disperse in their own little groups, whispering among themselves. Probably wondering who the person was who started everything and what exactly the consequences are going to be.

"It's good TV," Niamh says, leaning against the wall. "Right? They can't be that mad."

I think about what Chris said while we were hiding. Could she be right? Did Niamh start the food fight? I want to ask her, but I know that she'd probably just get annoyed that I'm making accusations.

"It *is* good TV," I say instead. "I think Galvin was probably annoyed because there was flour in his hair."

"He does love his hair. You can tell. There's a lot of product in it," Niamh says matter-of-factly.

"Well, he is a famous TV show host. His hair has to look good," I point out.

"Do you think they'll eliminate the person who started it?" Niamh asks. "Or anybody who participated?" She's nervously picking flour out of her hair, and it doesn't make her look less guilty.

"If they eliminated everyone who participated, half the contestants would be gone," I say. Because looking around, almost everyone is covered with a dusting of flour, some with other things that are all kinds of colors. I don't want to even want to think what exactly they've been hit with.

"It should be easy to figure out who was first, right?" Niamh says. "It's a TV show for God's sake. They have cameras everywhere."

"They do, but that would be a lot of footage to get through. Maybe it would be better if whoever started it just confessed," I say, glancing at Niamh with what I hope is reassurance. If it was Niamh who started this, maybe she can make amends. After all, her and Séan's antics have been getting the show buzz. They wouldn't just throw them out like that.

Would they?

TWENTY

Bake It Till You Make It

BY THE TIME EVERYTHING'S CLEANED UP, GALVIN IS BACK IN HIS seat, looking grumpy as ever.

As we all head back to our kitchen stations, Niamh squeezes my hand. When I meet her gaze, she just gives me a smile. And I'm not sure if it's because she's worried she's about to get into trouble or not.

I slip into my kitchen station, still feeling pretty happy about my bakhorkhani. And knowing that I didn't throw food at any-one. I catch Chris watching me, but she glances away almost as soon I catch her eyes.

I ignore the flip-flop of my stomach, the escalated beat of my heart, and turn toward the judges. One by one, they call each of us up.

It's . . . not pretty.

Chris steps forward with her half-burnt pineapple buns. She's tried to cover up the burnt sides with crushed strawberries and even sprinkled some sliced strawberries on the side of her plate, so they almost look like rose petals. Despite the presenta-tion, Galvin glares at Chris the entire time he chews the bread, like it's the worst experience of his life and he can't believe she is making him eat it.

Even from where I stand, I can tell Chris is terrified. I can't see her face, but the way she stands in front of the judges is not her usual cool and confident self. She could be eliminated. She could go home. And not because of anything she did or didn't do.

"I see you had a few problems," Padma says kindly once she's finished chewing. Her face betrays no emotion though.

"I was too long taking them out of the oven," Chris says so low that if it weren't for the mic taped to her, I probably wouldn't hear her at all.

"Well, despite that. It's got good flavor," Máire says with a smile.

"Good texture too, the parts that haven't burnt," Padma adds with a nod.

"Serving burnt food is really something you should think twice about" is all Galvin says. No feedback at all. Chris just nods and stares at the ground the entire walk back to her station. All of us watch her, knowing that her chances of being eliminated are high.

The next few judging rounds don't go much better. With the amount of time the food fight took up, everyone's dishes suffered, and nobody comes away with glowing compliments. Not even Niamh and Séan. The judges' disappointment in them is palpable.

"Even with the advantage that you were given, you didn't manage to deliver today," Galvin says to Séan. For once, Séan doesn't hold his head high with that annoying pride of his. Instead, he actually looks kind of disappointed too. Maybe it was Séan who started the food fight. It has to be.

"Shireen," Galvin says, clearly still in an awful mood after everything.

I grab hold of my plate of bakhorkhani and stumble forward.

"So, what do we have here?" Padma asks.

"Um, it's a dish from the region of Bangladesh my family is from," I offer. "It's called bakhorkhani."

"Looks like paratha," Galvin says, scrutinizing it closely as if I've lied to him or something.

"Yes, well, it is a little bit like that. But the taste is different," I explain.

"I've had bakhorkhani before," Padma says. "But none like this."

"There are regional differences?" I offer. "This recipe is from Sylhet. It's my mom's recipe I think." At least, it's the recipe from her cookbook.

The judges cut into it, and the texture is soft and flaky, just as I had wanted it to be. I breathe a sigh of relief, though I know I'm not out of the woods yet.

"Sweet, soft, flaky," Padma says, nodding her head. She's trying not to look too impressed, but I can tell that she is. I suppress a smile as she takes another bite.

"A really good mix of flavors," Máire adds. "Good job."

"Probably the only person without anything undercooked or overcooked so far," Galvin says. And if I'm not mistaken, his lips twitch. Like he wants to smile but is trying really hard not to. That's pretty much the highest compliment anyone can get from Galvin today.

I would skip back to my station if everyone weren't watching me. It's a little harder to stop grinning though. But thankfully, most people look too concerned about themselves to think about me and how well my judging went.

As soon as the judges leave the room for deliberation, I see Chris slump down on the counter in front of her. My heart tugs painfully. If this were just a few weeks ago—before we broke up—I would be there consoling her. But it's not a few weeks ago, and we *are* broken up.

But we're also supposed to be friends now. Tentatively.

Except I don't know what being friends with Chris looks like. Does it mean I get to comfort her, or would that just make her feel a million times worse?

I make a mental note to tell Fatima that she was so right about this whole thing. I know she'll probably gloat and rub it in my face and say I told you so, but . . .

As I stride forward to close the space between my and Chris's kitchen stations, I don't mind so much that Fatima was right.

"Hey," I say. "It's going to be okay."

"Right," Chris says with a humorless chuckle. It's not like Chris is always fun and happy, but I've never seen her like this. She seems so . . . down. So unhappy. During the start of the competition, when I was still reeling from our breakup, I think seeing her like this would have made me ecstatic. Like she deserved exactly what she was getting. Like her unhappiness was all tied up with our breakup and should make me feel superior.

But now I hate it. Because as much as I don't want to, I still care about Chris. As a friend.

Actually, as more than a friend—though nobody else has to know about that part.

"A lot of people had bad dishes today," I say to her. "And they're going to come down on the person who started the food fight, right? That's their top priority."

"I doubt they even care about that." Chris' voice sounds defeated.

"But Galvin was so—"

"It makes good TV, Shireen," Chris says. "I bet in our interviews for this episode we're all just going to be asked about who we thought started things and what happened."

I know she's right, but I don't want to give in to her dejection.

"You don't know that."

Chris looks up at me with a small smile. I think back to what she said at the pier the other day, about how one of the things she loves about me is that I see the best in everything. Just thinking about that—our conversation, our kiss, brief as it was—makes me flush.

"Your presentation was the best out of everyone. They have to give you points for that at least," I say.

"What's the point of presentation if the food sucks?"

I want to tell her that presentation can be just as important as taste. That we eat as much with our eyes as we do with our mouths. That nobody can be enticed to eat something they don't like the look of. But before I can even open my mouth, the judges stroll back in.

"They're already done?" I ask in a whisper.

"Must have been an easy decision," Chris says, like she already knows what the decision is.

I want to win this competition and beat everyone, Chris included. I should want to beat her specifically, after everything. But I don't. If she gets eliminated today, I'm not sure how I'll handle that.

"Well, the decision for best dish of the week was pretty simple," Galvin says, his eyes casting around us. He still doesn't look particularly happy, but he doesn't look as annoyed as he did after the food fight ended.

I feel this weird kind of anxiety mixed with hope. I know the judges loved what I made. I know Padma Bollywood definitely loved it. Could I win the best dish of this week? Could I get an advantage for the next round? I say a quick prayer under my breath, even though I'm usually not much for prayers.

"The best dish this week goes to . . ." I stare at Galvin, like if I stare hard enough, he'll know to look at me and to say my name. I know I shouldn't get my hopes up, but I can't help it. My hopes are up and I'm already imagining how proud Ammu and Abbu are going to be, how I'm going to relay the information to Fatima, and how annoyed all the assholes on Twitter will be. "Ruby!"

My heart sinks as the room bursts into polite applause. I raise my hands, too, but clapping feels like way too much effort, given how deflated I feel. The rest of the names get called out— including mine, Séan, Niamh—and even though Chris doesn't get called until almost the very end, she makes it through to the next round.

I should be grateful. I get to stay and win another day. But I can't help thinking this was my one shot to get best dish, and it's just slipped out from under me.

TWENTY-ONE

A Loaf Triangle?

IN THE CONFESSIONAL BOOTH THAT EVENING, ANDREW PREDICTABLY only questions me about the food fight. I kind of wish I could flip it around and ask him some questions. After all, the camera crew must know who started it. Who made it worse. They must know everything. They're like the all-seeing eye of this show.

"I don't know who started the food fight," I say to the camera for the umpteenth time, but Andrew doesn't seem satisfied with any of my answers today.

"There must be someone who you thought was acting suspicious?" Andrew asks. "Something you saw?"

"I was under my kitchen station the entire time. I couldn't have seen anything."

"Right. You and Christina were out of sight for a lot of the food fight," Andrew says. "Some of the other contestants found that suspicious."

I don't know if he's telling the truth or just egging me on. I don't know how to figure it out either.

"They did?" I ask. "But we didn't do anything. Chris's dessert got ruined. She almost didn't make it through."

"But a lot of the other contestants also had ruined dishes," Andrew says with a thoughtful nod. "And they also found it suspicious that yours was one of the only dishes to remain almost perfectly intact."

I'm not sure how to process this information. I wouldn't be surprised if some of the other contestants did talk about how my dish was perfectly intact but only because Andrew and the rest of the crew made it seem like I was the one to blame. In the same way he's trying to get me to implicate someone else.

"I think there must be some kind of footage that shows who started the food fight," I finally say to the camera, even though I know they're definitely not going to be using this footage. "And if you wanted to find out, you just have to dig a little deeper instead of asking us."

Andrew gives me a tight-lipped smile before moving on to talk about the rest of the episode. And I'm not sure if I should feel relieved or if the knot of anxiety in my stomach is warranted.

"YOU WERE RIGHT."

Fatima leans into the camera. "What are you talking about?"

It's the day after we finished filming the second episode. The day before the episode airs and too many days since I had a proper conversation with Fatima. I know she's mad at me, and maybe I was a little mad at her too. But I can't get through the rest of this competition without my best friend.

"Chris. It's harder being friends with her than I would have thought. I haven't hung out with her or anything but it's just . . . weird. I don't know."

"That took less time than I thought," Fatima says, though she doesn't really sound happy about it.

"It's not like I regret it," I rush to add, because I don't. I've just realized that Fatima is right. "It's just harder than I thought it would be."

Fatima rubs the bridge of her nose like this conversation is frustrating her. "So I'm right, but you're not going to do anything about the fact that you're setting yourself up for heartbreak?"

"I just wanted to say that I'm sorry. I was annoyed at you the other day for making very valid points," I say. "And we haven't really talked since then, and I don't want you to be angry at me." I can feel the resentment from her even through the phone screen and all the miles separating us. God, I wish there weren't all these miles in the way. Friendship is somehow so much easier when you're in the same country. In the same city. Most of the time in the same room, hanging out on the same bed, eating really delicious donuts.

"I'm not angry at you," Fatima says softly, though still looking kind of angry. "I guess I just . . . don't want to have this conversation about Chris over and over again. I don't want to go through the same steps, of you not being able to get over her."

"We don't have to talk about it," I say, even though I really do want to talk about it. "Let's talk about your trip."

Fatima eyes me for a moment, frowning like she doesn't really believe we're not going to segue into discussing my love life. Finally, she relaxes and lets her shoulders drop a little.

"Well, we went to Sri Mongol," she says. "I'll show you pictures when I come back, but it was beautiful. So many green hills full of tea leaves." There's a brightness that envelopes Fatima when she's excited—when she's happy—and it emanates from her now. She barely looks at me as she talks about her trip, about running up the hill tracts with her cousins, playing charades during the car ride, about the cool air in Sylhet, about visiting her bari and going fishing in the lake.

I try to ignore the jealousy I feel—Fatima is over in Bangladesh having the time of her life and maybe she doesn't even miss me as much as she says she does. And I'm stuck here.

After my phone call with her, I climb down the stairs to the kitchen, a familiar smell wafting through the air.

"What are you doing?" I ask Ammu, who's bent over the stove.

"Making food," she says dryly.

"I know that. Why are you making that?" I point to the bakhorkhani that she's adding syrup to.

"You're the only one who can make bakhorkhani?" Ammu asks, like I've personally offended her by asking questions about her cooking. I'd given Ammu and Abbu a play-by-play of what happened during the last filming. Ammu had listened observantly when I told her about my decision to make bakhorkhani. She hadn't commented then, and I'm not sure what to make of this.

"No. But . . . who are you making it for?" I ask.

"It's for when we watch the episode. I thought it'd be nice to have. Like we're eating what you're making." At that, she finally smiles. This is the way Ammu tells me she's proud of me. Not with words but through randomly making bakhorkhani.

But I also can't watch this episode with Ammu and Abbu, like it's not a surreal enough experience watching myself on television without having my parents ready to comment on everything and everyone by my side.

"Will you save me some for later?" I ask Ammu instead.

"I will save you as many as you want," says Ammu.

I FIND MYSELF AT Niamh's doorstep the next day. She invited me over to watch the next episode of the show together, and since I couldn't watch with my parents and I hate the idea of watching it by myself, I took her up on the offer.

So here I am against my better judgment—and definitely against Fatima's advisement . . . if I had told her. I ring the doorbell, expecting things to be much the same as they were last time. But when Niamh swings the door open everything is different.

There are no people behind her. There's no music playing. Even the lights seem brighter, and the house seems much bigger without so many people squashed inside.

"Hey!" Niamh's voice is bright as she ushers me in.

"Where's everybody else?" I ask.

"Oh. I didn't invite anyone else," Niamh says. "I thought . . . I don't know. It got kind of uncomfortable last time. We're all competing. We probably see enough of each other during the show."

I know she's right. It is uncomfortable—especially seeing Séan, who none of us are exactly big fans of. But at the same time, it's strange that Niamh never mentioned it would just be the two of us.

I follow Niamh into the sitting room.

"Do you want . . . you don't drink tea or coffee . . ." Niamh drifts off, not finishing her question.

I hide a smile. It's always a bit of a difficult thing when you visit an Irish person and don't drink tea or coffee. It's kind of the same if you visit a Bengali person, but at least they have snacks ready to fill you up to the brim, even while they make weird comments about your weight.

"It's okay, I'll just have some water," I say.

"There's orange juice," Niamh offers.

"Sure, I'll have some orange juice," I say.

By the time Niamh is back the show has started and Kathleen Keogh fills up the TV screen with her humongous smile. Niamh hands me my orange juice and sits herself and her cup of tea down on the other end of the couch—leaving plenty of room between us.

I'm not sure what to read into this, especially after she invited me here for just the two of us to watch this episode together. So I try not to think of it at all.

The show doesn't focus so much on me or Chris in this episode, but it focuses even more on Séan and Niamh. When the two of them start bickering, Niamh flushes red beside me. She casts me a glance, like she's worried about what I think of her. I shift around in my seat, made uncomfortable by the fact that I'm wearing a dress that's riding up on this too-deep sofa seat.

I give her a smile that I hope is reassuring, and we awkwardly keep watching.

My phone buzzes in my pocket as the show cuts to an ad break.

Chris: who do you think started the food fight? My money is on Niamh.

I glance at Niamh, not sure what to say to Chris.

"Who's that?" she asks.

"My friend," I say quickly.

"Fatima?" Niamh asks, which surprises me. I had spent so long not mentioning Niamh to Fatima that it's strange she knows Fatima's name. "Isn't it super late where she is right now?"

"Yeah, but, she's supportive," I say with a smile. It's technically not a lie.

I text Chris back as quickly as I can before tucking my phone away: definitely not Niamh. My money is on Séan.

"So, who do you think started the food fight?" I ask Niamh tentatively.

"No idea," she says. "And I guess the judges must not know either, right? Why else would they not have mentioned it during filming the other day?"

"Maybe."

The show comes back on. I watch myself hard at work, making the syrup for my bakhorkhani. It zooms all the way to me about to open up the cling-wrapped bowl, ready to start shaping and frying my dough.

That's when the first bit of food starts flying around. The camera pans all around, showing different angles of the contestants. Strangely, me and Chris show up on-screen too. The camera shows close-up shots of our faces, as if we're reacting to the food fight. In reality, I know that we were both already hidden under my kitchen station by now.

I shift uncomfortably in my seat, remembering the confessional I'd been subjected to at the end of this episode. I know from watching a bunch of reality TV shows that it doesn't always matter what the truth is. The producers can edit things to make you fit their version of the truth. But somehow, I didn't think I'd be a victim to that. I thought the *Junior Irish Baking Show* would be about baking, not about the drama.

Finally, they cut to a shot of me ducking, but the way it's presented it's as if we're already halfway through the food fight. Like I was, at the least, watching everything unfold. Maybe even participating.

"Good instincts," Niamh mutters beside me with an impressed grin. I shoot her a smile back before turning to the screen. It looks worse than it did when it was happening. Probably because I was hiding out with Chris the entire time. There's food flying everywhere, and everyone is covered with a light dusting of white—among other things. People are trying to defend themselves while blindly hurling things around too. It's complete and utter chaos.

It *is* great television.

In the confessional booth, all the contestants give their version of events. Everyone speculates about who was the first to start throwing food. And everyone accuses different people—though Séan and Niamh's names crop up quite a few times. Strangely, so do mine and Chris's, even though we were both hidden away from sight most of the time. My long confessional recording where I was asked so many questions about the fight doesn't air at all. Neither does Chris's, and I wonder if she went the same route as me: choosing not to accuse anyone.

"I think that whoever started the food fight deserved to go home," says Hannah, the contestant who was eliminated at the end of the episode. "I did the best I could with what I had, but that person sabotaged everyone."

The camera zooms a little closer on her face. Her expression sobers. "And I'm sure it was Chris and Shireen." The episode cuts out to the end credits.

I can only blink at the screen for a moment. How could Hannah accuse the two of us?

"I know it wasn't you two," Niamh says a little too quickly. "I mean . . . it *was* a little suspicious that you two were out of sight the entire time while the rest of us were fighting it out."

"We were just hiding. We didn't want to get hit," I say.

"Yeah, but you didn't hide until—"

"That's just how the show made us look," I interrupt. I know it's not Niamh's fault so I take a beat and a deep breath. "You didn't see us while we were filming, right? We hid from the very beginning."

"Sure, but I guess people are wondering how you managed not to get hit. And your dish was the one that wasn't affected at all. It came out exactly as you wanted it to."

"So, you think it was me?" I ask.

"No." Niamh shakes her head vigorously, like the harder she shakes it the more inclined I'll be to believe her. "I'm just trying to explain what other people are saying."

I let out a huff of breath and lean back in my seat. I should have seen this coming. The show is trying to paint me and Chris as the villains, even though we've given them absolutely nothing to work with.

"Can I ask you a question?" Niamh asks. She leans forward in her seat, until we're almost face-to-face. All the distance between us suddenly gone.

I can make out all the freckles dotted around her nose and cheeks and the way her eyes are the color of the sky on a perfect summer day.

"Sure," I say, leaning back a little to put some distance between us. I try not to think about the fact that my voice comes out a little too breathy.

"You and Chris . . . ," Niamh says slowly. "Did you use to . . . I mean, it's just you mentioned an ex-girlfriend and you have a history with her, and I just thought—"

"We did." I glance down at the wood floor instead of meeting her gaze. I knew I would have to tell Niamh at some point or that she would figure it out. I was just hoping we could breeze over it like it was nothing. "But we broke up."

"And now you're . . . ?"

"Exes?" I ask, but my voice rises a little too much for that to be believable.

"Exes who protect each other during a food fight and still hang out?" she asks.

"We don't hang out," I say hastily. "And we just . . . happened to find each other that day. Because of how close our stations are to each other." It sounds like a lie, but it's the truth. It's not like I sought out Chris.

"So you're not friends?" Niamh asks.

This time, I look up to meet her gaze. And she seems to genuinely be asking. I try not to think about why she's so curious. But I'm also not sure how to answer her question. Chris and I are supposed to be friends, but at the same time I have no idea where we really stand.

"We're kind of friends," I say. "But like, we're not getting back together," I add quickly.

"I didn't ask if you were," Niamh says with a chuckle. She rises, stretching her arms up above her head, like sitting and watching the show for the past hour has really done a number on her. "You want something to eat?"

"Um, I should probably—"

"Come on," Niamh says with a little whine in her voice.

"We can order in. I'm up here in Dublin all on my own. I barely know anyone. And you keep saying you're too busy to hang out with me."

I guess I hadn't really thought about the fact that Niamh isn't from here. We're kind of in the same boat this summer, since Fatima is gone and Chris is now my ex.

"Okay," I say. "But only for a little bit."

Niamh grins, and I hate the fact that such a small gesture makes butterflies flutter around my stomach. But there's really nothing I can do about that.

From: Clare Farrin <junioririshbakingshow@ietv.ie>
To: Shireen Malik <shireenbakescakes@gmail.com>

Dear Shireen,

Ms. Padma Bollywood would be delighted if you would join her for a cup of tea in the IETV studio's café at 10:30 A.M., before filming begins for the next episode of the show.

Kind regards,
Clare Farrin

TWENTY-TWO

A Legend in the Baking

WHEN I ARRIVE AT THE CAFÉ, MY CHEST TIGHT WITH NERVES, THE first thing I see is Chris. She's over by the counter, probably waiting for her coffee. She catches my eyes almost as soon as I spot her. She waves at me with a question on her face.

I wave back before turning to look for Padma Bollywood's familiar face. But I can't see her anywhere. Did I imagine that email from Clare Farrin? Did someone else write it as a prank?

As I let my mind run wild with all the possibilities, the door to the café flings open, and Padma Bollywood steps in. In a white blouse with puffy sleeves and jeans, she doesn't even look like a celebrity chef.

Recognition flashes in her eyes when she sees me. I have to try not to swoon because the little voice in my head is screaming, "Padma Bollywood recognizes you!!" over and over again, in a not-so-little-voice.

"Shireen!" Her pronunciation of my name is perfect. "Thank you so much for agreeing to join me today." She has a slight Indian accent as she speaks now, and there are a few words that she pronounces a little too thickly. It's almost like she's letting herself speak more freely in our presence.

"Thank you for, um, asking me to tea." I somehow stutter

out the words. Padma either doesn't notice my nervousness or is too kind to say anything. She just flashes me a smile and ushers me to one of the empty tables at the corner of the café. A moment after we sit down, Chris arrives.

"Hi." She sounds a little odd, her voice too high. When I glance up, I notice her cheeks are flushed pink.

"Christina!" Padma exclaims, like the two of them are best friends. "Please, sit."

Chris heads toward the other empty chair, looking at her mug of coffee instead of at either of us.

Before anybody can say a word, two servers bustle toward us with an entire trolley of confections. They lay empty cups in front of us, along with painted pink teapots and coffeepots. Then, they place a six-tiered tray filled with everything from finger sandwiches and macarons to shomuchas and mishtis.

I can only blink at all the choices—choices that I'm pretty sure didn't come from the café's selection of foods.

"I wasn't sure what you would enjoy so I thought a little of everything," Padma says with a smile directed at both of us. "Eat!"

She begins to pour herself a cup of tea, while Chris and I share a mystified look between us. I'm a little afraid to do anything for fear that I'll suddenly wake up from a dream. Because there's no way that this is really happening. There's no way I'm having tea with Padma Bollywood—and my ex-girlfriend.

But then Chris begins to pour herself tea and places some cakes and pastries on my plate before serving herself.

I can hardly just ignore what's right there in front of me.

There's an orange macaron with yellow filling, which is somehow better than any macaron I have ever tasted in my life. I'm delighting in the taste when Padma finally starts speaking.

"So, tell me." She leans forward eagerly. "How are you feeling about the show?"

Chris and I exchange another quick glance.

"Um, it's fun?" Chris says, sounding like she's very much not having any fun at all. Padma turns her smile to me.

"It's yeah, g-good," I stutter. I clear my throat. "It's, um—"

"I'm sorry, Ms. Bollywood." Chris cuts me off—probably saving me from making a fool of myself. "Why did you ask us to tea?"

Padma sits back, the brightness of her smile dimming. I wonder if Chris has offended her. I'm a bit annoyed at her for asking the question now, even though I want to know too.

"First of all, you can call me Padma," she says. "Second, I've been paying attention. Ever since the first episode aired and I saw the reactions on social media. I just wanted to see how you two were doing. How you were feeling about continuing on in the show. If there was anything that we could do to make you more comfortable."

"That's a very nice offer," Chris says. "But I don't think you can do much. People are going to say things if they want to. They always do."

Padma nods sagely. Her eyes settle on me once more. "I know it's not exactly easy to make it in this business as a person of color," she says. "What you said resonated with me, Shireen. About there not being a lot of people like us out there in the cooking world. I've definitely been where you are, but you have my support."

I try to compose myself, because this is a serious conversation, and I'm pretty sure screeching with joy because my idol said my words resonated with her is not an acceptable response.

"Thank you," I manage to squeak out somehow. "It means a lot to have your support."

"I've been trying to get the network to make a statement condemning the responses," Padma continues. "Because I don't like the increase in the harassment I've been seeing, but it hasn't exactly been easy to convince them."

It's strange to think about the fact that even *the* Padma Bollywood doesn't have the power to make a network like IETV put out a statement against racism. Supporting me and Chris as their only contestants of color on the whole show? But I guess I shouldn't really be surprised.

"Well, we appreciate the support," Chris says, leaning back in her seat. She doesn't sound happy. I wonder if she's gone through all the same stages I have, wondering why Padma wanted to meet for tea. I had been excited, elated—and a little nervous too. But now that we're here, it feels strange to be speaking to her about something so ordinary. Something that Chris and I have been dealing with our entire lives.

"I've dealt with it, too, you know," Padma says after a moment of silence. "I mean . . . I still deal with it. And there's really nothing I've been able to do to stop it."

She sounds dejected, but there's a kind of bravery in her

sharing that information with us at all. A strange warmth in it. It's not that I imagined Padma has never had racism leveled at her, but I don't think I've ever heard her speak about it. I guess it's not seen as the done thing if you want to make it. You're supposed to be the "bigger person," and for some reason that means bearing it in silence.

"I just want you to know that you both have my support, and anything that I can do to make this easier, better, I will try to do."

"Thank you," I mumble because there's nothing else really to say.

Padma parts her lips to say something else but just then a woman in a navy-blue suit approaches. "Ms. Bollywood, you're needed to prep before we start filming."

Padma gives a curt nod as she pushes back her chair and rises. "Please, enjoy the food and the tea," she says. "I'll see you both later."

As soon as Padma is out of sight, Chris lets out a sharp breath. "Wow, I can't believe your favorite baker in the entire world just gave us a pep talk," she says.

"And offered to support us in whatever way she could," I add, a smile finding its way to my lips. I take another bite of the heavenly macaron on my plate. "They say you should never meet your heroes, but mine turned out to be pretty amazing, huh?"

THE FILMING OF THE episode goes by in a blur. Unlike last time, no food fights break out and nobody messes up the challenge of baking half a dozen cupcakes "in a big way." At the end of the day, my apple crumble cupcake gets second-best dish of the day to David's chocolate-covered strawberry cupcakes. And while I'm happy to almost be at the top I can't help feeling a little bit resentful. At least I wasn't on the chopping block, unlike Samantha, who didn't make it into the next round.

"Our next filming location won't be here," Kathleen Keogh announces at the end of the day. "We'll see you bright and early to catch a bus out of Dublin in two days' time!"

I remember seeing something about this in the informational packet we got at the beginning of the competition, but I hadn't thought much about it. Now my curiosity is piqued.

"Where do you think we're going?" Niamh asks as the two of us walk out of IETV and toward the bus stop.

"I hope somewhere nice," I say, though it's not like we have many places to go in Ireland. The farthest we could travel is about four hours away. "But why do you think we're traveling? It's not like everything we need isn't right here in Dublin."

"I'm sure we can speculate for as long as we want and still not know exactly what they're up to," Niamh says.

Niamh and I walk the rest of the way in silence. Once we're at the bus stop, she glances at me like she wants to say something but isn't quite sure how to say it. I haven't known her for long, but she's never struck me as the kind of person who's afraid to speak her mind.

"What?" I ask, half-scared of what she'll say.

"Nothing, I just, I saw you and Chris today," she says.

"You saw us doing . . . ?"

"At the café, with Padma?" she says, though it sounds more like a question.

"Oh right, yeah . . ." I'm not sure I really want to share what Padma said to us with Niamh. I remember how she had initially been dismissive of the response on Twitter. To the things people were saying about me and Chris. I'm not sure Niamh would get it, but I try to explain anyway.

"She just wanted to check in with us I guess," I say. "It was kind of weird . . . out of the blue. But nice. It's because of, you know, the way people are speaking about us online."

"Yeah, it's awful," Niamh says with a nod, though she still doesn't look quite comfortable. I chalk it up to the fact that white people are always uncomfortable when race comes up in conversation, though she's the one who's prying.

"We were just having tea and talking about it," I say. "And that's really it."

"Right." Niamh gives a nod of her head, and when she looks up at me again some of that strange hesitation is gone from her expression. "So, maybe we can hang out until the next time we're supposed to film?"

I know I should say no. I'm not supposed to be hanging out with Niamh, not really. But I shrug and say, "Maybe."

TWENTY-THREE

Family Batters

I CALL FATIMA SO MANY TIMES THE NEXT DAY THAT I'M PRETTY SURE my fingers will cramp from hitting the CALL button. But she doesn't pick up. I even text her a few times about the show and almost getting the best dish of the day.

But since our last conversation, it feels like something is off between us. That's probably why I don't bother to mention Niamh or Chris in the texts—or the fact that I'm pretty sure I'm feeling things for both of them that I'm absolutely not supposed to be feeling.

I almost pick up my phone and text Niamh about hanging out. I know she'll probably say yes. But I think better of it at the last minute.

Instead, I go downstairs to the kitchen to look through Ammu's recipe books again. After all, that's what I should be focusing on.

"What are you making?" I ask, when I spot Ammu sitting at the dinner table with a bowl and rolling pin and board in front of her.

"Cheese bread rolls," Ammu says, not bothering to look up. She's taken a piece of bread and is rolling it flat. Then, she takes a handful of the mixture in her bowl and presses it into an oval shape. She places that onto the flattened piece of bread and rolls it out on top. Then she folds it up, presses the edges together tightly, and puts it away on another plate.

"Can I help?" I ask, sitting down next to her.

This time, Ammu looks up with a smile. "Having a star like you help me with my cooking? How can I ever—"

"Ammu," I say, rolling my eyes.

"Yes, of course, you can help," she says. "Here." She passes the bowl of mixture toward me. "Roll these up and hand them to me. I'll do the rest."

I put my hands into the bowl and take out the mixture. It's a bunch of different ingredients together and dark brown in color. I press it up, shape it into an oval, and pass it to Ammu.

"What did you put in here?" I ask.

"It's a cheese roll," Ammu repeats, like that answers my question.

"I know, but there's more than cheese here!" I say.

"Well, I put some cheese, some potatoes, some vegetables, chaat moshla, onions, coriander, and morich."

"You've never made these before," I say. "Are there guests coming over?"

"Not today."

"Tomorrow?"

"For the finale of your show," Ammu says. She doesn't look at me when she says this, like I should just expect that she'll have people over to watch that. And like there's no doubt in her mind I'll be in the finals.

"There's still a few episodes to go until then, Ammu," I say.

"Yes, but I'm going to make some for us and keep the rest for later. I'm not young anymore. I can't make all the snacks and food the day before a dawat," she says in a scolding voice, like I'm the one telling her to have a dawat and feed people for the finals of my show. Bengali parents really are something else.

"What if I don't make it in?" I ask.

Now Ammu looks at me, her brows furrowed together like I've asked a ridiculous question. "You're doing so well. Why wouldn't you?"

"Because everybody else who's made it this far is doing well too. It's reality TV. You don't know what could happen," I say.

"You'll get there," Ammu says with unflinching confidence. A little too much confidence for a woman who didn't even want to let me enter into the show a few weeks ago.

"You thought that it was a bad idea for me to even enter the show," I point out. "And now you think I'm definitely going to make it to the final."

"And probably win."

"Ammu."

She puts down the rolling pin, stares me right in the eyes, and says, "Shireen, I was worried about what would happen. Going on this TV tuvi in front of the entire world, when you were acting like . . . not yourself." She takes a deep breath, before returning to her work. I guess she was just peacefully making her cheese rolls until I came around. "But you were right. You're old enough to handle it by yourself, and every week your Abbu and I watch you working hard and trying your best. And it'll be good for all of us if you win. When you win."

"No pressure," I say under my breath, and even though it does feel like a lot of pressure to have Ammu and Abbu believe in me so intensely, it's also kind of nice. Motivating. I went into this competition believing I could do it and with my parents not really sure if I was up for it. And now that I'm doubting my abilities, it's Ammu and Abbu who believe in me without any qualms.

"Now stop daydreaming and finish the cheese rolls," Ammu says, shooting me a glare.

"Okay, Ammu," I say. I start my work again, grabbing bits of the mixture Ammu has made and rolling it into an oval, so she can flatten it with her rolling pin. And it's kind of nice. I've never really cooked like this with Ammu before. It's usually her. Or me. But I think I could get used to it being us.

TWENTY-FOUR

Get the Show on the Rocky Road

IT SHOULD BE ILLEGAL FOR ANYBODY TO BE FORCED TO WAKE UP AT 6:00 A.M. during your summer holidays. But on the next day of filming, I'm up at 6:00 A.M. to get ready. I don't know where exactly we're going, but I decide on a plain black blouse with puffed sleeves and a bright yellow knee-length skirt.

I traipse down the stairs only to find Abbu drinking a cup of tea with a very somber expression on his face.

"Why are you up so early?" I ask. Our shop doesn't open until 7:00 A.M. usually, and I'm pretty sure it's not even Abbu's turn to open.

"I'm driving you to get the bus," Abbu says, glancing at me from over his mug with a look that tells me that there's no arguing with him this time.

"I'll be okay," I say.

"I know you'll be okay," Abbu says. "But I'm dropping you off anyway."

Of course, I didn't realize that my definition of being dropped off and Abbu's are not exactly the same. Because when he pulls up the car at Donnybrook in the IETV car park, Abbu doesn't just wave goodbye and leave. He parks the car in a free spot and follows me out toward the bus, where all of the other contestants are standing around. Everyone—other than me—has a cup of coffee in their hands, whether it's one of those paper cups you get in the café or a thermos they're hungrily sipping from.

I try not to stare too hard at Chris's thermos, which is black and says GAME OVER in colorful letters on the front. It's something I gifted her months ago.

"Excuse me." When I glance away from Chris, I realize that Abbu is trying to get Kathleen Keogh's attention.

Kathleen does not look very happy to be approached by him. Her lips are pressed into a thin line as she glances at him. "Yes?"

"Where is this bus going?" Abbu asks.

"I'm sorry, who are you?" Kathleen asks.

"This is my dad," I say, rushing forward to avoid this conversation becoming extremely awkward. "And Abbu . . . they're not telling us where we're going. You *know* that. They can't—"

"Shireen can't go anywhere without her parents' permission," Abbu says.

"Sir, you did sign a permission slip that said we could—"

"For recording. And for a trip. Not a 'secret' trip to somewhere we don't know," Abbu insists. "We need to know our daughter is safe and sound."

"She will be. And unfortunately, the most we can say is we're going just two hours out of Dublin. To another city. And it's a completely safe environment. We promise."

For a moment, I'm afraid that won't be enough for Abbu, but finally he turns to me with an inkling of a smile.

"Text me when you get there," he says firmly.

"I will, I promise," I say.

"Okay, fine." Abbu nods. I'm not sure which one of us is more relieved—me or Kathleen.

Abbu waves me off with a khodahafez and slips into his car, and I join the crowd of contestants with their coffee cups, looking like this is the last place they want to be this early in the morning.

"I'm definitely getting some extra sleep on the bus," Niamh says, stifling a yawn.

I can see Chris watching the two of us, but I turn away from her. The conversation with Ammu yesterday solidified something for me. It reminded me that I can't be with Chris again, no matter how I may still feel about her. Because when we broke up, I was at the lowest point I've ever been. And I'm not going back to that.

Kathleen shuffles us all onto the bus a few moments later, and Niamh and I slip into seats next to each other.

"They're really not going to tell us where we're going?" Niamh asks as the driver starts the ignition.

"My dad tried to get it out of Kathleen, but even he had no luck," I say. "We're going about two hours outside of Dublin though. I know that much."

"Two hours of sleep," Niamh says. She closes her eyes and lays her head on my shoulder, snuggling so close that I can smell her rose-scented shampoo and the warm smell of the freshly

196

ground coffee she just drank. She doesn't ask for permission. She doesn't act like this is out of the ordinary. And I wonder for a moment if I should move away. Shrug her off.

But Niamh is warm, and I like that.

So I don't.

MOST OF OUR JOURNEY consists of being on the motorway and watching green pastures zoom by through the windows. But as we get close to our destination, things become more familiar. We take an exit, leaving the motorway behind, and enter the city. It's not like Dublin though. There are fewer cars and fewer people. It's much smaller, and through the open window I can smell the sea air.

The bus comes to a stop, and I realize that half the contestants have dozed off. I don't know how. I've been way too excited to fall asleep. I shake Niamh awake while my eyes are peeled to my window. The cool morning has given way to a warm, sunny day. Which is perfect because a) my cute outfit wouldn't really work in the rain and b) we're at the beach!

All of us pile out of the bus and onto the nearly deserted beach, where our three judges are waiting, along with another woman I don't recognize.

None of the judges look tired in the slightest, and I wouldn't be surprised if they were driven down here earlier and put up in the nicest hotel in town.

"Welcome to Galway!" Máire Cherry says as soon as all of us are standing in front of them. She has the biggest smile I've ever seen on her. I remember a little belatedly that Máire is actually Galwegian. "And welcome to the food festival that's going to take place here in just a few hours."

I try to catch Niamh's eye, because I'm wondering if I'm the only one concerned about the logistics of an open-air food festival in Ireland.

Niamh, though, is listening to Máire with rapt attention. Instead, the person that catches my eye is Chris. And the two of us look away almost as soon as our eyes meet.

"And here to welcome us is the founder of the festival herself," Máire says.

The woman I don't recognize steps forward with a smile. She has dark black hair, brown skin, and when she speaks it's with a Galwegian accent. "My name is Safiya Hassan," she says. "And this festival is called Seas the Day. Galway has quite a few food festivals, and we're hoping Seas the Day will be annually recurring. This is our inaugural year, and we're really excited to be joined by all of you from the *Junior Irish Baking Show*. Now, in a few hours there will be a lot of people here, including a lot of other vendors."

I'm not sure why, but I had just assumed we would be doing a simple challenge at the beach. Instead, we're going to be selling what we make. I try to ignore the pulse of anxiety that sends through me.

"So, I just ask you to be respectful of everyone," Safiya continues. "But we are very excited to have you be a part of this, and we're excited to see what you come up with for us today."

She steps back, while Galvin steps forward. Unlike Safiya and Máire, Galvin doesn't smile. So I guess even on the sunniest, warmest days, he's not exactly cheerful.

"Today's challenge is not going to be easy, but it's to see that you can work as teams and that you can work with customers. In the other challenges, you were in the studio, working behind the scenes. But now, you get to take everything you've learned and apply it practically. This is what the real world is about," Galvin explains. "Because at the end of the day, as bakers you have to think about more than yourself. You have to think about your customers. So you will be participating as vendors in this food festival."

"You're going to be split up into two teams," Padma adds. "Five on each team. And it's your job to come up with two unique desserts to serve during the festival. You'll also be responsible for settling on a name for your dessert stand and deciding pricing. Just like you would if you had your own bakery."

My palms are sweating a little at the idea of this, even though I really shouldn't be as nervous as I feel. I've worked with customers before. I've worked with them for a long time now. I'm used to being customer-facing. Used to helping Ammu and Abbu come up with new names for donuts and deciding on pricing. I think about Ammu and Abbu watching this on TV when it airs. They'll definitely be thinking that they've helped me prepare for this. That thought calms me down a little.

"There is one more thing," Máire says, the smile gone from her face now. She looks us in the eye, her lips set into a thin line. "The entire losing team will be eliminated."

TWENTY-FIVE

Love-Heat Relationship

I KNEW THAT THERE WEREN'T MANY EPISODES OF THE SHOW LEFT, but to go from ten to five so swiftly is a little wild. I can tell everyone else is thinking the same thing because there's complete silence after the judges reveal this. Still, we don't have long to process.

The next minute, Galvin is picking out team leaders.

"Since David had the best dish from last week, he'll be the first team leader," Galvin says, ushering David away from the rest of us contestants. "And he'll also get first pick."

"And since Shireen had the second-best dish, she'll be the second team leader," Máire says.

I try to paste a smile on my face as I step away from the other contestants too. I share a glance with David, and he looks a little panicked. Suddenly, we're tasked with choosing teams that will lead either to our success or our demise in this competition. By the end of today, one of us will continue, and one of us will go home.

No pressure at all.

"Um, I'm going to go with Ruby," David says, pointing to her. She seems pleased to be the first pick, but none of us are surprised since the two of them partnered up in the first episode, they've been doing well in the competition, and they obviously work well together.

I glance at the rest of the contestants. They're all talented, but at the very front stand Chris and Niamh. And no matter what the other contestants bring to the table, I know one of them has to be my first pick. It's like the choice I've been going over in my head for the past few weeks is solidified in front of me now. Like the universe is conspiring against me, forcing me to finally make a decision.

"Um," I mumble, not sure who to choose. Niamh is better at baking. She's talented, she's passionate, and she's hardworking. She's less likely to make mistakes. But I already know that Chris and I can work well together. She might not always excel at baking, but she's always been way more creative than me—and that's shown in her presentation in every challenge so far. And like me, she has experience working in her parents' donut shop. Invaluable experience.

"We don't have all day, Shireen," an exasperated Galvin glances at me.

"Niamh," I say. Niamh's face lights up as she joins me. Chris glances down at the ground instead of at me. I don't know what she's thinking. If I were in her position, would I be disappointed? Would I expect Chris to choose me? I'm not sure. Maybe she would be better off on David's team anyway.

"Emily," David says. My stomach plunges, because Ruby, Emily, and David have made some of the best dishes during this entire competition. They're favorites of the judges.

"Chris," I say. Chris doesn't even look at me as she joins our little group. Next to join us is Bridget, and surprisingly the last person left standing is Séan.

He doesn't look happy about this at all. And neither am I. Even though Séan has consistently done well in every challenge so far, everybody knows that he's difficult to work with and just an all-around arsehole. He's the last person I want to work with, but he's who I'm stuck with.

"You have one hour to plan and prepare before people start pouring in to the food festival," Kathleen Keogh announces. "And remember, at the end of this challenge only one of your teams will be left standing."

"WE SHOULD MAKE SOMETHING people wouldn't get at a food festival usually," Séan says as soon as we get to our kitchen station. "Like a soufflé or a tiramisu."

"You want to make soufflé in the middle of a beach-based food festival?" Niamh asks, sending him a death glare. "You might as well just say you want to be eliminated."

"I'm just thinking about ways that we can stand out as a team!" Séan says. "What do you suggest?"

"I don't know, something classy but also popular. Like macarons, which we are both good at making," Niamh says. She glances at me with a smile. "What do you think, Shireen?"

"I don't know," I say hesitantly. I never asked to be team

leader, and all I can think of are the worst-case scenarios. What if we decide to make macarons and so does the other team? What if people here hate macarons and they don't even want to try them?

"We should make donuts," Chris says. "And cupcakes."

"Seriously?" Niamh asks. "Donuts are like everywhere these days."

"That's exactly why we should make them," Chris says. She's not really looking at Niamh, but she doesn't outright ask me for my thoughts either.

"If they can get donuts everywhere, why would they buy them here?" Niamh presses. And I'm not sure if it's me, but I sense an edge of anger in her voice. I wonder if that's because of me. Because she knows now for sure that Chris is my ex and not just the daughter of my parents' competitors.

"It makes sense," I say. "They're popular. People will buy them. And we're going to make them our own way."

"They're also easy to make and not complicated," Chris adds.

"And Chris and I are experts at donuts," I say.

"You are?" Séan asks, glancing between us with a confused look.

"Our parents own donut shops," Chris explains.

"Are you sisters?" Séan looks between us once more, like he's trying to figure out the similarities between us.

"No." I sigh. "Chris's parents and my parents own donut shops. Different ones."

"So, we should go with what you know instead of what we're good at?" Niamh asks now, crossing her arms. "That doesn't really seem fair."

"You want to make Séan's ideas?" I ask Niamh. "Soufflé?"

"No. But I think we should entertain it," she says.

"I'm good with Niamh's idea of macarons. They're unique, unexpected at a place like this, and we're really good at making them," Séan says.

I look to our fifth member—Bridget—who has been quietly glancing back and forth during this whole conversation.

"Which idea do you prefer?" I ask.

She flushes as everybody's eyes turn to us. Technically she's the deciding vote.

"Doesn't it make sense to do both?" she says. "Séan and Niamh can work on macarons, and you and Chris can do the donuts. We need two desserts."

"And this way, we can also see who was right," Séan says with a smug smile. He obviously expects that people are going to go mad over his macarons.

"Okay, we need a name," Niamh says. "Maybe something simple, like Macarons and Donuts."

"No." Chris looks at me. Finally, her expression changes, a smile tugging at the corners of her lips. The familiarity of it sends tingles down my belly, which I ignore, because we have work to do. "Shireen?"

"Um, how about . . ." I glance up at the blue sky, thinking about all of the different donut names I've come up with since Ammu and Abbu opened You Drive Me Glazy. "Just Desserts?"

I expect some pushback when I glance back down, but everyone nods like they're on board.

"What about prices?" I ask, glancing around at everyone for ideas.

"Well, these are going to be really good quality. Gourmet," Séan says, somehow drawing out the word *gourmet* in a way that makes him sound incredibly pretentious.

"Nobody's going to pay ridiculously marked-up prices in the middle of a food festival," I point out. "There's a lot of competition."

"So our prices have to be competitive," Chris agrees.

"And what about our flavors?" I ask. "We can do two different flavors of donuts and the same for the macarons."

"So people have choices," Chris agrees.

"And also so that we can do a marked-down price if people buy two," I add.

"I guess," Séan mutters, and Bridget nods in agreement too. The only one who doesn't seem to be totally okay with this is Niamh. She's looking at me and Chris with narrowed eyes.

I try to breeze past it. Once we get started, I'm sure Niamh will be on board. Or at least, she'll be a little too busy competing to care.

THE PREPARATION TIME GOES by in the blink of an eye, even under the watchful eye of the cameras around us—and occasionally Kathleen Keogh. By the time she comes around to announce that it's ten minutes until people come pouring into the festival, our team is ready to go. We have two perfect summer-themed donuts that Chris and I came up with: John Lemonade and Vincent Man Gogh. And two macaron flavors that Niamh and Séan came up with: Very Berry and In a Hazelnut Shell.

We write everything in chalk on our menu board and place it outside our stall as people start strolling toward our end of the beach. We can already see so many other vendors set up across the space. There's a grilled cheese stall called Take It Cheesy just a little way from ours and a burger and hot dog stall on its right called Meat Your Heart Out. But of course they're not our competitors. They're not who we have to worry about.

"Did you see what the other team are serving?" Bridget asks us. Their stall is on the other end of the beach, so we can't really make them out.

"It's probably better if we don't know," I say. "Let's just keep our heads down and do what we have to do."

As customers begin to arrive at our stall, I'm feeling pretty good. Bridget handles taking orders while the rest of us work on the baking.

Making donuts with Chris feels like the easiest thing in the world. We find our rhythm way too easily, and even though we work silently, it's like we know each other so intimately we don't have to speak at all. I'm reminded again that this is what I loved about our relationship. That Chris knew me, inside and out. She could anticipate what I needed when I needed it.

I remember when I started my food blog and after every post went up and didn't do as well as I wanted it to, Chris would bring me treats. Sometimes my favorite flavor of bubble tea. Sometimes my favorite flavor of donuts or cupcakes or shaved ice. The treats were endless, and so was how much she cared for me. How much she loved me.

At least that's what I thought. Until the day she asked me not to send in my application for the show. Because if I entered, I would win. And *she* wanted to win.

I shake those memories off as the customers start lining up. There's a queue filling the beach toward our stall. Which is great, except . . .

"Guys, you need to hurry up with the macarons," Bridget urges Niamh and Séan.

"We can't speed them up when Niamh keeps breaking the shells," Séan says.

Niamh sends him a death glare. "Do you want to serve broken macaron shells to the customers?"

"At least we'll be serving them *something*," Séan says.

"Okay, we're all swapping jobs," I say, because I can't deal with any more of Séan and Niamh's bickering. "Séan, you can take the customers, Bridget can help Chris with the donuts, and I'll help with the macarons."

"No way." Séan stands up tall and scowls. "I'm the best baker you have, and you want me to handle the customers?"

"I want you to handle the customers because you're doing a pretty bad job at being part of the team," I say.

"I'm not," Séan says. "Niamh is the one who's making mistakes."

"Fine, then Niamh can go and—"

"No." Niamh cuts me off. "You're really going to listen to his ideas over mine? I'm way better at baking than him anyway. You know that."

Chris lets out a frustrated breath behind me. "If you guys want to be eliminated, keep arguing back and forth," she says. "Or you could just listen to Shireen."

Once Séan is away from the rest of us, things go a little bit smoother, though Niamh still doesn't seem very happy.

"Are you okay?" I ask after a few minutes of working in near complete silence.

"I'm fine," she says.

"I feel like you're mad at me."

She sighs but doesn't stop working on the macaron fillings. "It's just . . . I thought you'd be on my side today. Not Chris's." She says Chris's name like it's something bad. Like she's angry at Chris, though Niamh barely knows her. They've hardly spoken two sentences to each other.

"I wasn't trying to take sides," I say. I thought that should have been obvious. "I just think she was right. I mean, look at all our customers." I glance to the queue of people still waiting to get their macarons and donuts.

"I guess so," Niamh grumbles.

By the time the judges arrive at our stall, things are running a little more smoothly, and the bickering within our team has gone from constant to only occasional.

"Macarons and donuts . . . ," Galvin says as he examines the chalkboard menu in front of our stall. Padma is studying the queue of people waiting to order, looking impressed but trying not to look too impressed. I have a good feeling, but without knowing how the other team is doing there's really no way to say who's winning. Maybe the other team has an even longer queue and an even better menu.

"Do you mind if we try one of each?" Máire asks with a smile.

Séan for once has nothing to say and just smiles as he plates up the donuts and macarons and hands them to the judges. They eat at a leisurely pace, watching us work and serve our customers. Even as I'm working on the fillings for the macarons, I can't help but keep glancing at the judges over my shoulder every once in a while, trying to study their faces and expressions. This tasting could be make-or-break for us.

"An interesting combination of flavors," Padma finally leans forward to tell us, a smile dancing on her lips. She glances at me momentarily with a look that feels like a secret between us. But she looks away so fast that I'm not sure I haven't just imagined it. Then, the three judges take off once more, strolling past all the people in line and the families on the beach. Somehow even in the summer heat and sun, they look perfect. Not a bead of sweat on any of them. Not a hair out of place.

"That's it?" Séan asks, letting out a frustrated puff of air. "They didn't even give us any feedback!"

"They'll probably do that after we're done serving the customers," Chris says. "Like at the end of the day."

"But I want to know how we did!" Séan says, throwing his hands in the air.

"Me too," Bridget agrees meekly. "I wish they'd given us a little more to go on."

When we close up the stand, it's already afternoon. The crowds have thinned out a little, and we're all chilly from the ocean air.

The judges and Kathleen gather us into one corner of the beach, blocked off from the people attending the food festival.

"Well, good job to everyone," Máire Cherry says, beaming at all of us. "It couldn't have been easy running your own stall during such a popular festival right near Galway city."

"Though if you win this show and go on to work in the food industry, of course this is the kind of work you would be expected to do," Galvin adds.

"We've had a look at all of your sales," Padma says. "We've also tasted all of your desserts and seen how you've worked together as a team."

"Both teams faced challenges, and all of you worked hard," Máire says with a nod. "But unfortunately, there will only be one winner, and only one team will continue on in the competition to the semifinals of the show."

My stomach clenches as the judges stare down at us. Almost like they're trying to draw it out, test our patience, and make this as anxiety inducing as possible. It's working, because my heart beats faster, and my palms start to sweat. This could be the end.

"Fresh Baked"—Galvin glances at David's team—"your choice to make cupcakes and pies was an interesting one. We weren't sure if they were going to work together, but they did, though your choice in flavor was slightly limited."

"Both your desserts were delicious, but the presentation was just a little lacking," Máire adds.

"Unfortunately, the foot traffic to your stall was also a little shy, maybe because people weren't so interested in something as heavy as pie or cupcakes on quite such a warm, sunny day?" Padma asks.

"Just Desserts"—Galvin turns toward us, his expression never changing—"donuts and macarons are not necessarily something I would put together, but it worked. You also had a choice in flavors that definitely worked in your favor, even if it slowed down your production."

"Your desserts were also delicious, though the presentation at times could have been better," Máire says.

"Now, donuts and macarons also could have gone down the path of being a bit too heavy for people on a day like this, however you chose such light summery flavors and people seemed very drawn to that," Galvin says.

But were they drawn more to us or to the other team? I hold my breath as the judges share a glance. The two teams are close. I can tell. It must not have been an easy decision.

"David, I'm afraid your team just didn't make the cut," Máire says with a sympathetic smile.

Suddenly, a weight lifts off my shoulders as I try to process what Máire just said. We made it through to the next round. We're going to be in the semifinals. I'm going to be a semifinalist.

Niamh throws her arms around me, squeezing me tight. I hug her back. And when everybody else joins in, I don't even mind that I'm squashed into the weirdest group hug: between my ex, a girl that I may kind of have a crush on, Séan—who I definitely have a strong dislike of—and Bridget, who is still a virtual stranger.

When we pull away from each other, all of us are grinning. Because we did it. We're through.

Now . . . we just have to beat each other.

TWENTY-SIX

Quiche from a Rose

THAT NIGHT AS I'M TRYING TO SLEEP, I CAN'T HELP BUT START BUILD-ing up my dreams of the future where I'm the winner of the *Junior Irish Baking Show*.

In my dreams, my win catapults me to success—like Nadiya Hussain. With cookbooks and TV shows and BBC specials. And You Drive Me Glazy gets so much acclaim that my parents have to hire five extra people and build an expansion to handle the popularity. Most important—everyone suddenly knows Bangladesh is not India and that our food is the best food to exist in the history of the world.

My phone rings, pulling me out of my starry-eyed dreams. It's Fatima, reaching out to me after countless unanswered texts.

"Hey, stranger!" I say, picking up the phone.

Fatima looks tired. There are bags under her eyes, and she stifles a yawn. "Hey, Shireen."

"Where have you been?"

"Oh, don't get me started," she says, blinking slowly like she's having a hard time staying awake. I know that it must be pretty late in Bangladesh right now. "It's just been wedding after wed-ding here. I've barely had the time to check my phone."

"It must be fun though," I say.

"It's pretty good, yeah," Fatima says with a nod. "But enough about me. You got through to the next round of the competition!"

"The semifinals!" I exclaim.

"The semifinals!" she repeats, though she doesn't sound even half as enthused as I hoped she would be. "You can really win this thing, Shireen. Not that, you know, I ever had any doubts about that."

"Right," I scoff. "You want to help me pick out what outfit I'm going to wear when I inevitably win, or will we do that when you come back?"

"About that," Fatima says. She glances down and my excitement dissipates. Cold dread takes its place. "Ammu and Abbu decided to push back our flight by just a little bit."

"But why?" I ask.

"Well, they thought it's still a while until school starts, and we got a couple of wedding invites for next week. They just thought it made sense to stay a little bit longer." Fatima shrugs, and I can't tell if she's happy or sad about the extension. Considering how much fun she's been having with her cousins, I can't imagine that she's very upset about it.

"I thought you would come back and support me. That we could celebrate together and hang out in person. I miss you," I say.

"I miss you too, Shireen," Fatima says. "But I don't know when the next time I'll see my cousins will be. I know I'll see you when I come back to Dublin."

"You didn't even try to fight them to come back?" I ask, even though from Fatima's expression and explanations I already know the answer.

"Shireen, I couldn't," she says. "I wanted to stay longer too."

"But you've been there all summer, Fatima. And *this* is a once in a lifetime thing. I was counting on you to be there."

Fatima's eyebrows furrow. "So is this, Shireen. When else am I going to be able to buy an expensive ticket to Bangladesh and spend an entire summer with my family? I can still support you from here."

"It's not the same. You don't understand what it's been like here without you. I've been all on my own, and it's not just the show. It's also the breakup and everything that comes with it. I've been barely holding it together and I thought finally . . . finally I would have my best friend again and—"

"You have me!" Fatima exclaims a little too loudly. She glances behind like she's afraid someone's going to reprimand her for being too loud. When she turns back to me, she drops her voice to a whisper. "You're not being fair. I want to be there, and I've been here for you as much as I can, but I'm here spending time with my family for the first time in my life. I don't know when I'll get to do that again. I'm not going to miss out on that just because you love getting yourself into drama."

"I love getting myself into drama?" I ask. "How is being betrayed by my girlfriend and going through a breakup me getting myself into drama?"

"That's not, but the way you've been dealing with it all is. You should have been focusing on the competition, but all this stuff with that Niamh girl and trying to be friends with Chris . . ." Fatima gives me a disappointed look. Like she has the right to be disappointed when she's the person who's choosing to abandon me in my time of need. "That's you getting yourself into drama."

I can't believe I'm hearing any of this—from Fatima of all people.

"I thought that you would want to support me through my *drama* as you call it," I say. "You're supposed to be my best friend."

"I've been supporting you as best I can, but where is your support?" she asks. "I have to stay up until three A.M. to say, 'Hooray, Shireen got into the semifinals,' but you can't even pretend to be happy about me getting to spend more time with my family here?"

I take a deep breath and close my eyes. "Fine. I'm happy that you get to spend more time with your family in Bangladesh," I say. "And you should be happy, because I know better than to disturb your precious sleep and your precious time with your cousins."

Fatima takes a deep breath. "Shireen, you're—"

But I end the call before Fatima can finish her sentence because my blood is boiling. I can't believe I waited all this time to finally get the chance to talk to Fatima, and that was the conversation we had.

Still, I keep staring at my phone screen. Waiting for her to call back. To text. To try and make things better.

But she doesn't.

Me: What should we do to celebrate making it to the semifinals?

I send out the text the next day before I can think too much about it. I'd spent half of last night tossing and turning because of my conversation with Fatima. But I wasn't going to let her—or anyone else—take away from my achievements and my excitement.

Are you sure you want to celebrate with me?

My fingers fly across my phone, yes!

Meet up for dinner?

I send a thumbs-up emoji and fling open my wardrobe to find the perfect outfit to celebrate getting into the semifinals.

Since the sun is still out and the weather is still warm— probably the warmest it will be for the whole summer at 23 degrees—the perfect outfit is a blush-pink midi sundress with white flowers etched across it.

Niamh is waiting for me by the gates of St. Stephen's Green.

"Hey," she says a little hesitantly.

"Hey!" I say, trying to put the cheer into my voice that I'm definitely not feeling.

"I wasn't expecting to hear from you," she admits. She

studies me with a little too much precision, and it's almost like her electric blue eyes can see right through me.

"Why not?" I ask. "Aren't we friends?"

"Yeah, but . . . you haven't exactly been enthusiastic about the two of us hanging out this summer."

"Well, I'm enthusiastic about it now," I say with a smile. "And did you really think I would want to celebrate getting into the semifinals with my ex-girlfriend?"

Niamh looks like she wants to say more for a moment, but then she smiles and turns toward Grafton Street. "Let's go, then."

The two of us end up in a little restaurant with a beautiful garden area for dining. It has a makeshift roof adorned with fairy lights, giving the entire place a golden glow. I've never been here before, but it feels less like a place for a celebration and more like a place for a date. Especially when I spot all the couples occupying the tables.

"Right here," Niamh says, leading us to a table in a secluded corner.

"How did you hear about this place?" I ask, taking a seat opposite Niamh.

"My sister went to university in Dublin, so I asked her if she had any recommendations. She suggested this place. It's nice, right?" Niamh glances up at the fairy lights with a grin.

"Yeah, it is," I say, though I'm thinking about the fact that Niamh said she has a sister. Even though I've spent the last few weeks hanging out and competing against Niamh, there's really very little I know about her. And maybe that's what the problem is. I still feel at ease with Chris because we know each other. We spent an entire year in a relationship learning everything about each other. The only person who knows me better than Chris is Fatima. Maybe I just need to get to know Niamh better. And this is my chance to do it.

"So, you've got a sister?" I ask, leaning forward on our table.

Niamh glances back at me, that smile still on her face. I think again how she has a really nice smile. It illuminates her whole face, makes her look brighter somehow.

"Yeah, I've got one sister. It's just the two of us and our parents," she says. "What about you?"

"It's just me," I say.

"You're better off," Niamh says. "My sister and I used to fight so much when we were kids, she used to annoy the hell out of me. And I used to annoy the hell out of her. Now that we're older, things are better. We don't live together anymore, and I'm pretty sure that helps."

"Where does she live now?"

"She's in London. She works there as an HR manager for some company."

"That sounds—"

"Really boring, right?" Niamh asks. "That's definitely not what I want to do."

"You said you wanted to be an accountant," I point out.

"I'm good at maths, and accounting is practical. It'll be more interesting than being an HR manager," Niamh says with confidence.

"If you say so."

The waiter comes to take our orders, and I realize I can't remember the last time I've eaten at a restaurant like this. The dinner menu has dishes like pomegranate salmon gravlax, which is something I have never eaten before. Chris and I mostly ate Chinese, Indian, Vietnamese, Mexican—anything that had a lot of seasoning and a little bit of spice.

I end up ordering a risotto, while Niamh orders chicken. Once the waiter leaves, I lean forward again.

"Do you usually eat these kinds of foods at high-end restaurants?" I ask.

Niamh grins again. "No. I guess I was trying to impress you because you said you wanted to celebrate."

"I didn't even understand half the menu," I say.

"Honestly, me neither." We hold each other's gaze for one long moment before both of us burst out laughing.

"Okay, that's the last time you choose the restaurant," I say.

"No complaints here."

The food ends up being surprisingly good, and with the twinkling fairy lights and the soothing music, the evening is kind of perfect. For once, it doesn't feel like Niamh and I are competitors because we don't talk about the competition. Instead, Niamh tells me about growing up in Belfast and her family and how she wishes she could pursue food as a career.

"I feel like if I win this, maybe my parents would understand," Niamh says. "Like it'll show them how serious I really am."

"Getting to the semifinals won't show them that?"

"I mean . . . maybe it shows them how serious I am, but not that this can be an actual career. That I can make something of myself with my baking, you know. They just think my dreams are unrealistic, and I guess I don't blame them. They're trying to be practical. Trying to make sure I'll be able to take care of myself and keep a roof over my head."

"Yeah, I get that," I say, even though I'm not totally sure I do. After all, my parents are kind of dreamers themselves. What else can you be when you're two Bengali immigrants in Ireland setting up a donut shop of all things? And even when they don't want to see me crushed, they'd never try to put a stop to my dreams either. My parents are not the most practical people, and they've never asked me to be practical either. It's kind of lucky that I have them. Not everybody has parents like Ammu and Abbu.

Instead of getting dessert at the fancy restaurant, we slip outside into the cool summer evening. The sun is setting across the sky, and the colors are all the beautiful shades of pink, red, and orange. This is one of the things I love about Ireland. Sometimes you look out the window and see a sunset unlike anything you've ever seen before. Tonight is definitely one of those times.

"We could get ice cream?" Niamh suggests as the two of us make our way through the crowds of people in town.

"I want cake," I say definitively. "And I know exactly where to go. Come on."

I weave us through all the different shops, restaurants, hotels, past Luas lines and bus stops, past a lot of people, and into a tiny café in an alley off Capel Street.

"This place has the best, trust me," I insist, pulling Niamh toward their display. I haven't been here in a while but their selection is just as amazing as I remember. They have a beautiful carrot cake topped off with crushed nuts, raspberry cheesecake that is the most heavenly shade of soft pink I've seen in my entire life, and the most decadent chocolate cake decorated with reddest of red strawberries and frosting roses.

I order a piece of chocolate cake—obviously—while Niamh gets a slice of raspberry cheesecake with a scoop of ice cream on the side. The two of us slip into a booth in the corner and dig in.

"This really is one of the best desserts I've ever had," Niamh says after she swallows her first bite.

"Told you." I grin.

"Is this where you learned how to bake?" Niamh asks.

"No, but it's definitely a place to draw inspiration from."

"If you ever made me this, I'm pretty sure I'd have to propose marriage," Niamh says, scooping another forkful of cake into her mouth.

"Some say my cheesecake is even better," I say, though the only person who says that is Fatima, and I'm not sure she counts since she's my best friend.

But I don't want to think about Fatima, so I shake those thoughts off and finish my own dessert.

"You have something . . ." Niamh reaches forward with a napkin, dabbing at the edge of my lips. For a moment the two of us freeze—too aware of our closeness. And the fact that she's touching me, and it's sending butterflies fluttering around in my stomach. Niamh meets my eyes, and I can make out all of freckles along her nose and cheeks, even the ones that almost disappear into the pink of her face.

Niamh leans forward, and I know I should pull away. There's a little voice in my head—which I'm pretty sure belongs to Fatima—telling me to put a stop to this. But I don't listen to it.

Instead, I lean forward, too, until there's no space left between us. Until our lips meet, and I can taste the raspberry of her cheesecake, smell the roses from her shampoo, feel the goosebumps along her skin. When we pull apart Niamh is blushing a furious red, and I can feel heat rise up my cheeks too.

"Sorry, I didn't—"

"It's okay," I cut her off, and I'm not sure if that means the kiss was okay or that it was okay if it was a mistake. But Niamh doesn't make me explain. Instead, she finishes off her cheesecake and walks me to my bus stop. And when she says goodbye with a kiss on my cheek, I know which version of okay I meant.

TWENTY-SEVEN

Sweet Dreams Are Made of Cake

NIAMH AND I TEXT CONSTANTLY OVER THE NEXT FEW DAYS, AND even though it shouldn't be the start of something, it feels like the start of something. With Fatima still on the other side of the world, and Chris . . . being Chris, I accept that Niamh is the only person who's really in my corner. Even though we're competitors.

And maybe it's not so bad that she kissed me—and that I liked that she kissed me.

Have you seen what people have been saying on Twitter after the last episode aired? Niamh texts me the night before we're supposed to film the semifinals. She's attached a bunch of pictures alongside her texts. Screenshots of tweets about me and how I don't deserve to be in the semifinals. And apparently neither does Chris.

I take a deep breath because I don't care. And I've been staying away from social media since the first episode aired.

Me: I don't really want to talk about that
Niamh: are you sure? Because I'm here if you want to. It must be hard
Me: I'm fine . . . just nervous about tomorrow
Niamh: me too

I WAKE UP TO the smells of Ammu's porota and Abbu's aloo bhaji and almost float down the stairs.

"What's the occasion?" I ask, sitting down at the breakfast table ready to go.

Abbu brings out a pot of his aloo bhaji. He always mixes up the sliced potatoes with scrambled eggs and cheese, giving it that heavenly taste. And Ammu piles two porotas fresh from the pan onto my plate.

"We just thought with the semifinals today, you need a good start to the day," Ammu says, sharing a smile with Abbu.

"Well, this is definitely going to put me in a good mood for the show." I rip a piece of the porota and scoop up the aloo bhaji with it, while Abbu and Ammu do the same. This is actually the first meal the three of us have had together in a long time. Usually, one of them is at the donut shop, busy with work. We rarely get to have time together like this anymore. I miss spending time with them.

"Are you going to have the aunties and uncles over to watch the semifinal?" I ask.

"Of course," Ammu says, like she can't believe I would even think anything else.

"What about if I don't make it into the finals?" I ask hesitantly. It's not a possibility I want to consider, but I don't really want Bengali aunties and uncles to watch me lose either.

"You won't lose," Ammu says with all of her confidence.

Abbu, though, considers me for a moment. "Shireen, you know that we're proud of you right?"

"I know," I say through a mouthful of aloo bhaji, though I'm not entirely sure I really knew. In that moment neither of them looks particularly proud of my table manners. And I can't really blame them.

"It doesn't matter if you win or lose. We're proud of you, and that's why we want all the Bengali aunties and uncles to watch the show. To see how talented you are, to show them how proud we are . . . and so they can be proud too," Abbu says with a definitive nod of his head.

I know deep down Abbu is a total softie, but he's never told me he's proud of me in this way. It's not like Bengali people go around talking about their feelings all the time. In fact, I don't think Ammu and Abbu have ever even told me that they love me. I'm not sure we even have the right words in Bengali to express that kind of love. The love you feel for your family, for you parents or your daughter.

But they always show me that they do. Like with today's breakfast.

And apparently by forcing all the Bengali aunties and uncles to watch the *Junior Irish Baking Show*.

"Thanks, Abbu." It doesn't quite feel like enough. But I know he gets it from his smile—and that twinkle in his eye.

PADMA IS PACING BACK and forth in the front hallway of the studio when I arrive at IETV. She's on the phone, speaking in Hindi.

"Mujhe nehi pata, but please figure it out. Ye next week ke pehle zarurat hai," Padma says. I don't understand Hindi the way my parents do, thanks to their steady diet of Bollywood movies and Indian natoks, but I do pick up a few words here and there. She doesn't sound very happy.

I try to dash past her, but Padma catches my eye and makes a gesture for me to wait.

Her face softens as she goes back to her phone call. "Okay, okay . . . baad main kehta hoon. Mujhe abh kam hai."

She hangs up the phone and gives me a tight-lipped smile. "The wonders of working in this industry," she says.

"Oh, I didn't realize," I say.

"We're trying to open up this shop in Dublin, and it's a lot of work to do in not a lot of time," Padma says. "Anyway, I've been meaning to check in on you and Chris."

"You don't have to do that," I say, mostly just to be polite. And also because every time I speak to her, I feel like my heart is going to leap out of my chest. I'm not sure I can deal with that for prolonged periods of time.

"Well, I know things haven't been great online, but I'm glad that you and Chris are doing so well. You're both so talented, and I really want to see you both succeed."

I feel heat rising up my cheeks at her words. Padma Bollywood—my idol—thinks I'm talented. She wants to see me succeed.

"Th-thanks," I manage to get out.

"Well, I should let you go. Don't want either of us to be late." Padma pauses to gesture something to the receptionist in the hallway, who digs into one of the drawers at her desk and pulls out a set of keys. Padma grabs hold of them and flashes me a smile. "Apparently, we can't leave the premises with a set of keys. We always have to sign them in and out. Well, I'll see you up there!" With that, she dashes past me into the studio.

It takes me a moment to get myself together before I slip inside. Almost everyone is there but it feels kind of empty with only five of us left. We began with twenty-six, and now I'm in the top five.

Niamh slips in just a few minutes after me. She gives me a hesitant smile from her kitchen station, and I smile back. We don't have a chance to talk though, because the next moment the cameras start rolling and Kathleen begins her intro.

After all the judges are introduced, the cameras turn to Galvin Cramsey to tell us about our challenge for today. He's wearing a black suit jacket with a light blue button-up shirt.

He stares right at the camera with his solemn expression and begins to speak. "The challenge is pretty simple, but it won't be easy to carry out. You have to make a cake. Any cake at all, but we will be judging on all of its components. Flavor, structure, and presentation are key, so you want to make sure you're getting all of those right from the get-go. You have exactly two hours to bake this cake so make sure you use your time wisely." Galvin pauses, his eyes sweeping over the room. "Because at today's judging, two people will be eliminated."

Galvin's announcement fills the room with a sense of dread. Still, I can see everyone's expression shift as they try to think of what kind of a cake they can make. None of us can afford to get caught up in the worry of a double elimination. Not when there's a cake to bake.

My mind is running through a list of cakes. I have an entire section dedicated to cakes in my recipe book. But for some reason my mind keeps going back to the café I went to with Niamh just a few days ago. The chocolate cake I had was amazing, and Niamh had tasted like raspberry when we had kissed. The idea hits me like a light bulb moment: chocolate raspberry cake. The perfect combination.

Kathleen counts down the start of the timer, and once the red numbers appear everyone is on their feet and ready to go. I grab all of the ingredients I need from the pantry. Once everything is on my counter, I get right to work.

"Hi, Shireen, you look very hard at work here," Kathleen says in her sickly sweet voice a few minutes into the challenge. I glance up to see her and a cameraman following behind. She's wearing stark red lipstick once more and a white dress.

"Yep. Hard at work," I say, while mixing my batter.

"So, tell us what you're planning on serving the judges today?" Kathleen asks.

"Well, I'm going to make chocolate raspberry cake." I barely look up as I talk. I don't want to make any mistakes with this batter. I can't waste time starting over again. "Raspberry and chocolate pair really well together."

"Wow. Nothing special for Padma Bollywood today?" Kathleen asks.

I chuckle. "I'm sure Padma is a fan of chocolate cake, just like all the other judges."

"Feeling very confident today, I see." Kathleen raises an eyebrow toward the camera. "Do you think you'll get through to the finals? Do you think you'll get best dish today?"

"I think I have as good a chance as anyone," I say with a grin.

Thankfully, Kathleen moves on to bother Séan and leaves me to work in peace. Still, the distraction means that after I finish mixing my batter, I realize I've forgotten to turn on my oven. So I put my batter to one side and have to waste a few precious minutes on that. Once my cake is in the oven, I start to work on my icing and try to figure out exactly how I want this cake to look.

I'm so enthralled in my work that I barely notice anything that's happening around me. It's a good thing I'm a quick worker because there's always a chance I'll be so caught up that I'll completely forget the time limit.

I'm thickening up my icing when a yelp breaks my concentration. Everyone looks up and toward the noise. It came from right beside my workstation.

A moment later, a sheepish Chris stands up, brushing dirt off of her. "Sorry. I was running from the pantry, and I fell." She begins to pick up a jar of walnuts that she's dropped.

"Are you okay?" I ask.

Chris just shrugs it off. "Fine. Just need to get this done." She takes a big gulp of air before rushing back to her station— managing to stay on her feet this time.

I can't help my smile as I turn back to my icing. As I go back to work, it's just a little bit more difficult to concentrate.

THE CLOCK BUZZES TO announce that our time is up, and I grin from ear to ear. My cake is exactly as I wanted it to be. It's a two-layered chocolate cake with ganache and fudge chocolate frosting. I've topped it off with fresh raspberries, the color of which pops against the brown of the chocolate. I'm pretty sure this is one of the best cakes I've ever made—and I've made a lot of cake in my life. Mostly for Fatima's birthdays or when she wins the academic achievement award at the end of every school year.

I glance around at what the other contestants have made, and even though everybody's cake looks amazing, I'm feeling pretty good about my chances.

When Niamh catches me glancing at her Black Forest cake, she gives me a small smile. But she glances away a little too fast. I chalk it up to nervousness. In fact, there's definitely an air of nervousness in the very air as everybody finally looks up from their own desserts. At the end of this round only three people are going to continue on to compete in the finals.

It's a lot of pressure.

I try not to let that weigh down on me too much as the judging begins.

Séan is up first to present his toffee crunch cake. I watch as the judges nod, satisfied with what he's presented them with.

"I think maybe it's a little too sweet?" Padma is the only one who offers up any criticism. "It needs a little bit more balance in the flavor."

Séan frowns at the criticism but nods. Once he's finished, Niamh steps up. She shoots Séan a glare as she passes his station. I'm not sure if it's because of her dislike of him or because the cameras follow her movement.

"And what have you made for us today?" Máire Cherry asks with a kind smile toward Niamh.

"Black Forest cake. I thought I would go with something that's just traditional and try to really nail those flavors," Niamh explains with her hands tucked behind her back. She doesn't sound nervous, but I can see the way she's picking at the skin around her thumb behind her back.

The judges begin to cut into her cake and take bites. They nod slowly, exchanging glances with each other.

"I love this." Padma is the first to chime in. "The cake is soft, and the flavors are balanced perfectly."

Galvin nods in agreement. "Very delicious. You made a good

decision keeping it traditional because you really did nail the flavors."

Máire Cherry is all smiles too. "There's really nothing else to say. It's really a delectable Black Forest cake. Well done."

Niamh is grinning on the way back to her station. She basically skips over while the judges call up Bridget—whose salted caramel apple cake doesn't taste enough like apples, apparently.

After Bridget, it's Chris's turn. She glances over at me as she grabs hold of her plate. I can feel the nervous energy emanating from her. But she really didn't have to worry.

The judges only have rave things to say about her walnut coffee cake. How it's perfectly gooey and balances all of its complex flavors. Galvin even compliments the way she's decorated the top of the cake with glazed caramel dripping down the sides and topped it all off with a perfect sprinkle of crushed walnuts.

Finally, it's my turn. Despite all my precious confidence, my stomach flip-flops when I hear my name. I grab hold of the plate with my cake on it and shuffle toward the judges.

"Tell us about what you've made," Padma says, practically beaming at me.

"Chocolate raspberry cake. I thought the sweetness and slight acidity would work well together."

"It looks amazing," Galvin says, glancing at Padma and Máire on either side of him. "Let's try it, shall we?"

He cuts a slice of the cake for each of the judges and places it on their plates. Then he grabs a fork and takes a huge piece of cake with icing, a raspberry, and both layers joined together by the ganache.

My breath hitches in my throat as I watch all three of them chewing, knowing that what they say next could make or break me in this competition.

"Shireen . . ." Galvin is the first to speak. He looks at me with his lips in a thin line but knowing Galvin that's no indication of what he thinks of the cake.

"Yes, Galvin?"

"Did you try this yourself before serving it up to us?" he asks.

"Well, no. I mean . . . I couldn't obviously," I say.

"What about the batter?" Galvin asks. I'm pretty sure I did try the mixture, but being confronted with the question, I can't be sure.

Galvin waves me up to him. "Come here."

My stomach lurches as I step forward, not sure what all of this means.

Galvin picks up a fresh fork and hands it to me. I take it, my hands shaking, and cut a piece from the cake, slipping it into my mouth.

The taste is . . . overwhelming.

Overwhelmingly bad.

It's way too sweet.

Galvin looks at me with a raised eyebrow. "I thought you should try it, since you made us try it."

I want to say something, to defend myself. But my throat is

dry and I can feel the tears well up in my eyes. But I can't cry—I'm not going to cry—on national TV. I can't wrap my head around what happened. When I tasted my mixture—and I'm so sure I had—it tasted perfect. Not too sweet, not too savory.

"It is a little too sweet," Padma cuts in before Galvin can continue to berate me. "But . . . it has a great texture. It's very soft, just the way you want it to be. And just look at it. It's so beautiful."

"It is stunning to look at," Máire offers with a little smile that tells me she knows I'm ready to burst into tears. "It's really a shame about the sweetness, but all your other elements were excellent."

I nod, though I obviously don't deserve Padma or Máire's compliments. What is a dish if it doesn't taste good? If it's basically inedible because of how saccharine sweet it is?

I walk back to my station, my head low. I can't bear to look at anyone—definitely not Chris or Niamh. I'm fighting to keep my tears at bay.

It'll take a miracle for me to get to the final round now.

TWENTY-EIGHT

All Good Things Crumb to an End

AS SOON AS THE JUDGES LEAVE THE ROOM TO DELIBERATE, I RUSH out of my kitchen station and toward the bathroom at the very back of the hall. The last thing I want to do is sit in that room, watching people give me sympathetic smiles because they know there's no way I'm going to make it to the finals.

But as soon as I slip into the bathroom, my breath becomes short and stilted. My chest feels tight, and my vision becomes blurry. I've had panic attacks before, but this seems worse than the rest. I'm not sure if I'm even breathing anymore.

"Shireen, you're okay." Chris's voice seems to come from nowhere. When I look up, she's right in front of me, holding my hands. I'm not even sure when she got here.

I don't want to see her. I don't want anyone to see me here. But I can't pull away either. It feels like I'm barely in control of myself.

"You know what to do, Shireen," Chris says. "You just have to breathe."

But I'm not sure if I can.

Chris nods encouragingly, grasping my hands tighter. It feels so familiar and warm. Like a guiding light away from my panic attack.

"Just take a deep breath. I'll count with you," she says. I take in a breath and she counts me down and tells me to exhale. She counts that down too. And again and again, until things seem a little bit better. My heart is still beating a little too fast, but my breathing is back to normal. And I feel back in control of myself.

I pull my hands away from Chris's and wipe away my tears with the sleeve of my dress. "Thanks," I mutter, turning away from her.

"Are you okay?" she asks.

"I'm fine."

"Shireen . . . ," she says. "It's going to be okay. So you messed up one dessert. They didn't like Bridget's dessert either. You have a chance, and you're probably the best baker in this entire competition. Don't—"

"You're in denial." I cut her off. Her faith in me is kind of nice I guess, but it feels too much like pity all the same. "There's no way I'm getting into the finals. They loved what you made and Séan and Niamh. There are only three spots, and Galvin *hated* my cake. I can't even blame him."

I'm still trying to wrap my head around what happened. I just can't understand it. How did I make such a ridiculous mistake? I have never made something so atrocious in my entire life. The first thing I ever baked—a batch of muffins for our school's bake sale when I was a kid—was better than that cake.

"You're overexaggerating," Chris says. She really sounds like she believes that. "Look, let's go back and whatever happens, I'm sure that—"

"You were there," I say, turning to meet her gaze now.

Realization dawns on me finally, and I begin to piece things together. "You fell right near my station."

Chris steps back, her eyebrows drawn together.

"Yeah, I did fall," she says. "Because I was running from the pantry toward my station, and I should have been more careful."

"And very conveniently you were right by my station," I say.

"Are you accusing me of something?" Chris says, like she can't quite believe it. I'm not sure if I can believe it, either, but Chris looks and sounds defensive now. Just like that, all her concern is gone.

It reminds me of the night she asked me to not apply for the competition because she wanted to win. She didn't care that this was my dream. She only cared about herself. And isn't that who Chris is at the end of it all? Hasn't she been placing herself before me all this time?

She'd do anything to win. Maybe even sabotage me.

"I know things aren't easy with your parents' donut shop, but I can't believe you'd . . . you'd sabotage me like this. After everything. After we decided to be friends. After tea with Padma Bollywood. After—"

"I can't believe you would really think I'd do this. After everything, you really think I would sabotage you?"

I meet her eyes, but I'm not sure what I see in them anymore. They're unreadable. I can't tell if she's telling the truth or just trying to put me off her scent.

"You can't deny it!" I exclaim. "You were the only person near my station. And now you're just deflecting, turning it back on—"

"I didn't do this, Shireen." There's a finality to her tone now. "I would never do that to you. I would never do it to *anyone*, least of all you and . . ." She looks away from me. "I know I fucked up with asking you to not do the show. I know that. But I apologized. I'm trying to make it up to you. I'm trying to be your friend. For you to accuse me like this . . ." She pauses like she doesn't even have the words to finish her sentence.

Without giving me a chance to reply, Chris turns around and slips out the door.

I stay in the bathroom for a few more minutes, trying to sort through my fuzzy thoughts and wiping away the remnants of my tears. But I know I don't have much time. I have to go back out there and face the decision the judges have made. So I fix my makeup as best as I can, hoping the cameras don't focus on me too much, and leave. All the while I'm trying to look like I'm okay. But absolutely nothing is okay.

THE JUDGES COME BACK from deliberation with determined looks on their faces. I'm trying to look like I haven't spent the entire time crying my eyes out and having a panic attack. I know that I'll be on national TV, and I'm sure the people online getting a kick out of racially abusing me and Chris will get a good laugh if they see me upset.

"There were a lot of really great desserts presented to us today," Galvin begins, clapping his hands together. There's a hint of a smile on his face, though it doesn't quite shape into an actual smile. "So it was difficult to choose the *best* dish of this round. Ultimately, though, we all agreed. The best dish should go to Niamh Lynch for her terrific Black Forest cake."

In the station behind me, Niamh's face lights up, her smile stretching so wide it seems to take up her whole face. "Thank you so much!" she exclaims, sounding both extremely pleased and humble somehow.

"Unfortunately," Máire Cherry begins this time, "there were a few desserts that missed the mark by just a little. And only three people can continue to the final challenge."

Before Máire can say anything else, Padma cuts in.

"You should all be very proud of yourselves, regardless. Even if you don't make it into the finale, you've come so far and worked really hard."

Máire has a smile on her lips as she announces the contestants who didn't make the cut. "The junior bakers not continuing to the final round are Bridget . . ." On the other side of the room, Bridget's face falls. "And Shireen."

I had expected to hear my name—of course I had. But I guess there was still a little part that had held on to some hope. I try not to let my disappointment show on my face, but I don't think I do a great job of it.

As soon as the cameras turn off, Kathleen ushers Chris,

Niamh, and Séan—the three finalists—off the set. Probably to prepare them for the final round of the show.

I feel an odd sense of emptiness as I untie my apron and put it back on my workstation. It's not mine anymore. Not this apron, not this station. This will be my last time here.

"Shireen, are you okay?" I glance up to find Padma standing in front of me, pity written all over her face. It makes me feel even worse than I already did. I failed—in front of everyone. My ex-girlfriend, my new—something, my idol, my parents, all the Bengali aunties and uncles, the entirety of Ireland, and apparently even parts of Bangladesh.

"I'm fine," I say, trying to make my voice sound chipper. It just comes off too high-pitched. I clear my throat and say, "It's a competition, right? So I'm okay." Maybe if I say it enough times, it'll be true.

Padma nods, looking like she doesn't believe me at all. "It's a setback, but we all have them. I know I've had my fair share of them. But Shireen, you're so talented, and I know how passionate you are about this. Don't let this get you down."

It's easier said than done, because right now just pretending to be okay feels like more than I can handle. Especially knowing that I hadn't lost because I messed up, because I made a mistake . . . but because my ex-girlfriend sabotaged me. For a moment I wonder about what Padma would say if I told her my suspicions about Chris. I even consider it. I imagine a future where Chris is booted off the show for cheating and I'm let back in her place. Reality shows love scandals exactly like that.

But it's only for a moment. I can't do that. For one, I don't think Padma would even believe me. More important, no matter how much Chris hurt me, I'm not sure I can hurt her back so easily.

So I give Padma the best smile I can muster. "Thank you for everything," I say, knowing this is the last time I'll see her. "You don't know just how much I appreciate it."

TWENTY-NINE

Donut Fall in Love

AMMU AND ABBU ARE BOTH ON THE COUCH IN THE SITTING ROOM when I come home. They turn their heads to me as soon as I'm inside, eyes wide like they're surprised to see me walking in.

And I know they know. I'm not sure how, but they know.

"Shireen!" Before I can say anything, Ammu leaps off the couch and pulls me into an embrace. It's strange—not that Ammu never embraces me, but we're definitely not the type of people to hug as soon as I walk in the door. The warmth of her makes that lump form in my throat again and I blink back my tears.

"Are you okay?" Ammu asks.

"I'm . . . fine." It's a lie, and I tell it badly.

Ammu pulls away from the hug but leans close to cup my face in her hands. "The Huangs told us that their daughter got through to the finals and you . . . didn't."

"Oh." I had almost forgotten about how Abbu had said the best way to get back at the Huangs was for me to win against Chris. So on top of not achieving my dreams, I'm also letting my parents down.

"I know you really wanted to win—" Ammu begins.

"I'll be fine," I say, prising myself out of her grip. "I don't really want to talk about it right now."

"Do you want me to get you dinner? We can order in."

"No, I'm not hungry," I say, even though it's evening and I haven't eaten in hours. But I don't feel hungry. I just feel empty.

I slip off my shoes and head up the stairs, Ammu and Abbu's eyes following me the whole time. Honestly, it's a little creepy and I wish they'd stop staring at me.

I pause in the middle of the stairs. "Did . . . were . . . the Huangs happy?" I ask. "Like, they were rubbing it in your faces?"

"They were happy," Abbu says, "but not rubbing it in our faces."

"Okay," I say. At least they didn't try to humiliate Ammu and Abbu because I lost. The next question I want to ask gets stuck in my throat. *Are you disappointed?*

But Abbu gives me a smile and says, "Get some rest, Shireen," like he knows what I'm thinking.

I nod and head up the stairs and into my room.

OF COURSE, THAT NIGHT I have a good cry in my bedroom. After Ammu and Abbu go to sleep, I enter the kitchen to fill up on desserts. And like my parents can read my mind, I find an entire box of my favorite donut flavors from our shop and a tub of my favorite ice cream in the freezer. So at least I know that if I have nothing else, I'll always have the love and support of my parents.

Normally, this is the time I'd watch *The Great British Bake Off* and eat my desserts and feel sorry about my life. But I can't even watch the show anymore because it's just going to remind me of everything I've lost.

I wonder if I would be this heartbroken if I had lost the show on my own merits. If I had just made a bad dessert instead of having someone sabotage my work. I wonder if I would be this heartbroken if it had been someone other than Chris who had caused me to lose. If it were Séan . . . or even Niamh.

But I know the answer to all of those questions.

Somehow the hurt of everything got tangled up inside me— the breakup with Chris, losing the show—they're two sides of the same pain. Because in one fell swoop I lost both the girl that I love—because I do still love her no matter how much I want to have been over her a long time ago—and the dream I wanted to achieve.

Not only will I not be Ireland's first-ever *Junior Irish Baking Show* winner, taking ten thousand euros home to help Ammu and Abbu with You Drive Me Glazy, but I will also no longer have Chris. Not as a girlfriend and not as a friend.

Back in my room, I open up the drawer where I stuck the necklace Chris made me for our anniversary. It's cheesy—of course it is. But there's something wonderful about it. The brightness of the pink icing is the almost exact shade of the donut costume she was wearing the first time we met. She must have spent hours getting the details exactly right.

I grab a bin bag and throw the donut necklace into the bottom of it. There's something final about it. I don't know if it makes me feel fantastic or infinitely worse, but at least I'm doing something. And this needs to be done. I should have done it a long time ago—at the start of the summer, right after our breakup. Maybe then letting go would have been easier, and this would be less messy.

I begin to gather every remnant of Chris in my bedroom. The jumper she lent me on our first date when I was too cold in my half-sleeved yellow cotton dress. The birthday card where Chris had drawn both of us in ridiculous donut outfits. The photo of the two of us in Phoenix Park, cherry blossom trees blooming pink in the background and ice-cream cones—big and bright and dripping in our hands. I toss them all into the black bin bag. There's something poetic about it. Because our relationship now is definitely garbage.

THIRTY

A Friend in Knead Is a Friend Indeed

"I WAS LITERALLY ABOUT TO BOOK NEW FLIGHTS BACK TO DUBLIN!" That's the first thing Fatima says to me when I finally answer her call. It's been almost a week since the last challenge—and a day since it aired on IETV. I had spent the whole week brooding and feeling sorry for myself. As is my right as an official loser.

"I thought we weren't talking," I say.

"Where did you get that idea when I've been texting and calling you nonstop?" Fatima asks. "Just because we have a fight doesn't mean I'm not going to be there for you when you need me."

Her saying that makes me feel even worse for ignoring her calls and texts for the past week. I just knew on top of everything else, I couldn't deal with Fatima too. I know she's right. I had been selfish. But it's because I miss her, and without her I feel like I have no one.

I want to tell her all that, but instead I burst into tears, exactly what I had been trying to avoid by not picking up her calls.

"Shireen!" she cries.

"I'm sorry," I manage to choke out between sobs, rubbing at my eyes. "I've been such a bad friend lately. I couldn't even be happy because you're having a good time over there with your cousins. I've been jealous, and I miss you. And you're still here for me."

"Obviously, I am," she says. "And it's okay. Maybe if it was the other way around, I'd be feeling the same. I know things haven't been easy for you this summer, with Chris and the show and everything else."

"Still," I say, wiping away the last of my tears. "It's not really an excuse." I sniffle before looking at her properly. "You weren't really going to change your flights again, were you?"

Fatima shrugs. "I've been worried about you. Ammu and Abbu talked to your parents, and they said you're upset."

"You asked your parents to talk to mine?" I say. I'm not sure how much more embarrassing this could get.

"Well, you weren't talking to me. You didn't leave me with much of a choice." She takes a deep breath. "I would ask if you're okay, but I know you're not."

"I'm . . . doing better." My words don't sound convincing, even to me.

"Yeah, I can tell by the fact you burst into tears as soon as we started talking," Fatima says.

"Well, I'm trying to do better."

"By ignoring calls from your best friend? And writing the most depressing blog posts ever that are somehow also about baking cakes and making donuts?"

"I just didn't want to talk about it," I say. "I knew if I answered, we would have to talk about everything. Our fight, the show. I wanted to wait until the episode aired so that I wouldn't have to talk about that. Now everyone knows that I'm a failure."

Fatima lets out an exasperated breath. "You're not a failure just because you didn't win a ridiculous baking show. I know you're talented. Your parents know. Everyone with good sense knows. Winning this show doesn't mean anything. It doesn't make you more talented."

"If you say so," I say as I pull my duvet over my head so I can't see Fatima on my screen anymore.

"I know you don't want to talk about it," Fatima says.

"I don't." My voice comes out muffled.

"But not talking about it won't help you deal with it."

"I don't want to deal with." I know I sound like a child, but I don't care. If I'm not allowed throw a tantrum now, when will I ever be allowed to?

"So you're just planning to mope about like this for the rest of your life? You're going to give up on your dreams because of one setback? Because of—"

"It's not that," I groan, peeking out from under the duvet. I hate that her and Padma have this same idea—that this is just some setback. But they don't understand the reality. What actually happened.

"So what is it?" Fatima asks.

"It's . . . it's . . . Chris," I say, even though I don't really want to. But as soon as I do it feels like a weight is being lifted off of me.

"Okay," Fatima says hesitantly. "What did she do?"

"She's the reason I lost."

"Okay . . ." Fatima nods like she's trying to process this information. "Explain."

"Remember in the show Galvin said that my cake was way too sweet?"

"Yeah, I remember that."

"Well, it wasn't. At least not when I tasted it while I was still trying to get it perfect. It was exactly as sweet as I wanted it to be. So that means someone did something to my batter. It had to be Chris, because she fell right by my station during the challenge."

"You really think Chris did something to your cake?" Fatima doesn't sound like she quite believes me—which is exactly what I was worried about. Fatima has known Chris for almost as long as I have. She knows that Chris is not the type of person to do this. Except I guess we were both wrong about her.

"It had to be Chris!" I exclaim. "She was the only one who could have done it."

There's a pause as Fatima seems to take in what I've said.

"Shireen . . . did you watch the episode when it aired?"

"No . . ." I couldn't bear to sit through watching all of it only to see myself fail. It was humiliating enough to live through it. It would be worse to see it on TV, knowing that millions of people across the country—and I guess people who aren't even in this country—are watching my humiliation.

"Well, if you had watched it, you would see Chris couldn't have done anything to your cake. She really did fall. She was panicking about her cake, and she felt like she didn't have enough time. She messed up her cake batter and she had to start from scratch. That's why she had to go into the pantry and grab extra stuff. She was running back in a panicked rush and she fell."

"But how can you be—"

"They showed the whole thing," Fatima interrupts. "And they panned your kitchen station. Your cake was already in the oven when she fell, Shireen."

I blink at Fatima slowly. How can she be sure?

"What about my icing? Maybe that's where—"

Fatima cuts me off. "You were holding it, and you put it to one side when she fell to go over and ask if she was okay. And plus, Chris was way too stressed about her own cake to even think about sabotaging you."

"Oh." I'm not sure if I believe it completely. But Fatima wouldn't lie. Not about this.

"I mean, that doesn't mean somebody didn't do something. I just don't think it was Chris."

A thread of regret worms its way through me. I accused Chris without having any proof. She must be feeling the same as me—betrayed. Hurt. If I was Chris, I would hate me right now.

"You already accused her, didn't you?" When I look up she's massaging her forehead like my problems are giving her a bit of a headache again. I *have* had many of them this summer, and Fatima has been here for me even when she shouldn't be.

"I was angry," I say.

"You should apologize to her. She's probably feeling pretty shitty right now too."

"I don't know."

"You don't want to apologize to her?"

"Not before I understand what I'm feeling. I mean, I put all of her stuff in this bin bag and put it away. I was going to throw it away the next time the bin collection people came."

"Wow." Fatima leans back, observing me thoughtfully. "You were really going to throw away her stuff?"

"I was ready to move on. Or . . . to try. Or I was just angry. I don't know." I shake my head. "Anyway I . . . I kissed Niamh. So I should move on. I *am* moving on."

I expect Fatima to have a bigger reaction to this confession than she does, but she just says, "Interesting."

"Interesting? That's all you have to say?"

"I don't know much about this girl Niamh," Fatima says. "But if I remember correctly, isn't her kitchen station right behind yours on the show?"

"Yeah," I say, not sure what Fatima is getting at.

"So, you didn't think of her when you thought about being sabotaged?"

"Why would I?" I ask. "She's given me no reason to distrust her. She kissed me. We're friends. Maybe more than friends, and she was nowhere near my station."

"Wait. *She* kissed you?" Fatima asks.

"Well, yeah, but that doesn't mean anything," I say.

"When did she kiss you?" Fatima asks.

I'm not sure why it matters but I shrug and say, "After we got into the semifinals. We were celebrating and I don't know, it just kind of happened."

"Just the timing is weird," Fatima says. But she doesn't know Niamh, so of course she would think Niamh was to blame. But there were only two people who could have sabotaged my cake.

"You're sure that it wasn't Chris?" I ask, even though suddenly I'm sure too. Chris was in the station in front of me. If she had done something, I would have seen it.

"I'm sure," Fatima says.

I glance up to meet her gaze because I don't want to think it. I don't want to say it aloud. "Maybe it was Niamh."

With the idea of Niamh sabotaging me in my mind, I can't think of much else. After all, who else could have done it? Who else would have had the opportunity?

Plus, it's pretty strange that she hasn't texted me at all since the last day of filming. We barely even spoke *on* that day.

"We've been texting since we met but it's been radio silence since the day I got eliminated," I admit.

"She might have just realized she would be a bit of an asshole to be texting you and reminding you that she's still on the show when you're not anymore," Fatima points out.

I glare. "I thought you didn't like Niamh."

"I don't know Niamh!" she exclaims. "And I just think you need more proof before you decide she was the one who did something. You don't want to make another baseless accusation, do you?"

"No, I don't," I say. The last thing I want to do is spend more time thinking about the show when it's already caused me so much heartache. "Maybe I should just forget about it. What will proving that someone sabotaged me even do? What will happen if it turns out that Niamh did do something? I'm still out of the show, and Niamh is still going to be in the finale."

"Justice!" Fatima cries out louder than she should. It makes me nearly jump out of my skin.

"Ey, aste aste bolo," someone cries from behind Fatima.

"Sorry!" Fatima calls back before leaning forward and lowering her voice to a whisper. "Justice," she repeats softly, like I hadn't heard her loud and clear the first time.

"How?" I ask. "Do you really think the judges will do something if I can prove that Niamh sabotaged me?"

"They might!" Fatima is way more optimistic than I'm feeling. "You'll never know unless you try."

I think back to Padma and the two private conversations we've had. She wanted to support me, so maybe she would listen. Maybe there was still a chance.

"I'll think about it," I say finally.

"Seriously? You'll just think about it?"

"I need time to weigh all my options!" I say.

"Since when do you weigh options?" Fatima asks. "I leave for a few months and you start being reasonable instead of completely impulsive?"

A smile tugs at my lips. "I'm sorry, Fatima. I know I shouldn't be jealous of you over there with your cousins. I definitely shouldn't be angry that you decided to spend, like, a few extra days there, but I just . . . miss you."

"I know," Fatima says. "I miss you too. Like, a lot."

"Really?"

"Yeah, really," Fatima says with a laugh. "I love my cousins. Like, so much. But they're not you. And also they don't feed me the best desserts in the universe like you do. I'm pretty sure there will never be anybody in my life who does that, so you're basically irreplaceable."

I smile even wider if that's possible. "You're pretty irreplaceable, too, only because there is nobody else who'll tell me I'm being an eejit when I need to hear it."

"I'm always here to call you an eejit when you need me to." Fatima grins. And just like that, I know Fatima and I are going to be alright.

THIRTY-ONE
Believe It or Nut

AMMU AND ABBU DON'T PRESS ME TOO MUCH ABOUT ANYTHING since the day I came home from getting eliminated—and, well, a fair few days after that. They try to feed me a lot, which I appreciate. But I get tired of not doing anything pretty fast. I can't mope around in my room for the rest of the summer.

When I ask Ammu and Abbu when they want me at work, they just exchange sad glances and say that I don't have to worry about it.

But I get pretty tired of them covering shifts for me when they already work themselves to the bone. At least before the show, we had almost no customers. Our big flood of customers after that first episode aired didn't sustain itself, but we've had more and more people trawling in and out since I've been on the show. I know it's even more work for my parents than ever before. So the day after my call with Fatima, I decide to get my act together.

"Shireen?" Ammu is at the counter when I enter You Drive Me Glazy. She looks shell-shocked to see me. I'm shocked to see her—at the till. She usually gets too annoyed at the customers who take way too long to decide what they want. So if there's any one of us available to work the till during her shifts, they're the ones at the register.

"Ammu . . ." I let myself into the other side of the counter. "I can take it from here."

She stares at me like it's the first time she's seen me. "You're not supposed to be working today."

"I haven't been working for a little too long now. I thought I'd come and help out. Is that okay?"

For a moment, I'm afraid Ammu is going to make me go back home, but she gives a curt nod of her head and disappears into the back. If I'm not mistaken, I'm pretty sure I see a flash of relief in her eyes.

Almost as soon as Ammu's out of sight, a customer slips inside. She passes me a small smile while her eyes drift over the donuts in our display case.

"Can I have a . . . an Almond Einstein donut?" She points a perfectly painted nail at the chocolate glazed donut sprinkled with almond shavings.

"Of course!" With a pair of tongs, I slip one of the Almond Einsteins into a paper bag and hand it over to her. "That'll be three euros."

As she pays up and I bid her goodbye, Abbu walks in through the front door. He gives the customer a friendly smile as he passes her.

"What's that?" I point to the paper bag that Abbu is holding.

"You don't recognize our own bag?" He points to the obscured logo of the donut with a bite taken out of it.

"Why do you have it? Where were you?" He wasn't at home

when I had left, so I just assumed he was working in the back room of the shop.

"Across the street," he says, like that's where he always is. He busies himself by fiddling with the coffee machine, but he definitely hasn't given enough information to satisfy my curiosity.

"Where across the street?"

Abbu finally meets my gaze. "I was at the Baker's Dozen."

My heart sinks. "Why? What did you do?" Now, on top of having to apologize for accusing Chris of sabotaging me, I would also have to apologize for whatever Abbu just did. It's not that Chris and I aren't totally used to our parents messing with each other's businesses. But it was one thing when we were dating. I have a feeling it's going to be different now.

"I just brought them a box of donuts," Abbu says nonchalantly. Like we make a habit of sharing donuts with the Huangs. I'm not fooled though.

"And . . . you put chili powder in the donuts?"

"No."

"Laxatives?"

"No."

"You put naga morich!"

Abbu looks at me with a frown as he shakes his head. "No, but should we make a donut with naga morich in it?"

"In *Ireland?*" I ask. "Who would eat that?"

Abbu sighs sadly. "You're right."

"Abbu, why did you give the Huangs donuts?"

"To make peace."

I can only blink at him, trying to process this information.

I'm not entirely sure that this isn't Abbu's alien clone—because really, that's the only thing that makes sense in this instance. "Why would you do that? You hate the Huangs. Eirkom bodmash manush ami jiboneo dekhinai. That's what you said about the Huangs the week we opened this shop up and they stole our recipes."

"Yes, well. I guess we've done a little bit of bodmashi too."

I'm not going to disagree with him. We've done a *lot* of bodmashi, but I never expected so much perspective from my parents. They had been so hell-bent on getting back at the Huangs. I never thought there would be an end in sight for their rivalry.

"Did they take the donuts?" I ask. Considering the Huangs technically started the rivalry, I can't see them being very open to "peace." But if my parents are capable of it, after everything, why not them?

"They were suspicious, but they took them."

"They might have chucked them in the bin as soon as you left."

"It's a possibility." Abbu nods, but he doesn't seem too bothered about it. Somehow, though, I don't think they *have* tossed the donuts into the bin. I remember the conversation Chris and I had on the pier in Dún Laoghaire, about the reason why Chris had decided to enter the *Junior Irish Baking Show*.

"Has business really been that bad?" I ask. Abbu's eyes snap up to meet mine, like that was the last thing he expected me to say. "I mean, that's why you're trying to make peace with the Huangs, right? Because the rivalry ultimately hurts us."

Abbu slumps down into one of the chairs behind the counter.

"Starting a business is not easy. It takes a while to really start making profits. Your ammu and I knew that. We prepared for that. But we didn't plan for this rivalry. Sometimes, it helped us because we had to come up with bigger and better ideas. Mostly, it hurt us. And it hurt the Huangs too. Which is why it's better if we can agree to a truce."

I guess I shouldn't be surprised to hear that, but it still feels so heavy. Especially for my parents who made this shop out of their dreams and hard work. Nobody deserves success more than them.

"I thought things were getting better," I say, even if it probably makes me sound like a naive child to Abbu. He looks at me a little pityingly. I'm glad he's pitying me for having hopes and dreams for their shop and not for losing on the show.

"They are getting better," Abbu says. "The show helped a lot. You helped a lot."

"But now that I'm not there anymore, people won't care as much," I finish for him, the shame blooming in my chest. Even though I know it's not my fault, I can't help it. Is this how Chris felt about her parents' shop? Is that why she did what she did? Why she sacrificed our relationship for a chance at saving their shop?

"You can't go on a reality TV show every time our business is struggling, Abbu. That's not your responsibility," Abbu says.

He might say that, but I still feel the weight of it on my shoulders. If it feels this bad when Abbu tells me I shouldn't worry, I can't imagine how much worse it feels for Chris. Her parents love her to death but sometimes make her feel like she has to carry all of their burdens for them. I'd spent countless conversations where she told me about it all. She was their only daughter, just like I am my parents' only daughter. But things were different for us.

"Abbu, are we bankrupt?"

A wavering smile appears on his face. "No, Abbu, we are not bankrupt. And we won't be going bankrupt." He says that with so much surety that I have no choice but to believe him.

"It would be nice if we had the ten thousand euros from the *Junior Irish Baking Show* though."

"Shireen, this is nothing to do with you or that show. Your ammu and I knew this would be difficult. Running a business always is. And you don't have to worry about it."

Logically, I understand everything he's saying. I know that Ammu and Abbu would never put the burden of our struggling finances on me, but I can't help but feel as if I could have done something. I could have helped.

And maybe it's not too late.

From: Shireen Malik <shireenbakescakes@gmail.com>
To: Clare Farrin <junioririshbakingshow@ietv.ie>

Dear Clare,

I was wondering if I would be able to schedule a meeting with Padma Bollywood? ASAP . . . thank you.

Best wishes,
Shireen

From Clare Farrin <junioririshbakingshow@ietv.ie>
To: Shireen Malik <shireenbakescakes@gmail.com>

Dear Shireen,

Ms. Bollywood is extremely busy, but her assistant informed me she could meet you at her new bakery tomorrow morning, 9:00 A.M. sharp at Hume Street.

Kind regards,
Clare Farrin

From Shireen Malik <shireenbakescakes@gmail .com>
To: Clare Farrin <junioririshbakingshow@ietv.ie>

THANK YOU!!!!!

THIRTY-TWO

Don't Cake It Lying Down

IT WOULD HAVE BEEN HELPFUL IF CLARE FARRIN HAD GIVEN ME some contact details for Padma Bollywood—or even the name of her café. But since she didn't and multiple Google searches didn't turn anything up, I find myself walking down Hume Street, staring closely into every single window I pass. Hoping it's a bakery and that Padma will be inside.

Finally, at the very end of the street, I find a storefront that still looks under construction. But the sign at the top clearly says BOLLYWOOD DELIGHTS. This has to be Padma's bakery.

Even though the place looks closed, I knock on the door. But with the sound of construction inside, I don't think anybody hears me.

I glance back for a moment, having a little moment of crisis. Then, I take a deep breath, push the door open, and step inside.

"Hey, careful!"

"Sorry!" I say to the construction worker I nearly run into.

"Shireen!" Padma exclaims from the far end of the room. She waves me over, and I try my best to weave around all the construction people and toward her.

She's sitting at a round table and invites me to sit opposite her.

"You're a little late," she says, though she doesn't sound annoyed.

"Sorry," I mumble. "I didn't know what the shop was called so it took me a while to actually find it and also"—I place the bag I'm carrying on the table between us—"I brought donuts." My parents had taught me good Bengali manners: You don't visit someone without bringing treats.

"Wow, these look pretty amazing," Padma says, taking out the box of donuts from the bag.

"They're from my parents' shop," I say. "But I made them."

"Very impressive," Padma says. She takes out one of the Robert Brownie Jr. donuts and bites into it. She closes her eyes and seems to savor the taste for a second. That donut is one of the most chocolatey ones. And it's pretty amazing if I do say so myself.

"And probably one of the best donuts I have ever had," Padma says breezily, like there isn't ecstatic screeching suddenly going on in my brain at her words.

Externally, I pass her a smile that I hope doesn't make me look too deranged and say, "Thank you."

"So, you wanted to talk?" Padma asks.

"I wanted to talk," I repeat, taking a breath to get all the excited thoughts out of my head. I had practiced how I was going to tell Padma about the sabotage, but now that she's in front of me staring at me with her warm eyes and kind smile, my throat dries up, and all the words I'd rehearsed fly right out of my mind.

"I wanted to talk about the show," I manage to get out.

"Okay," Padma says, nodding encouragingly.

"About the last episode. When I got . . . when . . ." I gulp, close my eyes, and blurt out, "I was sabotaged!"

When I blink my eyes open, Padma looks thoughtful. Like even though I just had a minor outburst, she's considering what I said.

"Elaborate, please," she says.

"Well, it's just I know I didn't mess up my cake. I'm an experienced baker. I wouldn't make a silly mistake like dumping a bunch of sugar into my cake batter. That doesn't just happen," I say.

"You're right," Padma says.

"I am?"

"Yes, it doesn't just happen. And you are an experienced baker. You're really good at what you do, obviously." She points to the half-eaten donut in front of her.

"So you'll help me get back on the show?" I ask.

Padma's face falls. "I wish I could, Shireen. But my faith in you and your abilities are not proof. Unless we can definitively prove that somebody sabotaged your dish, my hands are tied."

I know I should have expected this, but somehow I had hoped that this would be easy. I would explain it to Padma, and if she believed me she would sort it out, no problem! But now I feel deflated again.

"I understand," I say, standing up and trying not to let my disappointment show. "I really appreciate you taking the time out of your busy schedule to meet with me, though."

"I wish I could be of more help, Shireen. I really do," she says. "But . . . here." She digs into her purse and pulls something out from it. A card. She extends it to me. "I want you to take this and keep in touch."

Normally, something like this would make me feel like I was floating on cloud nine. Padma Bollywood—*the* Padma Bollywood—wants me to keep in touch with her. But it doesn't change that I won't be back on the show and that I won't be able to help my parents out with the prize money. Still, I take the card and mumble my thank-you before slipping out.

Outside, it's a warm summer's day. There's not a cloud in the blue sky, and the sun is shining bright. And as soon as I step past the entrance of Padma's bakery, I run right into someone.

"Sorry, sorry," I say quietly.

"That's okay. Kind of my fault." I look up to find Chris staring back at me, the sunshine making her glow a little too brightly.

"What are you doing here?" I ask.

"Fatima told me you'd be here," she says. "She told me everything. And I saw you inside. I didn't want to interrupt. But I was curious and I was kind of hovering and not paying attention and—"

"Wait, go back. She told you everything?"

"All your theories about who sabotaged you," Chris says. "And from the look on your face, I'm guessing Padma Bollywood can't help you."

"No, she can't." I sigh.

"Well, it's a good thing I found you because I have an idea."

THE IETV STUDIOS LOOK different under the blanket of night. Usually, it's wildly busy here. The car park is always full, the café is buzzing with people, and there's always staff running around trying to get things done.

But now, the place is nearly empty.

"Why are you wearing all black?" Chris asks when I join her by the studio where they film the show.

I glance down at myself. I don't own a lot of black outfits, so even the black leggings and black dress I had ultimately chosen to wear have red cherries dotted all around them. It's not exactly the best disguise for blending in to the surroundings, but I don't think anything in my wardrobe has ever helped me "blend in."

"Isn't black what you're supposed to wear when you're breaking in to a place like this?" I ask.

"I feel like you think we're on a Disney Channel original movie or something," Chris says. "And anyway, we're not breaking in. I told the producers I had to pick something up from here. I have permission to be here."

"You have permission to be in the room with all their tapes and cameras and other expensive equipment?"

Chris pauses at that. "Okay, no."

"So we *are* breaking in. And I'm wearing the perfect outfit for it."

"I'm pretty sure criminals don't wear cherry dresses," Chris points out, but she leaves it at that. She leads us into the studio and past the hallway where we usually film episodes.

"I've definitely seen the crew bringing equipment in from here," Chris says, stopping in front of a door that says CREW ONLY. It's at the very back of the hall and not the double door the judges use to leave the room for deliberation. It's on the other side—so small and inconsequential that I hadn't even noticed it before.

Chris twists the handle and tries to pull it open, but the door doesn't budge. She steps back with a frown, like if she gives the door a sour enough look it'll swing open.

"You didn't expect they'd just leave the room with all their footage and camera equipment open for all to access, did you?" I ask, even though clearly she did.

"Well, I could hardly ask them to hand over the keys to the place," Chris says.

"How do we get in here then?" I ask, looking all around for some way to access it. But there's only this one door, and unless Chris is a master lock picker, we're not getting in. I can't believe I came all the way here for nothing.

"They must have the keys around here somewhere. We just have to find them." Chris sounds far more confident than I'm feeling. But the mention of keys reminds me of the last day of filming and Padma.

"I think I have an idea," I say after a moment. "I know where the keys are kept. I saw the secretary hand a set of keys to Padma, and she looked in one of the drawers in the front desk."

"So, we just have to find a way to get into the drawers?"

Chris asks. She almost makes it sound like an easy task, but my mind is going a mile a minute running through every single scenario. After all, we don't know which drawer in the desk they keep the keys in or even if they have the ones we're looking for. The drawers themselves might even be locked. I'm thinking of all the things that can go wrong and every worst-case scenario I can imagine.

But Chris is already leaving the room. I follow behind as fast as I can. We reach the front hall of the building, where the woman who signed us in on our first day is speaking on the phone.

"Absolutely, we can arrange that for you," she says. "And that will be on the . . . fourteenth." She types something into the computer, while Chris and I watch from a secluded corner. She doesn't notice us.

"Do you remember where exactly she got the keys from?" Chris asks.

"I wasn't paying attention. It's not like I could have known we'd have to break in here," I say, my voice slightly defensive.

"We have permission," Chris says again, though she doesn't quite sound like she believes it.

"How are we going to search the drawers without being noticed?" I ask.

"You distract her, and I'll handle the rest," Chris says.

"But—" Before I can begin my protest, Chris is already gently shoving me forward. I stumble over my own feet for a second. The receptionist at the desk is done with her phone conversation now, so she has plenty of time to observe me try my hardest not to fall on my face. Once I regain my balance and composure and curse Chris inside my head, I turn to the receptionist with the brightest smile I can muster.

"Hi!" I say a little too loud.

"Hi, can I help you?" the woman asks.

"Yes, my friend booked a hall here for her birthday party, and I thought it was this hall down there so I came here, but nobody's there. So I'm pretty sure that's not it. Do you know where it could be?" I ask, trying to look innocent. I need to find a way to move her away from her reception desk so Chris can get to the drawers.

"There are no birthday parties booked here," she says.

"I know, but it's somewhere here. She said it was like down the road from the café," I say.

The receptionist frowns, and for a moment I'm sure she doesn't believe me. But I know for a fact that people book birthday parties here all the time. A girl at my school had a big eighteenth birthday bash in one of the halls inside the IETV studios. It was probably super expensive to book the place, but she did it.

"Well, the café is outside this building," the woman says. "And there are a few places just down from there. I think I might know the place she meant. You just need to walk straight down and take a right and it should be the building in front of you."

"I'm really bad at directions. Can you show me which way?"

The woman looks at me like I've grown two heads. I don't blame her. Who can't follow such simple directions? But I try to look naïve as I say, "I have really bad spatial awareness. Did you say turn right and then—"

"I'll show you," she says, probably realizing she'll waste less time just showing me than repeating her directions to me over and over again. She slips out from behind the reception desk and leads me outside.

"There's the café," she says, pointing at it. I nod sagely, trying really hard not to look over my shoulder to see what Chris is doing. "So you just have to go straight down this road," the woman says. "And turn right at that building there," she continues. "And then the building right in front should be what you're looking for."

"Oh, okay!" I say, like I totally get it, even though I was barely paying attention to what she was saying. "Thank you so much!"

The woman stares at me for a long moment, and I realize she's waiting for me to jet off to my imaginary friend's imaginary birthday party. I should probably have thought things through a little better.

"I just have to use the bathroom before I go," I say. "That's through here, right?"

The receptionist gives me a clipped smile. "Yes, just down the hall."

I glance back and see that the hall is empty. Chris either found what she was looking for, or she couldn't get into the drawers at all.

"Thanks!" I say again, before walking down the hall and away from sight.

Chris is waiting by the door, dangling the keys in front of her like a prize. "Good thinking on your feet," she says.

"It would have been better if I had some kind of warning

before being shoved in front of the receptionist," I say. But I can't really complain. We got the keys. That's the most important thing. "Won't she notice them missing?"

"No way," Chris says. "We'll get them back before she knows they're gone."

We return to the door that says CREW ONLY. Chris slips out the keys and flips through them until she finds one with a little white label that says STUDIO 1: EDITING ROOM. She slips the key into the lock and turns it. It gives a satisfactory click. Chris grins as she pulls the door open. It's the room we were looking for. It has a bunch of camera equipment that looks ridiculously expensive and multiple computers set up.

Chris slips into one of the chairs in front of the computer. The screen comes on, but it requires a password.

"Do you know how to hack into a computer?" Chris says, turning to me.

I take the seat next to her, leaning forward to look at the screen.

"It must be something super obvious," I say. "Like . . . the JuniorIrishBakingShow."

Chris looks at me with her lips in a thin line, but she types the password in. It's rejected.

"JIBS?"

"Why would anyone have a password that easy?" Chris asks even as she types it in. Rejected again.

"Padma Bollywood?"

This time Chris looks at me with a tilt in her head. "That would be your password, not the camera crew's."

"What if someone in the camera crew is also a huge Padma Bollywood fan?" I ask, even though I know that's almost definitely not the password.

Chris tries a few more combinations—the name of the studio, every single judge on the show, even Kathleen Keogh. Thankfully, just as we're about ready to give up, a button appears at the bottom of the screen asking if we want a password hint. Chris and I exchange a triumphant grin. For a moment, it almost feels like we're back to before the summer, when everything was perfect.

"I hope this actually helps us figure it out," Chris says. She clicks on the password hint and a sentence appears: "You are as sweet as _ _ _."

Chris glances at me, eyebrows furrowed. "You are as sweet as . . ."

"Chocolate?" I try.

"It's three letters." Chris points out.

"As sweet as . . ." I think about it. There are a few too many sweet things in the world, and Chris and I should know, being contestants on a nationally televised baking show. "Pie!" I say finally. "That's how the saying goes, right?"

"Right." Chris types it in, but the computer still doesn't open up. Chris lets out a grunt of frustration, and I feel like our luck may have just run out.

"Maybe this wasn't such a good idea. I mean, maybe this is the universe telling us that we should just—"

"No." Chris's voice is firm. "The only thing the universe is telling us is that you didn't deserve to get kicked out of the show. We just have to . . ." Chris drifts off. There's a spark of something in her eyes—like she's just been hit with the most brilliant idea ever. The expression is a little too familiar to me.

"You are as sweet as . . . ," Chris mumbles. "314 . . . pi." She shoots me a grin before hitting ENTER. I'm about to tell her that she shouldn't be so cocky after all of our failed attempts, especially when nothing happens. But then, after a moment, the computer opens up to the desktop. We're in!

I try not to let excitement get too tight a hold on me. Just because we got in doesn't mean we'll find something.

THIRTY-THREE
A Calculated Whisk

"HERE WE GO...EPISODE FIVE, *JUNIOR IRISH BAKING SHOW*." Chris double-clicks into the folder, and hundreds of little image icons of recordings start to load up.

My heart sinks. When Chris suggested trying to find all the recordings of the last episode, I'd imagined it would be easy. There would be a few clips we would have to go through and we would catch Niamh red-handed!

Chris glances at me with a sympathetic smile. "We have a lot of time," she says. "It's only like ten o'clock. We can stay in here for hours."

"What about the receptionist?" I ask. "She thinks I'm in the bathroom. What if she comes looking for me?"

"Once she sees you're not there, I'm sure she'll figure you left out the back door to your friend's birthday party or something. She won't come looking for you."

Chris is right. The receptionist didn't even seem like she wanted to be having a conversation with me earlier.

"You don't have to go home?" I ask. "Your parents are suddenly cool with you being out at all hours of the night?"

"I told them that I was going to be staying over at Alyssa Chen's house today."

"And they believed you?" I ask. Alyssa Chen is the only other Taiwanese girl that goes to Chris's school, and despite their parents always trying to orchestrate them into a friendship, they've never quite seen eye to eye. Alyssa is all about schoolwork and grades, but that's never really been Chris's priority. She's more about her video games and art. That's probably why her parents wanted her to be friends with Alyssa.

"They believe what they want to believe," Chris says. "Now, we have a lot of tape to get through." She clicks into the first clip, which starts with Kathleen Keogh introducing herself, the show, and the judges. The second is the exact same thing from a different angle. The third is a confessional of Séan where he spends five minutes talking himself up.

"They didn't include this in the episode," Chris says as we watch. Almost like she knows I didn't watch the episode.

I wait for a moment as she closes out of the clip and opens another one before asking the question that's been weighing on my mind.

"How come you're helping me?" I ask.

Chris turns to me. "Is that a serious question?"

"Yeah, I mean, last time we spoke . . . well, *last*, last time. It wasn't . . . I wasn't exactly. And you were—"

"You were in the middle of a panic attack," Chris says. "You were in a bad place. And I was in a bad place too. I wasn't going to hold that against you." She turns back to the computer screen, which shows a close-up of Séan mixing batter, and clicks into another clip, which is a wide shot of all of us hard at work. I'm not ready to let this go, though.

"I would have held it against you," I say. "I am still holding things against you. I'm holding our breakup against you. I'm holding everything you've ever said against you. But you wouldn't hold this against me?"

"You really want me to be angry at you, Shireen?" Chris asks.

"Yes. Because you should be angry at me," I say. "I shouldn't have accused you like that without proof. Doesn't it bother you that I said all of those things to you, but I'm choosing not to say anything to Niamh until I have proof?"

Chris takes a deep breath and leans back in her seat. "Yes, it bothers me. But it just means you learned from accusing me without thinking it through properly. It's growth."

"Seriously? I haven't even apologized to you!" I say, because I can't believe Chris is being real right now.

Chris turns to me once more, looking kind of exasperated. Like she really doesn't want to be having this conversation right now. "Maybe I'm trying to make up for what I did before," she says. "I'm trying to be . . . the girlfriend that I wasn't before."

"But you're not my girlfriend."

"I know." She turns back to the screen and clicks into another video. We watch silently for what feels like hours. We go through at least two dozen clips without finding a single piece of evidence against Niamh.

"Maybe it *was* me," I say. "What if after all this, all we find is me dumping a bag of sugar into my own cake batter?"

"We won't."

"How do you know?"

"Because I know you. You don't . . . you don't mess up like that," Chris says. "You never have. You're hard on yourself, and you push yourself. You're like totally concentrated when you're working because it's what you love to do. It always shows. You would never make such a ridiculous mistake. This is your dream, and you wouldn't sabotage yourself like that." She pauses and glances at me, like she's considering if she should say the next words. "And I'm really sorry that I sabotaged you. Not . . . not now. With this. But before. When I was supposed to be your number one supporter. When I was supposed to—"

"*I'm* sorry." I cut her off, looking down at my shoes instead of at her. "Just because of what happened before doesn't mean I should have assumed you were the person who sabotaged my cake. I just thought that—"

"I know why you thought it." When I look up, Chris is staring at the screen once more, though her eyes are distant. "If I were you, I would have thought the same thing. I haven't given you reason to trust me. I don't blame you for not trusting me."

"But we agreed to be friends and—"

"When I asked you to do that, I was being selfish," Chris says. "I just missed you and I wanted to have you in my life, even if it was at your expense. Even though what happened between us was still too recent. Even though I know there was something going on with you and Niamh. And I never even did anything to earn your trust." She glances at me now. "I guess *that's* why I'm doing this. Because I wanted to make things right, and this might be my only chance to do that."

"Well, shouldn't I also be doing something to make things

right?" I ask. I'm already thinking of all of Chris's favorite baked goods, but I'm pretty sure that's not exactly forgiveness-worthy material.

"You could give me another chance," Chris says. And when I meet her gaze—her warm brown eyes and the hope sparkling in them—I know she's being serious.

This feels different somehow from the day at the pier. And maybe it's because of what Chris said. She had done something to make things right. And she had made things right.

Suddenly, I'm all too aware of the fact that our chairs are basically on top of each other. There's barely any space between us at all. One of us would have to lean forward just a little bit to close the gap between us.

And the thing is—I want Chris to lean forward. I want to kiss her this time.

"Look!" Chris says all of a sudden, whipping her head around to the computer screen. I try to bring my heart rate back to normal as I follow her gaze.

On the screen, I see me at my kitchen station. I'm in front of the oven, checking the temperature, and there's someone on the other side of the station. They're almost out of view of the camera, but I can see them add something to the bowl I've abandoned for a moment. They stir it in—so quickly that if I blinked I might have missed the whole thing.

I exchange a glance with Chris, my heart in my throat.

Because nobody else at the *Junior Irish Baking Show* has red hair like that.

"Niamh," we say at the same time.

"How did nobody notice this?" I ask, staring at the screen with wide eyes. "They had to edit the footage!"

"Maybe they noticed and decided not to do anything about it," Chris says. But I can't really believe that—can I? I know reality TV doesn't always tell the truth but hiding this seems like a step too far.

"Why would anybody do that?"

"I don't know. Why did we never find out who started the food fight?" Chris asks with a raised eyebrow.

She's right. It would have been easy to figure it out. There were cameras everywhere. Somebody started it, and the producers of the show didn't want them to be punished. They wanted to play out the story line in a different way. And it's the same thing here. Me being eliminated had more to do with what the producers wanted.

I think back to the confessional on the day I was eliminated. I was so dejected, barely able to keep my tears at bay. Andrew McNamara had asked me how I felt making such a big mistake. A mistake that got me eliminated. Maybe he knew all along that I hadn't made a mistake at all.

Chris leans forward and starts to email the video clip to herself.

"What are you doing?" I ask.

"We need to show the judges proof that Niamh sabotaged you," Chris says.

"And how are you going to explain how we got this video?" I ask.

Chris leans back in her chair. "Good question."

"We need to find a way to tell them to look at these videos," I say. "But I don't even know if they'll listen to me. If this is what they wanted and the finale is tomorrow—"

"We didn't do all of this for nothing," Chris says. "You need to talk to Padma. Show her the video."

"When she asks—"

"We'll tell her it was me." And without waiting for me to agree she leans forward and begins typing.

From: Christina Huang <chrishuang2412@gmail
.com>
To: Clare Farrin <junioririshbakingshow@ietv.ie>

Dear Clare,

Please forward this on to Padma.

Here's proof that Shireen was sabotaged on the show. Hope you and the other judges can do something to fix it.

Chris

"Chris, you can't—"

But before I can say another word, she's already hit SEND.

"What if they kick you out for breaking into these computers?" I ask, eyes wide as I stare at Chris. Who seems way too chill about all of this.

"I mean, you can hardly call this 'breaking into' a computer. We just guessed the really easy password. It's almost like they wanted us to—"

"Chris," I say.

She turns to me with a smile. "I don't care if I win this competition, or if I get kicked out."

"But the money that your parents need is—"

"Important, but they're going to be okay. We're going to figure out another way if we have to. Anyway, if your parents and my parents both put down the hatchet, I think we'll already be saving a lot," Chris says.

"You don't have to do this for me."

"I'm not doing it for you," Chris says. I give her a look because I definitely do not believe her.

"Okay, I'm doing it a little for you. But I never even wanted to be in this competition. My mom teaches me how to bake new things every single day. That's how I've been spending my summer, and I'm so tired of it. The money would be nice but winning this competition . . . it doesn't mean anything to me. Not like it does to you," she says.

I try to hold back a smile, but I don't do a good job because I'm kind of already smiling. "You've really been learning how to bake with your mom this whole summer?"

Chris nods. "It's been hell. She is not a good teacher, and she gets so mad when I mess up. And I mess up a lot."

"You've gotten really good though."

"Yeah, because you used to let me help you in the kitchen. We were always a good team."

"Yeah, we were."

We exchange a smile, but the moment from before is gone. Chris closes the files on the computer and stands up.

"We should get out of here before we get caught and get the

keys back before anyone notices they're missing," she says, leading me out of the editing room. There's still so much I want to say her, but also there's nothing I want to say to her at the same time. Whatever is between us now doesn't feel like old feelings coming back. It feels . . . fresh. Butterflies in my stomach and sweaty hands. Like a brand-new crush but on the same old person. Chris feels brand-new too, somehow. And maybe that's how she thinks of me as well.

Like all that time apart has made us into new people. Like maybe if I did give her another chance—if she gave me another chance too—our relationship would be different. Better.

I don't say any of this to her though, because if Padma uses our video, tomorrow we might be competitors again.

From: Padma Bollywood <padmabollywood@padmabollywood.com>
To: Shireen Malik <shireenbakescakes@gmail.com>

Shireen,

Please come to the IETV studios at 9:00 A.M. tomorrow morning, before filming starts. Thank you.

Kind regards,
Padma

THIRTY-FOUR

I Knew You Were Truffle When You Walked In

I ARRIVE AT THE IETV STUDIOS THE NEXT MORNING WITH MY HEART beating a little too fast. I know whatever Padma has to say has something to do with the video clip that Chris sent Clare last night. I'm not sure if I'm about to be tried for committing a crime—breaking into the studio and looking through their footage—or if I'm about to get justice for what happened during the last episode.

I take a deep breath to stabilize all my runaway thoughts, and then I push the door open and step into our recording studio.

The first thing I spot is Niamh's red hair at the far side of the hall. My anxiety spikes. What if Niamh accuses me of sabotaging *her*? What if even with the evidence the judges don't believe me? What if, what if, what if . . . ?

But there's nothing I can do about the what ifs. I think about Chris and how she risked everything for me with no hesitation. Like she didn't even have to think twice about potentially sacrificing her position in the competition for my sake. I take one more deep breath and march to the front of the room.

"Ah, Shireen, you're here." Galvin is the one who says this. He waves me forward and toward a chair beside Niamh.

I sit down, trying my hardest not to look at her. I fear what I'll feel if I look at her. The last time we spoke—really spoke— was the day we celebrated the semifinals. The day she kissed me and I let her. And I thought that was good. That I was leaving Chris behind, someone who had hurt me. But now things are so different in the space of just a few short days.

"Can you please tell us why you've called us in here today?" Niamh asks. Normally, she's nervous around the judges. Like me, she knows exactly how important they are. What they can mean for our careers in this industry. But today, she seems different. Still nervous but in a completely different way.

"Niamh, we've found some . . . worrying footage of the show," Galvin says, his voice grim. This time, I do sneak a quick look at Niamh. Her legs are bouncing up and down— something I've never seen her do before—but her expression doesn't change in the slightest.

"What kind of worrying footage?" Niamh asks. "I don't remember seeing anything on the episode that aired."

"That's just the thing. It wasn't included in the episode, but someone came across it after it aired," Máire Cherry says. Despite the seriousness of the situation, she is still all smiles. "It's, well, can we just show it?"

Galvin nods, before pulling out a tablet and setting it on the judges' table so we can all see. It's the same clip from the night before, but it feels different watching it here with Niamh beside me and the judges in front. Like this is a judgment being made . . . and there *must* be a judgments. Last night felt safe. Like I knew no matter what happened, Chris had my back.

The clip continues for a full minute showing me working and putting aside my cake batter to check the oven. It's only in the last few seconds that Niamh's red blob of hair shows up at the edge. We see a hand pouring something in and mixing it all together. Then the clip ends, and the screen turns black.

We all wait in silence for a moment. Honestly, I expect Niamh to say something, but she doesn't. She just sits there, expressionless. Never looking at me.

"Niamh, we have reason to believe that this is you," Galvin says, putting his tablet away and peering at her closely. "Can you explain yourself?"

"It's not me," Niamh says with a completely straight face. Galvin exchanges a glance with the other judges.

"Niamh, in the video footage—"

"You can't see anybody's face," Niamh says, her voice completely stable despite the way her legs are bouncing up and down. "Unless my face shows up on your camera, how is that any kind of proof?"

"Nobody else has red hair in the competition." For a moment, I'm not sure who said those words. But from the way everybody's looking at me, it must have been me. "Who else could it have been?"

"I don't know," Niamh says, turning to me. She's never looked at me like this before—like she barely knows me. Like we weren't friends. Like she hasn't spent all her time flirting with me since the very day we met. I wonder if it was all an act to get close to me and sabotage me. How could she have known that I was someone she needed to watch out for? Would she have

287

moved on to befriend someone else to sabotage if I had been eliminated early on?

"It was you. You *know* it was you," I say, and even though I know I'm supposed to stay calm and collected, I can't keep the hurt from my voice.

Niamh's face still gives nothing away. "It could have been someone from the crew. It could have been someone who happened to walk in on set. I might be the only competitor with red hair, but that doesn't mean I'm the only one on set with it," she says. "I shouldn't be penalized for being a redhead. I thought you'd understand that, Shireen."

My words get stuck in my throat, because if I'm not mistaken she's really comparing this to the racial abuse that Chris and I have been facing since the start of the competition.

"You don't even—"

"Okay, enough." Galvin doesn't raise his voice when he interrupts me, but it's enough to shut both me and Niamh up. He looks like he wants to be anywhere but here right now. I do, too, but probably for completely different reasons.

"I suggest that Shireen be allowed back in the competition, since it's clear that her work *was* sabotaged," Galvin says. "And the dish that was served to us wasn't what she intended it to be. And it wasn't in her control."

Niamh crosses her arms but doesn't say anything.

"I think Niamh should be eliminated in her stead," Padma chimes in.

"That's not fair," Niamh says.

"What if Niamh and Shireen do another baking round to see who should stay on in the finale?" Máire asks.

"How is that fair?" Niamh says, leaning forward and narrowing her eyes at the judges. "I got into the finals fair and square."

"Well, that 'fair and square' part is what we're here to discuss, Niamh," Padma says. I can tell she's trying very hard to keep the annoyance and anger out of her voice.

Galvin clenches his jaw like he's tiring of this continuous back-and-forth. "Give us a minute to discuss."

The three of them slip into the backroom while Niamh and I sit in stony silence. When they come back, their faces are somber. "We think the best solution would be if Shireen is reinstated and Niamh stays on in the competition too," Galvin says. "Then Shireen would get another chance to prove herself, and Niamh, since you say this wasn't you, you should be able to beat Shireen. Fair and square."

"I can," Niamh says, as if she hasn't been caught cheating red-handed.

"So it's settled," Galvin says. "Four contestants will enter the live show, but only *one* will be the winner."

NIAMH STORMS OUT OF the studio almost as soon as the judges dismiss us, but I gingerly make my way out. I'm not sure exactly how I'm supposed to be feeling. On the one hand, I have one last shot at winning the competition. On the other, Niamh isn't being punished despite being clearly guilty. But the worst part of it all is the fact that Niamh seems so unflinchingly comfortable with everything that's just happened. Because she's that desperate to win the *Junior Irish Baking Show*?

> Me: I'm back in.
> Chris: yay!
> Me: But . . . Niamh is still in the competition too.
> Chris: seriously?
> Me: It's . . . complicated. Are you here?
> Chris: Almost. 15 mins away.

I tuck my phone away and take a deep steadying breath, but I'm not sure if it steadies me at all. Because when I turn, I spot Niamh in the café, ordering.

I'm not sure exactly what compels me. But one minute, I'm standing by myself trying to calm my nerves and the next I'm marching toward Niamh.

"Why did you do it?" The words are out of my mouth before I've even thought them through properly. Like everything jumbled up inside my head is tumbling out.

Niamh barely glances at me—almost like she expected me to come over to her. Almost like she wanted me to. That infuriates me even more.

"I don't know what you're talking about," she says. "But you probably shouldn't make a scene." She takes a sip from the coffee cup in her hands, glancing at me over the top of it. I see something in her eyes—a flash of fear? Nervousness? Regret?

"I thought we were friends," I say. "I thought I could trust you. But you, you—"

"I should be saying that to you," Niamh says. Now I recognize that flash in her eyes. She isn't regretful or nervous or even afraid. She's angry. Like I'm the one who wronged her somehow and not the other way around.

"What are you talking about?"

"You've always known you were going to win. You already had an advantage. You started sucking up to Padma Bollywood from the first episode. Everybody knew that you loved her, and obviously she loved you too. She's Indian and so are you, so you have your little bond. I saw you and Chris and her having your little tea party. I saw her talking to you outside the recording studio. I know how she sees you. I can tell she wants you to win, no matter what. How's that fair, that you get to win just because you and Padma are the same race?"

For a moment, I don't even have any words. I can only stare at her with wide eyes because there's no way Niamh really believes that. She can't really believe that I'm getting preferential treatment, that the odds are stacked against her, when she can see how people have been acting toward me and Chris since the day the show started airing.

"Padma is just . . . she's just been looking out for us. Not because I'm 'Indian,' which I'm not. I'm from Bangladesh, which is a completely different country. But because I'm . . . I'm . . . because things are more difficult for us."

Niamh scoffs. "I was trying to balance things out. Tip the scales in my favor. Give someone else a chance at winning."

"Do you want to know *why* Chris and I were having tea with Padma?"

Niamh sends me a glare like it doesn't matter what I say, like she's made up her mind about us—about the way we're getting advantages because of our race that she never will.

But I speak anyway, because if I don't say this to her now—if we don't have this conversation—I'm not sure how long I'll hold on to my anger for Niamh. "Because of the things people were saying about us. Maybe you missed it," I say, even though I know for sure she hasn't missed any of it. "But people were calling us slurs. They were saying that we didn't belong in the show. They were saying, well, really awful things that I'd rather not repeat. Padma was just making sure we knew that she supported us, and would try to get the producers to as well. It wasn't about giving us an advantage. It wasn't even about balancing the scales. It was just about telling us that even though us being on the show seems to piss people off, even though we would come up against stuff like this again and again, we had someone who supported us."

Niamh tilts her head to one side, like she's having a difficult time understanding exactly what I'm trying to tell her. "It's just a couple of tweets."

"Hundreds of them," I say.

"It's still not fair," Niamh says. "You know it's not fair and you're still—"

"You ruined my dish. You got me kicked out of the competition. *That's* fair? That's how you want to win?"

Niamh doesn't reply to that. Instead she looks away, like she's done having this conversation.

I'm done too—because it's clear to me all of a sudden that whatever safety or comfort I ever felt around her was a farce. I misjudged her from the beginning.

"Was everything between us because of how desperate you were to win?" I ask. Only because I have to know. Because my feelings for her were real, even if my feelings for Chris were stronger.

She looks back at me, and she almost seems sad. "No," she says, her voice low. "I . . . I liked you. Everything was genuine. I like spending time with you, getting to know you. But you were playing me—flirting with me one second and hanging out with your ex the next. Lying to me about what was going on with Padma."

"I never—"

"You don't have feelings for Chris?" she asks.

And that, at least, I can't refute. Not that that makes any of it okay.

"I had feelings for you too," I say. "But I guess I was wrong about the kind of person you are."

"I guess I was wrong too," Niamh says, like somehow we're on the same level. Like I've betrayed her, same as she's betrayed me.

With that, she turns around and slips out of the café and out of my sight.

THIRTY-FIVE

At the Eleventh Flour

THE FINALE BEING A LIVE SHOW MEANS THAT THERE IS A LIVE AUDI-
ence. I can see Séan and Niamh's families encouraging them as
soon as I walk back into the studio. Even some of the eliminated
contestants are in the audience, probably thinking I'm here to
watch the finale just like them. Chris is still nowhere in sight.

I know I should probably have told Ammu and Abbu as
soon as I was reinstated in the competition, but I'm not sure if I
can handle disappointing them all over again. So even though I
could definitely use some of the support that Niamh and Séan's
parents seem to be giving them, I hold my head up high and
walk straight to my kitchen station. I'm ready to win this, even
if I wasn't meant to be here in the first place.

I pull out my phone and text Fatima, filling her in on my con-
frontation with Niamh. I've been texting her updates ever since
we talked it out, but she's barely responded. I'm trying not to be
annoyed or jealous. I know she's busy in Bangladesh with her
cousins. Still, I can't help but hope that she'll at least take the time
to watch the finale live now that I've clawed my way back here.

It's only five minutes until filming is about to start, and Chris
is still not here.

I glance all around, hoping she's just hiding somewhere. But of course, she's nowhere to be seen.

What if . . . what if she's been kicked out for sending the video in the first place? None of the judges told us where they got it or how they got it. Would they really tell us if Chris was disqualified? What if that's whose spot I'm taking?

But then the door swings open, and Chris walks in, her gaze almost instantly snapping to me. She smiles, but I'm barely even looking at her. Because behind her are my parents in deep conversation with hers. And . . .

Fatima!

"What are you doing here?" I ask, rushing over to them. "I've been texting you constantly and—"

"I literally just got off my flight," Fatima says. "It was a struggle making it here in time."

"You didn't tell us you got back into the competition," Ammu says chidingly. "You think we didn't want to come and support you?"

"Well, yes, but—"

"Bakers, please get to your kitchen stations."

I cast a longing glance at my best friend, who I haven't seen in months now, and my family, who I definitely owe some kind of an explanation. But there's no time.

"Come on, you can talk to them all after this is over," Chris says, taking my hand and pulling me away from them.

"Are our parents friends now?" I whisper as we march toward our kitchen stations.

"They're definitely . . . something," Chris says. She glances down at me and adds, "I didn't know if you'd have time to let your parents know about the finale with everything that was going on, but I wasn't going to let you do this without them. I know how much this means to them . . . and to you."

That rush of emotions I felt for her yesterday feels even stronger now. If I could, I would reach over and wrap my arms around her. Tell her how much I've missed her and all of this. The care and love that was always between us. But I can't.

Instead, we go our separate ways. Chris to her kitchen station and me to mine. But as the cameras start rolling, Chris looks back at me. A smile dancing on her lips. And I know that it's not the same as it was before. We may be competitors still, but it doesn't change how we feel about each other. It never had to.

"Welcome to the *Junior Irish Baking Show*," Kathleen says into the camera. "Where we're coming to you live for the *final* episode. Only one winner will take away the title of Junior Irish Baker and ten thousand euros at the end of tonight's challenge. Let's see what the judges have to say, shall we?"

After the judges are introduced, a grim-faced Galvin informs them that as a surprise for the finale, I've been brought back on the show. It's not exactly how I would have gone about introducing me—especially considering people like Niamh apparently think I'm already getting "special treatment," but I guess it's the best that anyone can do when Niamh is refusing to admit guilt.

"Shireen, how do you feel about being back in the competition?" Kathleen asks with a sympathetic look on her face. I wonder if she knows the real reason I'm back here.

"I'm grateful for the opportunity," I say. "And ready to win."

Once they move on from the news of my return, Máire Cherry announces the final round of the competition.

"Tonight's challenge is simple. It's a chance to tell us exactly who you are and what you can do. You can create anything that you want, but it has to be something meaningful to you. Something that tells us your story."

The countdown clock starts, and everybody runs to the pantry to get their ingredients. But I'm still trying to think through what I actually want to make.

Something that tells them exactly who I am and what I can do. The idea comes to me perfectly formed, but I'm not sure if it's too ambitious.

Then again, if I'm not ambitious now, when else will I have the chance? On the side of the room, I can see Fatima flashing me an encouraging smile, almost like she knows exactly what I'm thinking. I dash into the pantry, knowing that this is what I have to do. And there's no room for me to mess it up either.

Once I have my ingredients I start to work, focusing only on me and nobody else. At least this time I know that everybody's eyes are on us. There's no way Niamh would dare try and sabotage anyone.

I start with mixing everything together for the dough before putting it aside to chill. I quickly make the ganache and whipped cream as I wait for the dough to rise.

Once the dough is ready I begin to shape it and fry it. I'm so used to making donuts on my own that this is probably the most natural thing I've done during the whole competition. Making donuts is second nature to me. When I've fried all the donuts, I glance at the red countdown clock.

"Ten minutes left, bakers!" Kathleen cries, almost as soon as I look. Only ten minutes to assemble this thing—but it's definitely doable.

I start stacking donuts and cream as quickly as I can. One layer of cream, one layer of donuts and on and on and on, until I'm at the top of the cake. I rush it into the fridge to set and top the last of my donuts with chocolate glaze, lemon glaze, strawberry glaze, and lots and lots of sprinkles.

Then I pull my set cake out of the fridge, pour vanilla glaze on top, and decorate it with the last of my donuts. I'm putting the final touch of sprinkles when the buzzer sounds and I step back.

I grin at the cake in front of me. It's nothing I've ever made before but I feel pretty proud of it.

"Shireen, can you bring us your dessert?" Galvin asks almost as soon as the judging begins. I guess I'm first on the chopping block.

I pick up my dish and carry it to the judges' table, head held high for once. I've already been eliminated once, and this time I really have nothing to lose.

"Can you tell us a little bit about what you've made?" Máire asks with a smile. I can't tell from the judges' expressions if they're impressed or not.

"Well, you said to make something that tells you about who we are. And really, donuts are who I am."

"Because of your parents' donut shop?" Padma asks with an encouraging nod.

"Kind of," I say. "My parents do have a donut shop, and it's kind of the place where they've stuck all their hopes and dreams. It's where I work, but it's also where I met someone who's special to me. Without donuts, I'm not sure if I would even be here today."

"Well, let's try it then," Galvin says. "Structurally it looks sound," he comments as he cuts into the cake with a knife. He takes a big slice for himself and cuts slices for Padma and Máire too. My chest feels heavy as the judges chew. Even though the studio is filled with people, there is complete silence. We're all waiting with bated breath.

"With a cake like this," Máire begins, "there's such a possibility of it being a little too doughy or bready or even oily. But you've managed to avoid that."

"There's also the possibility of it being too heavy," Padma adds with a nod. "But actually the donuts themselves are quite light. There's a great balance in there."

"And you've chosen your flavors well," says Galvin. "The chocolate and the mocha complement each other but don't overpower. The hint of lemon and strawberry from the top . . . it shouldn't work, but it really does."

I nearly skip back to my station with my cake. I don't care

if nobody agrees, but I feel like I've redeemed myself after the failure of the last challenge. Even if I don't win, at least I'll know that I've done everything I can.

Séan is next to present his dish.

"I decided to make a hot raspberry soufflé for today because, well, a soufflé is one of the first desserts I ever made, so it almost feels like coming full circle making one here in this kitchen." Séan says it all with an easy smile, but I can see that he's shifting his balance from one leg to the other.

"A soufflé is the first dessert you made?" Galvin says in disbelief.

"Um, yeah."

"Well, how did it go when you first made it?" Galvin presses.

"Pretty terrible. I somehow managed to undercook it, it didn't rise properly, and on top of all of that it was too sweet." Séan admits. "Which is why I've worked hard at, you know, perfecting and elevating it." He nods at the soufflé on the plate in front of him.

"Okay, let's give it a try." With that, Galvin cuts into the dessert slowly. All three judges pick up a piece with their forks, chewing and exchanging difficult to decipher glances.

"Well, you've certainly come a long way since you made your first soufflé. I can tell you that. It's perfectly cooked, just the right amount of sweet, and absolutely beautiful to look at," Galvin says. Séan visibly relaxes, but my stomach lurches.

Niamh is next, and she steps forward with a plate of short-bread, topped with chocolate and caramel.

"I made gingerbread millionaire's shortbread," Niamh

explains. "Because this has always been a staple in my home. And it's very Irish too."

The judges bite into her shortbread, nodding in appreciation. "It's not too hard as millionaire's shortbread can sometimes be. It's got the exact kind of texture you want it to have," Máire says.

"And it has a great balance of flavors," Galvin adds.

Padma gives a wan smile and simply says, "I agree." Like she's not willing to indulge Niamh with compliments after everything.

Chris is called up next. She walks with ease and places a plate of decadent heart-shaped donuts in front of the judges.

"Chris, why don't you tell us a little about what you've made for us today?" Padma asks.

"Well, they're cappuccino-flavored donuts. They have coffee icing and cappuccino cream filling," Chris explains. "I made them because my ex-girlfriend made me this exact donut— except hers weren't heart shaped—after our second date. She's obsessed with baking. She loves it. It means everything to her. And back then, it was the best thing I had ever tasted in my life. Because she had made it but also because it was just amazing. Obviously, since then she's made me so many different desserts that I don't even know how this compares. But this was always special to me."

"So your ex was the inspiration for this?" Máire asks.

"Yes."

"And are you hoping she's seeing this today?" Galvin asks.

Chris's face flushes at the question, but she just shrugs.

The three judges each take one of the donuts onto their

plates, cutting into them and taking a bite. Once more—and probably for the last time on this show—they exchange indecipherable glances.

"Well, I think that's probably one of the most delicious donuts I've ever eaten." Padma says.

I know that it should make me feel tense. But it doesn't. Instead, I feel a warm bubble of happiness, because if I don't win this, Chris definitely deserves it. Maybe she deserves it even more than I do.

"It does have a great balance between the dough, the icing, and the filling." Máire Cherry agrees with a nod.

"But . . . I think it might have been a bit too simple of a dessert to make in the final round of this competition," Galvin says. "Delicious, but is it enough for you to win the competition?"

THE JUDGES' DELIBERATION THIS time seems too quick. They arrive back in the studio within the space of a few minutes, serious expressions on all their faces.

"This was a very difficult decision," Galvin starts off.

"You should all be very proud of yourselves," Máire adds. "You've done an amazing job in this competition."

"Unfortunately, there can only be one winner," Padma says finally.

"Chris, your cappuccino donut was certainly one of the most delicious donuts we've ever tasted, and as always, your presentation was top-notch. But your dish didn't have the kind of creativity we wanted to see. It wasn't elevated in a way that told us you really know your stuff. It felt too basic for the finale of the competition. Unfortunately, you are not the next Junior Irish Baker," Galvin says.

Chris nods solemnly, head still held up high. But my stomach clenches.

"Niamh, " Máire says, "your millionaire's shortbread was impressive and it was classic. But again, it didn't exactly have the kind of creativity we wanted to see. We wanted to see you elevate the dessert, make it your own. Show us why it was so important to you. You're not the next Junior Irish Baker."

Niamh gulps, her expression crestfallen. For a moment, I almost feel bad for her. I know how much she wanted this. She thought winning this show would really prove to her parents her talents, her skills. How important this was to her.

"Shireen . . ."

My heart begins to thump loudly, the blood rushing in my ear, almost drowning out Padma's words.

"Your donut cake was the first of its kind that we've seen," she says. "And we could tell that it was something important to you. The taste, the texture, it was all amazing. And Séan, your soufflé was simple and classic but it was elevated. The flavors were marvelous, and you made it your own. You added your own touches and really showed us how far you've come in this competition."

Séan takes a deep breath and so do I. It's between the two of us now. One of us is going to be crowned the winner.

"The winner of the first *Junior Irish Baking Show* is . . ." Everything seems to still at Maire's words. As if the very air has been sucked out of this room.

"Séan Brennan!"

THIRTY-SIX

My Heart Will Dough On

ALL OF SÉAN'S FRIENDS AND FAMILY BURST ONTO THE SET, CHEERS interrupting the stillness and silence of the room. While they're celebrating, the rest of us shake hands with the judges and mutter our goodbyes. Padma gives me a meaningful glance as we shake hands, like there's something she really wants to say to me but can't on camera.

I take off my apron and place it on the counter of my kitchen station. It definitely feels like the end of an era, even though we've only really been here for a few weeks.

"Shireen." Padma appears next to me with a smile. "I'm sorry that you went through all of this and still . . ."

She doesn't have to finish the sentence. We both know what she wants to say.

"At least he won fair and square." That's really the only consolation I have.

"I know you already have a job at your parents' donut shop," Padma says. "But if you wanted to come and work with me at least for the rest of the summer, as I set up my bakery here, I would really like that."

I take a step back, examining Padma closely. She seems sincere. Padma Bollywood is actually offering me a job.

"This would be like . . . being your assistant?" I ask.

"Hmm." She seems to think about it for a moment. "Something like that. Helping me figure out exactly what's best for the bakery. Helping me come up with recipes. And maybe some assistant things too."

I want to pinch myself because I'm sure this has to be a dream. Never in my life would I have imagined that Padma Bollywood would be offering me a job like this.

"Yes!" I say, a little too loudly.

Padma grins.

"Well, I have to check with my parents, but . . . yes, yes!"

Padma doesn't take back her offer after seeing my overenthusiasm. Her grin doesn't lessen. "You talk to your parents and let me know your final decision."

For a moment, I can only stand at my kitchen station, trying to take it all in. I may have lost the show but working with Padma may be even better than what the show had to offer. I'm about to turn around to find my parents and Fatima when the last person I expect stops by my kitchen station.

"Hey," Séan says, not quite looking me in the eye. "I just wanted to say I heard what happened with Niamh and the last elimination. I'm glad they let you come back so you could beat her fairly."

"Thanks," I mumble, not really sure why we're having this conversation, even if it feels nice to have someone other than Chris acknowledge that Niamh did something wrong. "I know you're not her biggest fan."

"It was all for show, you know," Séan says. "The bickering

and all of that. I mean, don't get me wrong. Niamh is unbearable, and I know she didn't find me easy to work with. But the whole thing with me stealing her recipe? I was okay minding my own business most of the time. She clearly thought we needed to do a little more to keep people's interest."

I blink at Séan, not sure if I'm even correctly understanding what he's saying. "But you took the bait," I say. "I mean, you were arguing with her. You were arguing with everyone."

"So was she," Séan says. "Well, she was arguing with people, starting food fights, then also having a whirlwind romance with you. She was playing the game."

I can feel heat rise up my cheeks at the suggestion of our romance. I never realized that Chris wasn't the only person who noticed what was going on with us. But all I can ask is, "You think she started the food fight?"

Séan shrugs his shoulder, like who's ever to know. "It doesn't matter now anyway. But it should never have gotten to where she sabotaged anyone." Séan almost sounds levelheaded. Like someone who is thoughtful and actually a nice person. Then he adds, "Of course, the real reason it doesn't matter is because I was always going to win and really, I never had to play any games. Niamh just knew I was her biggest competition, so she had to—"

"Congrats on winning, Séan," I say, cutting off what was sure to be a long tirade about his talents and accomplishments. "I hope you do good things with your winnings."

I turn around and nearly run to where Ammu, Abbu, and Fatima are. I have so many questions for Fatima, so much to tell her, but before I get the chance to even open my mouth, the three of them pounce on me. Embracing me in what is probably the biggest, warmest hug I've ever experienced.

"How did you get back here?" I ask, turning to Fatima.

"We were supposed to fly back tomorrow, but we changed our flights by just a little bit. I wasn't going to let you do this without me," she says.

I lean forward and pull her into another hug. This time just Fatima and me. Because finally—my best friend is back home.

"SO, LET ME GET this straight," Fatima says. "She kissed you, but the entire time she thought that there was something still going on with you and Chris *and* that you were getting unfair special advantage from Padma?" It's a few hours after my loss, and Fatima and I are sitting on my bed, finishing off a box of donuts from You Drive Me Glazy and catching up on everything we've missed in each other's lives. Which—it turns out—is actually a lot.

"Yeah, I bet if you had been here, you would have talked me out of that."

"The moment you mentioned her, I would have set you straight," Fatima says.

"I mean, you kind of tried to," I point out.

"Well, if I were here, I would have restrained you from making stupid decisions," Fatima says with a determined huff of breath.

I have to smile. "I missed you," I say, leaning forward on the bed between us and wrapping my arms around her. Even though we haven't seen each other for the entire summer, it feels like she hasn't been gone at all. Like we didn't have a major fight in her absence. Like everything that happened was almost inconsequential. It feels like things are back to normal.

"Okay, okay." Fatima pushes me off of her and adjusts her dark red hijab over her head. "So, what are you going to do next?"

"What do you mean? I lost the competition," I say.

"Yeah, but come on. Chris helped you out big-time. She made so many sacrifices for you. You're not going to talk to her? Get back together with her?" she asks.

"You really are team Chris, huh?"

Fatima rolls her eyes. "Please. I like Chris just fine, but I am and always will be #TeamShireen."

I can't help my smile, but there's still something niggling at me. "It's just . . . I couldn't trust her for a long time. And now everything feels different. She's shown me over and over that I *can* trust her now, even if I couldn't before. But I'm not sure if she knows that."

"She knows that," Fatima says, with a little too much confidence. "She wouldn't have done all this for you if she didn't."

I know it's true, but there's still something making our reconciliation seem difficult. Almost impossible. I can't put my finger on it, and I'm not sure how to deal with it.

"I think you're scared," Fatima says. "Chris hurt you, and so did Niamh, but this might be different."

"Might be?" I ask.

"Well, there are no guarantees, obviously. But Chris loves you, and you love her, right?"

I'm not sure what to say. Even throughout all of this, I did love Chris. I didn't want to, but I did. It's the reason I kept coming back to her. The reason it was so difficult for anything to happen between me and Niamh. Now I'm happy about it. After all, how much worse would everything have been if I had actually been in a relationship with Niamh? If I had trusted her the way I trusted Chris? If I was in love with her?

"I do," I say.

"That's all that matters, then," Fatima says.

"Since when did you become such a hopeless romantic?" I ask, bumping Fatima's shoulder with my own.

"Well, somebody has to be the hopeless romantic in our friendship. And if you're going to get a little dejected, then I have to pick up the mantle."

"I'll talk to Chris." Though I'm still figuring out exactly what I want to say. "But today is all about you."

"It should be about you," Fatima says.

"Well, it's not." Instead of spending the rest of the day together talking about the baking show and my love life, I dig out all of the baked goods I had frozen for Fatima while I was practicing for the show. And the two of us talk about Fatima and Bangladesh, and I listen with rapt attention.

THIRTY-SEVEN

Love Is a Batterfield

CHRIS AND I HAVE ALWAYS HAD OUR SPOT. IT'S NOT THE PLACE WE met, but it's where we saw each other most frequently. Where we would hang out after work, after school—away from our parents' watchful gaze.

And when I get to our spot the next day, the gazebo at Stephen's Green overlooking the pond, Chris is already there. There's a book propped open in front of her, but as soon as she spots me approaching, she closes it and tucks it away.

"Hey." She hops off the ledge and inches toward me hesitantly. Like she's still unsure exactly where we stand. We definitely still have a few things to sort out. "How are you doing?"

"I'm doing good," I say.

"Really?" She actually seems surprised. I guess I had made it seem like this competition was the only thing that mattered in the world. At some point, I'm pretty sure I even believed that.

"Yeah, really. I mean, I'm disappointed but fine." I hop onto wooden ledge of the gazebo. A moment later, Chris joins me, climbing up beside me until we're sitting side by side, swinging our legs back and forth. We sit in silence for a minute, taking in the way the sunshine illuminates the pond in front of us and how the trees are still that bright green of summer.

"I can't believe summer is almost over," Chris finally says. "I thought this summer was going to be different."

"You didn't anticipate going on a nationally televised baking show and becoming one of the runners-up?"

Chris chuckles. "More like I didn't anticipate us not spending the summer together."

"Yeah, me neither."

Chris turns to face me now, a seriousness etched on her face that wasn't there before. "I hope this is the last time I say this, but I really *am* sorry. There was stuff with the donut shop and my parents were desperate for me to win the show and I guess I just felt that responsibility a little too heavily. I shouldn't have put that on you, especially without even talking to you about what was going on."

"Your parents shouldn't have given you that responsibility, but I get it. I felt a little of that, too, with my parents' donut shop," I say. "*I'm* sorry, for lashing out at you and not . . . I don't know, really giving you a chance to explain. I wanted to make you the villain. It was easier to deal with our breakup that way."

"You remember when we broke up and I said, 'You don't have to go on the *Junior Irish Baking Show*, because you're much bigger than some TV show'?"

I don't really want to think about our breakup, because all I remember is how awful it was and how terrible I felt after it. How everything seemed tinged with a strange kind of sadness and heartbreak that I wanted to avoid at all costs. Still, I nod my head. I've played that conversation out in my head so many times I could produce it from memory.

"Well, I was being an asshole when I said it, but it's true. You are much bigger than a TV show. And your dreams are bigger too. I know all of the things you're capable of, and not winning this one show is not going to hold you back. I couldn't hold you back. Niamh couldn't hold you back. I'm not sure there's anyone or anything that can."

I bite back a smile. Not because what Chris said is true—but because I did take each one of my failures pretty hard.

"You know the things I'm capable of are only because I have you and Fatima and my parents to see me through it. Even when I can't see things clearly."

"Yeah," Chris says. "You *are* pretty clueless without us."

"Hey!" I bump her shoulders with mine, but Chris just grins.

Sitting here with her in Stephen's Green Park, it feels like the summer I wanted to have. Not the depressing, sometimes chaotic summer that I did have.

So with a deep breath, I take Chris's hand in mine. The familiarity of it fills me up with warmth.

Chris's smile widens—seems to take up her entire face. "You do trust me, right?" she asks. "Because I don't want you to—"

Chris doesn't have a chance to finish before I lean forward and press my lips to hers. It's a tentative kiss—so different from the ones we shared when we were together for one whole year.

"Of course I trust you," I whisper as I pull away.

"Good." Chris smiles, brushing a strand of hair away from my face. "Because I trust you too."

And even though neither of us says it right then, I can hear the undertone of it in Chris's words. In mine. Even though this is something new, it's something familiar too. It's all the parts of a new relationship—the butterflies in our stomachs and the excitement—and the comfort of something that we've known before.

THIRTY-EIGHT

Winner Bakes All

"WE NEED AT LEAST ONE DONUT." PADMA HAS A VERY SERIOUS LOOK on her face as she contemplates what kind of a donut dish she can serve in her bakery, Bollywood Delights.

"I mean, you really don't have to, Ms. Bollywood," I say.

"Padma," Padma says sternly for the umpteenth time. If we hadn't met through the *Junior Irish Baking Show*, I'm sure I'd be calling her Padma Aunty. But I don't think either of us want that since she's not even my mom's age—definitely not aunty age.

"Padma," I say hesitantly, even though it feels really weird to call any South Asian person older than me by their given name. "You really don't have to add a donut dish."

"How can I have an entire bakery in Dublin, where a runner-up of the *Junior Irish Baking Show* is helping me set up, and not even have a dish that honors her?" Padma asks.

"Donuts aren't exactly high end and they're so—"

"Your cake!" Padma says, clapping her hands together. "The donut cake you made during the finale. A variation of that. People will recognize it. They'll flock to it. And it was delicious. We need a name though." She looks at me thoughtfully.

Names are obviously my specialty, and I've been mulling

315

over what I could call my donut creation for a long time. Since the day I decided to make it on the show, actually. I'd gone through a lot of possibilities, but I finally arrived at the perfect one. "I've been calling it the Leaning Tower of Donut."

Padma gives me an impressed glance and writes it down in her little notebook before closing it up and shooting me the biggest grin I've ever seen on her.

For the past few weeks, working with Padma has been hectic. I went from one high-stakes competition to, well, a kind of high-stakes job. Though Padma has been nothing but supportive, working in a bakery like hers is no walk in the park.

"I think that's the entire menu," Padma says.

"Wow." It feels surreal in many ways as I look around at the bakery. All the interior design is finished. The place is furnished with lush pink chairs and tables, the walls are painted salmon pink, and the glass counters glitter in their newness. I helped set everything up, and I definitely helped create the menu.

"In a few days, we'll be ready to open things up," Padma says. "And obviously, you'll be here, helping me out, right?"

"Yeah . . . yes!" I say. "The only thing is school will be starting in just a few days, and I'm still supposed to help out with my parents' shop so—"

Padma waves her hand like that's of no concern. "I've spoken to your parents, and they're happy for you to alternate days between here and their shop. After all, with the Huangs and Chris, I think they already have quite a bit of help."

"Well, then. I'm ready to be put to work," I say with the biggest grin I can muster.

I leave Padma's bakery a few hours later to stroll into Ammu and Abbu's shop. Or, well, the *new* shop. It still has a CLOSED sign in front, but inside the place is buzzing. There are workers setting things up, and Ammu is arguing with Mrs. Huang in one corner.

"Hi Ammu," I say.

"Shireen, you're here. Good, we need your opinion." She waves me over, and I'm pretty sure I don't want to get involved. But it's not like I have a choice.

"For our big opening weekend, we need four-star desserts," she says. She shows me the box in her hands filled with Bengali desserts. There's kalo jam, shondesh, and chomchom.

"These should all be part of the lineup, right? How can you sell Bengali mishti and not have all of these?" Ammu asks. She scowls at Mrs. Huang like she's personally stopping Ammu from serving these to customers.

"All I said is we have two of your mom's and two of mine. So it's balanced. Equal," Mrs. Huang says. She's holding her own box of desserts, lined with sesame balls, pineapple short-cake, and yóutiáo. I have to agree with her. Mrs. Huang is being reasonable and Ammu not so much. Which is not exactly out of the ordinary.

"Ammu, sorry. You have to give up one for the big opening weekend."

Ammu makes an annoyed sound in the back of her throat, and says something under her breath, which I'm sure is not very pleasant. But she points to the chomchoms and says, "Fine. No chomchoms opening weekend."

"Good idea," I say. "Anyway, as soon as people have your kalo jam and shondesh, they'll be running back for more after the opening weekend," I assure her.

She smiles, convinced of her own talents obviously, and saunters off to do some more preparation for our opening weekend.

"You should always be mediator between me and your mom," Mrs. Huang says as soon as Ammu is out of earshot.

"She just takes a little while to warm up," I say. "Trust me, she likes you. She wouldn't let you sell your Taiwanese desserts right next to her mishti if she didn't."

With that, I leave Mrs. Huang behind and find Chris, where she's teaching our dads about the new shop website that she designed.

"You click here . . . and full menu, see?" Chris says, showing the screen to both of our dads. There's a glow to her as she navigates the website and instructs our dads, like this was something she was born to do. It feels like Chris is finally seeing that she has a lot to contribute to her parents' shop and their lives, even if she doesn't follow in their exact footsteps.

Our dads nod back and forth as Chris explains, exchanging impressed glances. It's a strange sight to behold, since just a few months earlier we definitely weren't allies. But with both our donut shops struggling in this economy, Abbu came up with this plan. A new shop between the Huangs and the Maliks. Not because they're friends—they're far from it. But because if nothing else, Abbu respects the Huangs' business savvy. And I guess they felt the same way.

And now they kind of are something resembling friends.

Chris and I even came up with the perfect name for the new shop: Where Sweets Meet, to represent the fusion of our two cuisines.

I clear my throat to get their attention. "Chris, are you ready?"

"Oh yeah," Chris says, putting the laptop down. "Sorry Uncle, sorry Baba. I'll finish this later, okay?"

"Okay, go," Mr. Huang says, though he's clearly not super happy about it. "We have lots to do anyway."

I don't wait for them to try and rope us into helping them with their lots to do and hurry out the door. Chris follows behind with a grin.

"You know, when my parents told me about this idea, I was so sure it was going to fail. I thought they'd be at each other's throats by now," she says.

"I think they kind of are, but they know they have to deal with it," I say.

"Right, almost like their dislike for each other makes them have more respect," Chris says, shaking her head like she doesn't really understand it. "It definitely helped once my parents knew that you were the ex-girlfriend I was talking about on the show."

"I still can't believe they know." It's definitely strange to have our parents know about our relationship after being forced to hide it for so long because of their feud.

It's almost surreal. And weirdly Ammu and Abbu love Chris—almost as much as they love complaining about the Huangs. Almost as much as they loved their ridiculous feud.

"We should probably hurry," I say, when my phone buzzes with an angry text from Fatima. "Fatima is getting fed up with us always being late."

"She'll get used to it," Chris says dismissively, but she starts walking faster anyway. Fatima may be my best friend, but she can be a little scary sometimes—especially when she's angry.

"Do you know just how long I was waiting for you?" she cries when we get to her. "You said eight!"

"I'm sorry. I do have a job," I say.

"Two jobs, actually. And that's not even counting your blog," Chris points out. Ever since the start of the show, my blog has been getting more and more views. I thought it would all end once the show ended, but it seems there are still people interested. Weirdly, the blog doesn't feel as important to me now as it once did, but it's still nice to see that people care about my recipes.

Chris and I sit down on the grass beside Fatima, soaking in the sun's last bit of golden rays.

"I would have thought after a whole summer apart, you would sacrifice anything to spend time with me," Fatima huffs. I can tell she's not being serious though. Still, I reach into my handbag and pull out the cupcake I made for her at Padma's bakery.

"Here," I say. "It's Oreo flavored. Your favorite."

Fatima eyes the cupcake suspiciously for a minute before grabbing it. She takes a bite and almost swoons. "This is the best cupcake I've ever had in my whole entire life," she says. "Okay. You're forgiven."

The three of us sit there together side by side, watching the horizon, where everything is a blend of different colors. Even the pond has turned a shade of orange from the reflection of the sky.

Right here, between the two most important people in my life (well, except Ammu and Abbu of course), I feel safe. Protected. In a way I'm not sure I ever have before. Definitely not during this summer with the *Junior Irish Baking Show*.

But I know that what Chris said a few weeks ago was true: my dreams are more than a TV show, and so am I.

It's the end of the summer, but sitting here with Chris and Fatima, it feels like the start of something new.

Author's Note

When I first sat down to write *The Dos and Donuts of Love*, I knew three things: This book was going to be about donuts. It was going to star a fat Bangladeshi protagonist. And for the life of me I could not imagine writing it without a heavy dose of fatphobia from the main character's family and friends.

The last fact probably shouldn't have surprised me as much as it did, considering I had grown up surrounded by very extreme fatphobia. As a teen, I was put through the wringer of diet culture, which led to many years of fluctuating weight, self-doubt, and very serious self-esteem issues. Worst of all, it resulted in an abhorrent relationship to food and my body, which is something I struggle with to this day.

Sadly, I suspect a lot of fat teens can relate to this experience and probably especially fat South Asian teens.

You see, South Asian, and specifically Bangladeshi, culture has a very interesting relationship with food and body. One that can make even the most secure person develop some serious self-image issues. Our culture gives two very confusing and conflicting messages about food. On the one hand, food is celebratory and community-building. Almost all of our cultural events revolve around food, and food is one of the most revered parts of who we are. When I visit Bangladesh, or visit Bangladeshi family friends in Ireland, everybody's main goal seems to be to feed me as much as they possibly can. And if I don't eat the food they have offered, it's impolite.

On the other hand, food and our bodies are seen as a source of shame. It's common for strangers, friends, and family alike to comment on how much weight you have gained or lost. Talk of diets is rife among our people. Even as you are being handed a plate of food with the insistence that you must eat all of it, you are being told that you weigh too much, you're too fat, and you must do something about it.

These are the conflicting messages that I and a lot of other Bangladeshis grew up with, and it's one of the reasons why many of us have an unhealthy attitude to food and how we view our bodies well into adulthood, and (for some) our whole entire lives.

Sadly, this is the baggage I was bringing with myself into the first draft of this book. Thankfully, it's not what's on the pages of its final draft.

While I may have grown up surrounded by a lot of fatphobia, as I wrote this book, I realized that writing about fatphobia is not necessarily the way to empower and represent fat South Asian characters. Instead, I asked myself what I wish I had read when I was a teen. And the answer was definitely not all my struggles reflected back at me.

The answer was much simpler than that: It was fat characters getting to exist as they were. Getting to have an uncomplicated relationship with food and their bodies. Getting to celebrate who they were, exactly as they were. And having supportive friends and family who loved them just the way they were.

So I tried to take all of my baggage and turn it on its head, to something a little bit more positive, something perhaps a little aspirational. But definitely into what I needed when I was a teenager, and maybe even need to this day.

I know there are still so many people out there who have experiences similar to mine: those who haven't felt at home in their own bodies because of the way fatphobia operates in our society.

I wrote this book for you.

And I wrote it for myself.

Acknowledgments

An amazing team of people made this book possible. Thank you to each and every one of you:

To my agent, Uwe Stender, for your endless support.

To my editor, Foyinsi Adegbonmire, for shaping this book into its best and punniest version.

To everyone at Feiwel and Friends/Macmillan for all your hard work including Mallory Grigg and Maria Williams (designers), Lelia Mander (production editor), and Jean Feiwel (publisher).

To Nabi H Ali, for the stunning cover. I am forever grateful to you for bringing my characters to life so perfectly.

To all my friends and family, who make every book possible because of what they do to make my life as a writer possible.

To my Bengali squad, Priyanka and Tammi, for always being there.

To Faridah, for always being a friend and a listening ear, especially when things get hard.

To Gayatri, for being a kindred spirit, and for all you do for the desi book community.

To my readers, because without you I wouldn't be here writing the books that I do. There are always too many readers to name, but a special thank-you to Sami (@samisbookshelf), Maya (@mnmbooks), and Tazrin (@tazisbooked), for the work you do to uplift marginalized authors and books, and specifically South Asian ones.

To Dublin's weird obsession with donuts, because without it, I never would have come up with the idea for this book.

To you, the reader, for giving this book a chance.